Retter

A Novel of the Mountains

Amy Garza

Amy Garza

Winston-Derek Publishers, Inc.
Pennywell Drive—Post Office Box 90883
Nashville, Tennessee 37209

Second printing 1989

PUBLISHED BY WINSTON-DEREK PUBLISHERS, INC.
Nashville, Tennessee 37205

Library of Congress Catalog Card No: 87-40251
ISBN: 1-55523-092-X

Printed in the United States of America

To Corie,

whose home has become a haven for
the Ammons family on the road to
eternal peace,

and

To Professor Charles Tinkham,
who believed in me.

Contents

Prologue

My breath was almost gone, yet the excitement inside me grew. Just ahead was the crest of the mountain—my link with the past.

It had been years since I'd climbed this trail cut deep into the heavy forest of the mountain. But I had to return!

Lately, something curious had crept into my dreams, and into my innermost thoughts. There had been nights that I'd awakened, and lying in my bed, in the dark, I'd seen a light. From the back of my eye came a flickering light to cast shadows on the walls of my memory.

Little by little, each night the light had grown brighter—until I could see that in the depths of my soul, I wasn't alone. There in my dream, in the flickering light of a fireplace, sat Grandpa. I could see him, plain as lightning during a thunderstorm—his small form resting in the chair he had whittled one cold winter, his hands resting on his cane. Near him, on his tree-trunk table, was his checkerboard—the checkerboard he had used to entertain me, especially on rainy days.

Night after night, the dream returned, until one night, he finally began to speak to me. His dark eyes stared deep into my own, as he told me to write it down—write it all down. He wanted me to tell all the stories that he had once told me.

At first, I was frightened. I tried to turn away. I could not.

His image drew closer still, and again he spoke, "Tell it all—you are my voice."

I began to cry, "Oh, Grandpa! Tell me how!"

"Go back to the beginning. Start from the beginning," he said.

Well, here I am—topping the mountain where it all began.

The once worn path is now covered with brush, tangled grapevines, and overgrown weeds. I watch the side of the trail carefully, for a sudden movement in the grass could foretell the lurking of a rattlesnake.

Now, at the top, I walk on level ground and large flat rocks. In the past, wagons, horses, and logging trucks had used this narrow road. Life had been scattered about on this land as abundantly as life is now scattered down on the river bottom.

Once this mountain had belonged to my grandparents, Tom and Retter Ammons. They had cultivated life and love on one hundred and eighty-six acres of mountain land.

Boughs of heavy-leafed laurel touch my shoulders as I make my way forward. Ahead is an old log bridge that crosses Grassy Creek. I test the log gingerly, and then cross over, the thrill of an old memory awaiting me on the other side.

The path now is covered with decaying chips of wood. Laughing, I remember that Grandpa cut wood for the fireplace in this very spot. Stooping, I retrieve a chip—it smells of cedar.

A rock wall begins to my left, and directly across from the wall are fragments of red, yellow, and pink tucked in among the weeds. A strand of golden dahlias testified to what is left of Grandma's flower garden. Bumblebees dance in the fresh air, changing partners in the dusty pollen—then fly, heavily laden, to their mortared nest in the old chimney.

Turning the corner, I stop and I look. My heart is full at the sight of the cabin that once housed a family of eleven. The frame still stands, but two of the walls and the roof have fallen in, and the floorboards have decayed.

I stand in the open doorway, looking over the fallen door, and see unmistakable evidence of a long-ago life.

There's a broken mirror hanging on what's left of a wall in the bedroom; there's a rusted tin of Prince Albert tobacco on the mantle; there are pages from a Sears and Roebuck catalog, yellowed with age, covering most of one standing wall; there are blackened river rocks from the fireplace still intact—and Grandpa's handmade chair still sits beside the fireplace.

Grandpa's chair!

I can feel my eyes grow large with expectation and my skin begin to tingle. But no one is there. I had almost expected to see grandpa waiting to greet me.

I was only a child when I sat on his knee before this very fireplace on cold wintry nights. It had been during these nights that he had told me almost all the tales of his and Grandma's early life together on the mountain. It was as if each word had found its own place somewhere in my mind, and had been stored away until it was time for me to say it.

Standing here in the doorway, for a moment I go back in time, to the sights and sounds of the late 1800's—to the time when Grandma first met Grandpa.

I shiver! Shadows roam this cabin—the cabin that is almost no more, whispering to me that time is not gone forever—it is only waiting.

The wind whistles through the pines outside, a few brown needles dropping on the fallen, rusted tin roof.

Once again, I look at the old chair. I wonder if I can sit in it.

Slowly, I maneuver my way across the decayed floor and sit in Grandpa's chair. There's a musty smell, and the bark of the white oak squeaks with age—but the crisscrossed strips hold my weight. I rest my feet on the hearth of the fireplace.

Grandpa is here—I can feel his presence. He's within me, warm and gentle.

The words are ready now.

And so, the story begins . . .

CHAPTER ONE

The Beginning

"Papa, kin I have some cornbread and buttermilk?" said Retter.

Absorbed in finding his tobacco on the shelf high on the wall near the wood stove, the father didn't notice the child as she stood below him.

A young man, smiling softly, was sitting at the supper table. He watched the little girl with amusement.

The child was five years old, she had long dark hair that hung in ringlets, and she was wearing a light woolen dress that almost reached the floor. A white cotton apron covered the top of the dark blue dress.

The young man was fascinated with the little beauty.

"Papa! Papa! Please, kin I have some CORNBREAD AND BUTTERMILK!"

The pleading grew louder as she tugged at her father's pant leg, bending her head back as far as possible, trying to see her father's face.

Having found his tobacco, Jim Coggins looked down at his youngest daughter, Retter.

"Shore, you kin help yoreself, chile."

Jim Coggins sat down at the table, and pulling his pipe out of his shirt pocket, began to fill the bowl with tobacco.

"But, Papa! I cain't reach it. It's way up on top of the stove!"

The young man sitting at the table opposite her father smiled at Retter. "Sit still, Mr. Coggins," he said, "I'll help her, and fill our coffee cups whilst I'm at it."

The young man was tall, with dark wavy hair falling over the collar of his shirt. His worn woolen pants were tucked into his boots, and he wore red suspenders in place of a belt.

As he reached for the cornbread in the warmer of the wood stove, the muscles in his shoulders tightened against his shirt. There was the calm of the mountains in his movements.

Retter watched this man with awe in her eyes. Her papa had called him Tom. She had never seen him until tonight. Before she came into the room, she had peeped at him through a crack in the door. Whoever he was, she knew that she liked him—liked him very much.

Tom brought the cornbread and the coffeepot to the table. As he filled two cups, the steam rising from the hot coffee forced him to lean to the side, closer to Retter. His eyes met hers, and he grinned, then winked at her. She blushed.

"Jest a minute. I'll fetch some buttermilk," he said.

Tom put the porcelain coffeepot back on the stove. Then, getting a glass out of the cupboard, he went to the table near the door, and filled the glass with buttermilk.

With long steps he crossed the wooden floor and then sat down at the table.

"Come on over here, sweetheart, and sit with me."

Her hands linked behind her back, Retter slowly edged her way over to his side, smiling timidly.

With large strong hands, Tom swung Retter up on his knee.

Jim Coggins watched with smiling eyes as the young man broke off a piece of cornbread and gave it to Retter. Her large hazel eyes were fixed on Tom's face.

"Thank you, sir," she said.

Tom laughed and began to talk to her father. Retter suppressed a longing to touch his face. She could sense the kindness in this man. He was like her papa, warm and caring.

Slowly, Retter ate the cornbread and drank her buttermilk. Then, as she wiped her mouth on her sleeve, she noticed the disapproving look on her father's face, and quickly rubbed the milk into the fabric of her dress.

Shaking his head, Jim smiled and turned his attention back

to his guest. He was interested in what this young man was saying.

"Daddy says that it's really pretty over there—jest like it is here. The mountains are big and the sky's real blue. I think the only difference is the rain. It shore does rain a lot, he says!" Tom's coffee was fast getting cold, so he set the cup down. He began to unconsciously run his hand down Retter's raven black hair.

The fire in the wood stove popped as the burning wood shifted, and the cold wind outside could be heard as a low undercurrent to the conversation going on at the table. Winter was on its way to the North Carolina mountains. The light from the oil lamp on the table cast shadows on the wooden slat walls covered with old newspaper clippings and pages out of the Sears and Roebuck catalog.

The conversation went on at length between the two men. Her stomach full, and with the warmth of the room, Retter began to get sleepy. Without realizing it, she slumped over onto Tom's chest, her eyes closing.

Tom, hesitating in his conversation, glanced down at the dark head against his shoulder. Outside, in the black of the night came the distant cry of a wildcat. He put his arm around the child.

"Tom, when are you gonna leave?" Jim asked as he leaned forward to tap his pipe on the battered lid he used for an ashtray.

"Soon. More than likely, tomorrow. I'm gonna hitch a ride to Asheville and catch the west bound. The snow ain't too far off now."

"Wish I was going, too!" said Jim, looking at the sleeping little girl across from him. "But, with my family and all, I jest cain't see my way clear."

Following the gaze of the man across from him, Tom looked down at Retter again. He understood.

"Wal, Mr. Coggins, I git your point. Yore family's mighty important. But I'm only twenty years old, and I have a lot of seeing to do before I settle down."

"Yep—you got the right idea. This here land's big! A feller

could jest git lost in it. I dreamed on it once myself." Jim leaned back in his chair and relit his pipe. His mind began to wander. Puffing absently, he lost himself in his thoughts.

The light from the lamp flickered, growing a little dim. The oil must be getting low, Tom thought.

Tom had come to visit his friend tonight to talk about his job at the lumber camp. Jim had told him that the work was finished for the winter. He decided then that it was time for him to join his folks in the state of Washington. He'd been away from them too long. At least he would visit them, and see part of these United States. Maybe he'd travel around a little before settling down. Nothing was holding him here.

Tom, moving his chair back, startled Jim out of his thoughts.

"Mr. Coggins, I'm much obliged fer all the help you gave me these months since Momma and Daddy left. But, I'm going tomorrow fer sure and fer certain. My mind's made up!"

Jim nodded his head as Tom spoke. He could see the gleam in the boy's eyes. "Okay, my boy, lessus git a good night's sleep, and I'll help git you ready in the morning." Jim rose slowly from his chair, his work-worn hands on the table, steadying him as he stood.

"Your back still bad, Mr. Coggins?" Tom asked as he saw the older man's look.

"Fair to middlin', Tom. Warn't fer Retter there, I'd feel it more than I do. She's jest a young'un, but she seems to have a way with her hands. She likes to take care of her old Pop!"

Laying his pipe down on the table, Jim walked over to the water bucket, drew the dipper full of spring water, and drank deeply. Then with a spark in his eyes, he turned to Tom, saying, "Want a good strong snort, Tom? Got a bottle in the shed."

Tom got up shaking his head, shifting Retter so that she lay with her head on his shoulder.

"No, sir! There's time for that later on. Jest now, I think I'll turn in."

Retter stirred, beginning to wake.

"Yore right, yore right, son." Jim moved closer to Tom, reaching for his daughter. "Retter, let's go now, time fer bed."

"No! Let me be!" came the muffled cry. Retter clung to Tom: her sleep-filled eyes looked up pleadingly at him. "No, Papa, I want to stay here!"

"That's okay, pretty little lady," Tom said. "I'll still be here in the morning to say good-bye before I leave."

"Please don't go." Retter's arms went around Tom's neck as she buried her face against his shoulder.

Tom grinned at Jim over the top of her head, as he removed her arms from around his neck.

"I gotta go, Retter. But, I'll tell you what! Someday—sooner than you think—I'll be back!" Tom said, smiling broadly. "I'll jest come back and . . . make you my sweetheart forever!"

Retter's heart pounded at these words! "You will? You'll be my very own sweetheart?"

"Yep—why, I jest might even marry you!"

The little girl's eyes were bright as he hugged her, and kissed her on the cheek. Then Tom placed her in Jim's waiting arms. "Don't fergit, now. I'll be back," Tom smiled. He looked at Jim and nodded. "You've got a sweet little girl, Jim," he said.

Jim carried her off, smiling and shaking his head.

Big hazel eyes watched Tom from over strong shoulders—eyes that never left his face until her father turned the corner into the darkened hallway, and she could no longer see him.

She would long remember the handsome young man called Tom. He was coming back someday to marry her!

CHAPTER TWO

Coming Home

(The year is now 1908—nine years have passed.)

The valley below was wide, with balsams scattered abundantly here and there on the rhythmic flowing hills. Sunlight danced brilliantly on the waters of the Tuckasegee River as it wound its way through the middle of the valley.

Across the river, smoke was rising from the chimney of the weatherworn cabin nestled among a grove of fruit trees at the bottom of the hill. The colorful leaves of the fruit trees could be seen from a great distance, shining up in contrast to the green balsams.

In a pasture near the cabin grazed a few scattered cows, a horse, and a couple of spotted goats. The crowing of a rooster from the old barn behind the cabin broke the stillness of the morning.

Tom Ammons sat, slumped over slightly, on the saddle of his horse, gazing down at the scene below him. He inhaled deeply, drawing on his cigarette, as his horse stamped its front hooves, shaking its head. The breath from the horse's nostrils rose like steam in the crisp air.

It was early morning—the sun had just come up. Tom thought it must be close to milking time because the smoke from the chimney told him that someone was up.

Since Tom had no gloves, his hands were dry and cracked as he drew the fur collar of his heavy canvas coat closer around his chin. With these rough hands, he stroked the mustache that curved down on either side of his mouth.

It had been a long hard trip from Asheville, where his train ride on the Western North Carolina Railroad had ended. After purchasing his mount, he must have ridden fifty miles straight up and down these dense mountains on his way to this quiet cabin. But he had loved the ride through the bath of the autumn colors surrounding him. He was home!

As Tom sat there, his thoughts traveled back to the time he had left Jim Coggins' cabin just about this time—late fall—and had gone on to Washington to see his parents. The state had indeed been beautiful, and had reminded him of North Carolina, but it hadn't been the same.

The home of his mother and father in Washington had been small and crowded. With two brothers and two sisters, all younger than he, sleeping in the same room, Tom had felt hemmed in. Before the year had passed, he had reached his twenty-first birthday, and his long lanky frame had taken up a lot of room. Eventually he had moved out of the house into the barn, sleeping in the straw.

Then, a friend of his had coaxed Tom into going with him to the notorious town of New Orleans. Pushing aside the protests of his father, Tom left.

New Orleans was a river town, and full of a fast and loose life. Tom had joined right in—gambling on the riverboats, drinking, carousing with beautiful women—living from day to day.

Now that he was home, it seemed the past nine years of his life had flown by.

Straightening his back and shifting a little in the saddle, Tom brought his thoughts back to the purpose for his return to these mountains.

A few months back, he'd received a letter from his brother, Robert. Their father, Jim Ammons, had moved his family back to his old homestead in North Carolina. His health was still good, but the acreage was large, and since there were only the two of them to work the land, they needed him. There was no mention of Frank, his other brother, or of his two sisters.

"Tom," the letter said, "Daddy wants you to know he's

going to give you his land here at the old place, if you want it. All you have to do is come home."

Tom knew that his father was trying to get him away from his "lively" life in New Orleans, but this letter had been exactly what Tom had needed. Unknown to his father, he had been at a time in his life when he'd begun to realize that the people and things around him were things he had no love for. They were not real to him. Home and family began to draw him, pulling with gentle strings—strings that had never been broken.

The horse moved a little and snorted. A return neigh could be heard from the horse in the pasture below them. The horse began to paw at the pine needles covering the ground beneath him.

The stillness of the quiet beauty surrounding Tom seemed to give him inner strength. He'd forgotten this deep love in his soul for the tall mountains and the smell of the pines as he rode among them.

A door slammed!

Tom watched below with heightened interest, straining to catch a glimpse of his father or his brother.

Carrying a bucket in each hand, with a hat pulled down over his face, Tom's brother appeared and strode toward the spring near the rear of the cabin.

Urging the horse forward with a touch of his knees, Tom slowly began his descent, warm expectation filling him.

On his way back from the spring, both buckets full of cold water, Robert came around the corner of the house, and spied Tom and his horse. He stopped and watched intently as Tom reined in the horse and swung down.

As Tom slowly turned to face his brother, Robert began to think he recognized this tall rugged-looking man with the handlebar mustache.

"Hello, Robert. It's good to see you."

His mouth falling open, Robert set the buckets down and then, smiling broadly, began to hurry toward his brother. "Tom! Wal, I'll be!"

The two men threw their arms around each other, pounding each other's backs as they laughed. The homecoming had started out well.

"Wal, Tom! Yore a sight fer sore eyes! Damn good to see you!" Robert had one arm over Tom's shoulders as they began to walk toward the porch of the old cabin.

"Robert, are Daddy and Momma up and around the house yit? How are they doing?" Tom asked.

"Daddy's rheumatism has been acting up here lately. And Momma's been down in the back a mite, but they're fine now. They're in the kitchen. Momma jest baked some mouthwatering buttermilk biscuits, and Daddy's reading the Bible a bit before starting his chores."

"Robert, where's the girls? In yore letters, you never did talk about them. And where's Frank?"

They had reached the steps to the porch, and Tom stood with one foot on the bottom step as he looked down at the shorter man.

"Wal, both our sisters done got hitched back in Washington. They seem to be as happy as a grizzly bear with his paws crammed in a honey tree!"

Laughing, the two men came up on the old rickety porch.

"And Frank?" Tom asked, pausing just in front of the door.

"He's staying with Lillie fer a spell. Doing okay, I reckon. He's one that shore did like that Washington state."

"You know, Robert, it does feel good to be home! I've missed these here mountains more than I knowed."

Tom looked contentedly out over the vast valley before him. The sky was deep blue, with a scattering of puffy white clouds, while the mountains rose high and blue-green against the horizon.

"Come on in now, Tom. Say hello to Momma and Daddy."

Robert pulled a leather strap, lifting the small wooden bar that allowed the door to swing open, creaking softly. Tom followed his brother into the warmth of home.

At the kitchen table, with her back to the door, stood his mother. She was dishing out the fatback, fried golden brown, onto a plate. She was a small stocky woman with gray streaks in her hair and always a twinkle in her eyes. Her cotton dress was covered with a white apron.

Across from her sat his father, leaning forward, his head bowed over the open Bible lying on the table. Jim Ammons had white hair and was almost completely bald on top, but his bushy white beard made up for the lack of hair. His features were thin, and he looked even thinner because of the broadness of his shoulders. He wore overalls and a red and blue plaid shirt.

As the door opened, Tom's parents looked up at the two men who came in. Their faces broke into wide grins as they recognized their oldest son. The touch of a work-worn hand on Tom's back, the sweet kiss from his mother, and the tears that flowed down wrinkled cheeks were all signs to Tom that this was where he belonged.

Time flew. The family sat together, ate breakfast, drank coffee, and relived the past few years. An hour passed.

Suddenly, Jim exclaimed, "My God, I've not milked old Betsy yit!"

To the sound of scraping chairs, the men all stood up—chores had to be completed before any more talking could be done.

"Sit still, Tom. You've traveled a fer piece. Talk to Ma there. It'll be good fer you both. Robert'll take care of yore horse."

Jim took a dipper of spring water and rinsed out the two milk buckets that had been sitting on an old table near the wood stove. Opening the wooden window slat, he threw the water out the window.

Tom had reseated himself, taking another sip of coffee.

Reaching for his heavy coat hanging on the wall near the door, Jim said, "You shore do look different, Tom. Yore a full-growned man now!"

Tom laughed as he leaned back in the chair, his eyes on his father. "Wal, it's about time the calf growed into a bull!"

Jim smiled, and turned to leave, calling over his shoulder, "Robert, maybe you'd better slop them hogs, too!"

Robert got up and carried his plate and cup over to the half-filled dishpan on the table near the stove. Usually the men of the mountains left dishes to the womenfolk, but Robert had always been thoughtful of his mother, and helped her all he could.

"Tom, you've come home in good time fer the git-together tomorrow. Remember the harvest social down to the school house?" Robert began pulling his coat on as he spoke. "There's the prettiest little thing you've ever saw gonna be there—little Dovey Coggins!"

Robert was out the door with that last comment, lugging the table scraps in the pail that had sat underneath the window near the table.

Tom pondered Robert's last statement. Dovey Coggins? The name seemed familiar.

The quiet mother watched Tom's face as he was deep in thought. It was so nice to look at him, her oldest child. He looked so much like her Jim when she'd first met him. Jim hadn't been in the United States very long when they'd met. To her, a man from Ireland was a novelty, especially such a nice-looking one! Jim Ammons had been a dashing young man with a trade, a surveyor of land, and a farmer. Jim had made her very happy these many long years. She'd lost count of the number—it didn't matter anyway.

"Momma, do you know of a Dovey Coggins? Seems to me that I know the name, but it don't sound jest right. I do think I remember Jim Coggins had a daughter, but I thought her name was Retter."

"Yes, son. Jim Coggins does have girls. Dovey's about twenty years old, and Retter's around fourteen or so. Right nice girls, it appears to me."

Tom's thoughts then flashed back to that last night he'd spent in North Carolina, years ago. He smiled. In his mind, he could see a child being carried off to bed—with her big eyes watching him until she could no longer see him. He hadn't thought of her in ages.

The child vanished from his thoughts as Tom's mind drifted back to himself. He was twenty-nine years old now, and ready for a home of his own. Before now, in his travels, he'd become world-wise and had had no intention of ever settling down.

But now, all that had changed. He was home to stay. Tomorrow he would go down to the sawmill at Tuckasegee Valley, and try for a job for the winter months.

Yes, and maybe he would go to that social at the schoolhouse. Dovey seemed just the right age for him, and just maybe the cards would be stacked in his favor.

A few mountains over, in another log cabin, sat another mother with her daughter. The daughter held a blue cotton dress in her lap as she talked to her dark-haired mother.

"What do you think, Ma? Do I need to do more to it?

"No, Dovey, it's fine. By the way, where's yore sister?"

"Don't know jest what yore gonna do with that girl, Ma. She's riding that ole smelly goat agin! I told her to git her dress mended, but no! Off she went with that goat!"

"My land! Fourteen years old, and still flittering around! She's shore gonna be a handful fer some pore feller someday. OH! MY GOD, look at that!" exclaimed the mother.

There stood Retter in the doorway, mud from top to bottom, a wide grin on her face. Dirty water dripped from the tail of her dress into a puddle on the floor.

"Ma, Henry threw me, and I rolled down the hill into the hog trough."

"Retter, git that dress off'n you this minute! What will I do with you? Oh, my Lord! Dovey, what will I do with yore sister?"

"It's okay, Ma! I'm gonna git washed up in the creek. I'll even wash my hair! I'm fixing to be ready to go to that social tomorrow. You wait and see—I'll fix up, Ma!"

Off skipped the tall, lanky mess of a girl, trailing mud and water behind her.

The two women at the table looked at each other, shaking their heads.

CHAPTER THREE

The Social

Retter was shivering. The water in the creek had been icy cold. After her escapade with Henry, the goat, she'd bathed in the creek, and had half frozen to death!

As she sat shivering on the edge of her bed, she gazed at her reflection in the cracked mirror that hung on the wall, and ran her fingers through her long wet hair. Then, taking the mirror down from the wall, and covering herself with a worn quilt, she huddled against the iron bed post. The face looking back at her in the cracked mirror was fair, she thought. Her young, soft ivory skin was blemish free and smooth. Her nose was straight, and her mouth was full and promising. But it was her wide hazel eyes that intrigued her.

At this particular moment, the hazel eyes reflected a question—what would she wear to the harvest social tomorrow night? Retter had only two dresses. The one she had just taken off was out of the question, and the other one was too short.

During the recent months, she had grown at least two extra inches, and nothing seemed to fit anymore. Her mother hadn't noticed the changes that were taking place in her daughter, for the canning season had just passed, and the work had been heavy from sunup until sundown. Harvesting the crops had taken all her parents' time and attention. Retter had been left to help when needed, and to explore the mountains at other times—when she could slip away.

Exploring the mountains was an education in itself. Without telling anyone, Retter had found a good and reliable friend in the deep dark valley over near Cherry Gap. She called him Charlie, because she could not pronounce his Cherokee Indian name, Cooweesucoowee.

When she'd found him that day, he'd been digging up the roots of a plant. She had silently walked upon him, and had watched him from afar—until he had stopped what he was doing and looked directly at her. Promptly, Retter had asked him what he was doing, and if she could learn it too. She had been without fear, and she tried to show the Indian her sincerity. He was old and lonely, and something seemed to tell her that here was someone special. They had become instant friends.

The Cherokee lived alone in a cave, and nature provided him with all of his needs. As time went on Retter grew to love the old Indian, and realized how wise and mystic he was. He became her teacher, showing her the medicine of the Indian. Retter learned fast and willingly.

And as Charlie spent more time with the girl, the Indian silently watched her with wonder. She was a child who seemed to be old beyond her years. Charlie's gaze would follow Retter whenever they were together, a quiet smile lighting the darkness of his thoughts. Someday he would tell the little girl the secret he carried deep within him—someday when she was old enough to understand.

Fascinated by Charlie's knowledge of the herbs of the forest, Retter watched and learned and soon grew to be adept at the art. The special talent had helped her lack of confidence.

Now, as Retter stared at the reflection in the mirror, her emotions were mixed. Her sister was twenty years old and a tiny slip of a girl, quite lovely, and would make some man a perfect wife, but Dovey had been sick for a long time and hadn't gone out much in the last few years. Thus her mother thought it was time that Dovey found herself a husband and gave her some grandchildren. She knew her mother's favorite was Dovey.

Retter told herself it didn't matter, that she could take care of herself, but deep down inside, she did feel hurt.

Her two older brothers, Sam and Elik, were off working with cabbage farmers, so they were no help to Retter. If it hadn't been for John, her youngest brother, and her papa, she'd have felt even more alone.

John and Retter were only a year apart, and did just about everything together. Her only secret from John was Charlie. She told no one about her bond with this noble Cherokee.

Her papa was not only her father, but also her friend. In the cold evenings, they would sit together in front of the fireplace, he in his rocker with his sweet-smelling pipe, and she at his feet, saying little—just being together. That was one of the warmest parts of her life.

"Retter! What are you doing?" Her mother stood looking at her with raised eyebrows, her hands on her hips.

Startled at the abrupt interruption of her thoughts, Retter was slow in answering.

"Retter! Do you hear me?" Her mother's voice grew louder.

"Yes, Ma. I'm jest a bit cold. I washed my hair in the creek." Retter drew the quilt closer around her, continuing, "Ma, kin I ask you something?"

Her mother, her face relaxing, walked over to the bed, and smoothing back Retter's wet hair, she answered, "Don't catch yore death of cold, now. What do you want to ask me?"

"Ma, I need a new dress fer the social. That pok-e-dot dress is too short fer me! I haven't asked fer anyting fer quite a spell. Please, Ma?"

There was no immediate answer from her mother. Instead she was gazing at her youngest daughter with something like surprise on her face. Stepping forward, her mother took Retter's face in her hand and looked at the budding of a strikingly attractive young lady.

"My goodness, chile! My baby's most growed! The way you ride Henry around, I hadn't noticed that there wuz such a pretty thing under them chile's clothes!" Her mother was suddenly smiling. "Wal, I guess I'd better get busy—now that I have two pretty girls to sew fer!"

She began to rummage around in an old chest as she spoke, never seeing the glorious look of happiness on her youngest daughter's face.

Her mother did care after all! That meant more to her than any dress. Retter hugged her knees to her chest with happiness as she watched her mother fling clothes out of the chest. These dresses were her mother's and her sister's—ones they no longer wore. That didn't matter to Retter. Her mother would make the clothes fit.

"Wal, now! Here's one I could let the bottom out . . . it'll see many a day of wearing yet. What do you think, Retter?"

"I like it! I'm much obliged fer it, Ma," said Retter.

"Stand up, Retter, and let me see," her mother said.

Retter dropped the quilt and stood before her mother in her petticoat.

The dress was a faded red, princess-style, with the waistline going down in a "v" in the front and back. As her mother held it up to her, the musty smell filled Retter's nose. The dress had been stored for quite awhile. But even though it was old and faded, the color brought out the darkness of Retter's long hair and her ivory complexion.

"This one is jest the thing, Retter. You're lovely!" Her mother hugged her, dress and all. Tears began to form in her mother's eyes as she stood back again and looked at her daughter. "Honey, you're so tall now, and skinny as a rail. You put me in mind of my mother. You have her dark hair and brown skin." As she laid the dress over her arm, she took a wadded-up handkerchief out of her apron pocket, and wiped her eyes. "I'll git to sewing now—not much time before tomorrow gits here."

As her mother hurried out of the room, Retter sank to the bed, the quilt again wrapped around her. She was no longer shivering. The social was gone from her mind. She was marveling at the love she had seen on her mother's face. Looking back at the antics she'd pulled, she began to understand the reason she had been so wrong in her estimation of her mother's feelings.

You can't show love to someone who continually scares you—by falling out of an oak tree, by crying in pain from eating too many green apples, by losing your only pair of shoes while wading in quicksand, even if you were only curious—and by bringing home a sick-looking bat!

Retter began to laugh, her thoughts racing. What a handful she had been. Well, things were going to change now—she was growing up! Life around the Coggins' cabin was going to be as dull as Aunt Eller's yearly visit! And that was dull!

Jumping up, Retter found her only other dress, and pulled it over her head. It was even tight through her shoulders, but she squirmed and tugged at the dress until she had adjusted it as well as possible, and then pulled her woolen socks up over the slender calves of her long legs.

The new hightop shoes her papa had gotten her were still splattered with mud, so she wiped them with the tail of the discarded muddy dress. The pieces of caked mud fell around her on the floor. With her hand down inside her shoe, she held it up, gazing at her blurred image in the toe of the shoe, saying aloud, "Retter, tomorrow maybe you'll see him—tall, dark and handsome. Yore one and only—and he'll carry you off to some place where you'll live happily ever after!"

She laughed again softly, and then, with a wistful look, she sighed, "Shucks! Who'd want the likes of me!"

It had been a good day for Tom Ammons. The foreman at the sawmill down in Tuckasegee Valley was happy to see him, and had hired him on the spot. He would start work on Monday morning. It seemed as if his luck was changing for the better.

On his way back from the sawmill, Tom had hauled a load of rough-cut boards, and had begun work on the old barn as soon as he'd arrived home. The barn had not been repaired in quite awhile, and if left untended, the broken rotting boards of the stalls would not keep the snow out this winter. He'd been working for a couple of hours, and had almost two complete stalls patched. It was exhilarating.

The bawling of the milk cows coming down the lane toward the barn could be heard as he finished nailing the last board of the stall. It was feeding time.

Going over to the door, Tom pushed it open to allow the cows to come into the barn. Creaking loudly, the door banged against the outside wall of the barn.

Through the double doors came three cows and a calf, nudging each other and Tom as they filed into their stalls.

He climbed up into the loft, and tossed hay down to the cows. As they began to chew, Tom climbed halfway down the ladder, and jumped the rest of the way. Talking softly to the cattle, he filled their feed boxes on the far wall.

"Wal, Tom. You've got it all set up fer me, I see. Much obliged, son!" said Jim Ammons as he came in with his milk pails. "You'd better git on up to the house. Robert's about ready fer that git-together down to the schoolhouse. I'll do the rest here. Now, git!" Laughing, Jim hit his son on the seat of his pants with one of the empty milk buckets. "Have a good time with the gals at the social," he called after Tom.

Tom was brushing straw off his pant legs as he left the barn, shaking his head and grinning. He opened the door to the kitchen. As usual, his mother was standing at the cookstove. "Momma, you got a bar of soap? I need to wash up a bit."

"Look there in the cabinet, beneath the jar of dried beans." She kept on stirring her stew as she nodded her head in the direction of the cabinet near the door.

"Momma, I'll be back directly. I'm gonna fix up fer some pretty little thing!" Tom laughingly teased his mother as he went out the door carrying a bar of lye soap and an old worn towel.

"Good idea, Tom. You should be thinking on gittin' hitched, anyways." Her voice trailed off as Tom softly closed the door on his way out.

Hitched! Well, it wouldn't be too bad to have someone soft and sweet at home. Tom grinned at the thought. He was sure looking forward to the dance tonight.

A little while later, two sons stood for their mother's inspection. The short woman looked up at them with pride. Their hair was slicked back, and their worn woolen coats were covering white shirts with black ribbon ties. Tom was taller than his brother, and his handlebar mustache gave him a much older look, even though he was only four years older than his brother.

"Sons, you both look right nice," their mother smiled her approval. "Have a good time."

She watched them go with a wistful look. Her days of dancing were over.

Twice a year, the mountain people had a social—once in the spring and then again in the fall. Each time, they came out in force, happy to see one another and catch up on all the happenings. This one was no exception. There were horses, wagons, and buggies all over the grounds around the small schoolhouse. Children of all ages ran hither and yon, in among, and in between the wagons and buggies, their happy expressions glowing.

Tom and Robert Ammons reined their horses in at the hitching rail and swung down.

"There's a right nice crowd already, Tom," said Robert as he looked around.

"I spect yo're right, Robert. Do you see the Coggins family anywhere yet?"

"No, I shore don't. I reckon we showed up a mite early. Lessus go check out that there—uh, lemonade jar." Robert was laughing as he led the way toward the schoolhouse.

"Howdy! Wal, looka here! DAMN! If'n it ain't Tom Ammons! FELLERS! Come shake old Tom's hand!"

"Where you been fer so long, Tom?"

Tom was besieged with well-wishers and old friends, all talking at the same time. He had been a popular boy in the mountains before he left.

Robert slipped away from the crowd, and went directly to

the lemonade bowl. As he dipped a cupful out with the ladle, he glanced up, and his gaze fell on Dovey Coggins as she walked through the door. Her mother had come with her, and had followed her through the doorway.

Dressed all in blue, Dovey was a vision. All around him, Robert heard favorable comments, and almost immediately she was surrounded by boys, all clamoring for her attention.

Dovey was flattered by all the attention she was getting, but as her eyes flitted around the room, she spied Tom talking among his friends. She immediately made up her mind—the tall one with the mustache was the one she wanted, and Dovey usually got what she wanted.

Just then, Tom also spied Dovey. Well, he thought, that's a pretty one. She had to be the one Robert had called Dovey. Excusing himself from his friends, Tom walked over to Robert.

"Robert, won't you help me make the acquaintance of Miss Coggins over there."

Dragging his feet a little, Robert reluctantly led the way over to Dovey's side. Some of the neighbor girls were now talking to her, but her eyes still followed Tom, until the Ammons boys got close. Then she pretended not to notice him.

"Dovey . . . Dovey! I want you to meet my brother, Tom," Robert said as they came up to her.

"Wal, I shore would like to make his acquaintance, Robert." Dovey's voice was overly sweet, and she coyly smiled in Tom's direction. "It's a great pleasure to meet you." She held out one hand to Tom, and patted her hair with the other. Dovey's eyes traveled up to his sun-tanned face as her small hand was lost in his. It had been a long time since any man had held her attention for any length of time. This one seemed promising. Again, she smiled. "You musta jest come home, Tom. I don't call to mind ever seeing you before now," came the sweet voice of Dovey.

Tom's eyes twinkled. He'd met all kinds of women in his travels, and could just about read by their talk and actions what they had in mind. Dovey liked him, he could tell, and was flirting openly with him. He figured he might as well go along with the game—she was pretty and he liked her.

"No, if'n I'd met you before, Dovey, I'd shore have remembered it! I have a fondness fer pretty faces."

Dovey's face lit up with Tom's compliment. "Why, thank you, Tom Ammons! You do have a way with words," said Dovey as she moved toward the edge of the crowd—Tom walking beside her, and Robert following. Over her shoulder she called back to Robert, "Robert, why didn't you tell me about your good-looking brother here?"

"I shore did tell you about him, Dovey! Jest last week when I seen you over to Nickelson's store. I told you he wuz comin' home soon." Robert was talking too fast, trying to keep Dovey's attention. But it didn't work. She hadn't even looked at him as she'd spoken. Her eyes still watched Tom, and she hardly even heard Robert's stammering voice.

"Come to think about it, I guess you did tell me, Robert," she said absently. Then, placing her hand on Tom's arm, she swung her dress out a little and tilted her head. "Oh, Tom, you are gonna dance with me tonight, ain't you? I do feel like tapping my feet!"

"Why shore, I am! Jest try to keep me from it! I ain't been to a good old timey social in a month of Sundays! It'll be a pleasure to swing you about!"

As he spoke, Tom had suddenly remembered that Robert had told him that Dovey hadn't been able to come to the socials the last few times because of illness. The two of them had something in common then—this was their catching-up night.

Laughing aloud, Tom caught Dovey's hands in his and swung her around. "Yup! We'll cut a rug, Dovey!"

There were pink spots in Dovey's cheeks as she laughed along with Tom, and leaned against his arm.

Across the room from the young couple, two dark eyes watched Dovey intently. The man who stared was tall, with a dark beard that covered most of his face. He was backed up against the wall of the schoolhouse, his hands in his pockets.

From the time Dovey had entered the room, his eyes had never strayed from her. There was no emotion visible on the man's face—only his dark eyes following Dovey's every movement.

Then, as Tom twirled Dovey about, the dark eyes left her to settle on Tom. The muscles underneath his jacket seemed to tense—he moved involuntarily away from the wall—then, glancing around, he slowly settled back, swallowing his jealousy. His burning eyes returned to rest upon Dovey's pretty face. He relaxed.

"Tom, I'd be much obliged if'n you'd fetch me a glass of lemonade," Dovey was saying, still flirting with her eyes.

Robert watched the game that Dovey and Tom were playing. He thought to himself that Tom better watch out, she looked like she'd already set her cap for him. Nor did Robert like the flirting ways Dovey was displaying. She had never acted this way to him. He stood back and really looked at his brother. Tom was tall and good-looking. Also he was older, and there was a confident air about him. Well, that must be it. Robert himself had never been very confident. For a minute, he felt a twinge of jealousy, but then, as Tom smiled at him, it vanished. Tom was his brother—that was all that mattered.

The small talk between Tom and Dovey continued as Robert moved farther away from them. Then, from the corner of his eye, he caught sight of something that almost made him gasp! Without a sound, another girl had come into the room, a tall slender form dressed in red. With dark hair that hung down almost to her waist, her striking beauty was lost to all in the room, except Robert, for the present. She stood back from everyone, in the shadows. There was a graceful, pleasing look about her.

Her eyes were on Dovey and Tom, a small smile lighting her face. She seemed to be happy seeing them together. Suddenly, her gaze fell upon Robert, and as he stood there with his mouth partially open, she smiled again and beckoned to him.

Without even thinking, he moved as fast as he could to get

to her side. She was as tall as he, and her big hazel eyes twinkled as she saw his expression.

"Robert, the flies are a-waiting to fly right inside yore mouth, if'n yo're not careful!" Retter was enjoying Robert's bewildered condition. For a minute, he still wasn't sure if he was seeing right.

"Uh—Retter? It cain't be! No, it jest cain't be!" Robert pulled a handkerchief from his pocket and wiped his forehead.

"Yes, it kin, Robert Ammons! I ain't seen you fer a coon's age. I growed some since then." Retter laid her hand on Robert's arm, and laughed softly as she looked into his eyes, still full of questions.

"I'm so glad to see you, Robert," she continued. "You still have Henry's kids? Yore taking care of them, ain't you?"

Robert suddenly laughed also—this was really his friend, Retter! What a change had taken place. With growing awe, Robert took in her smooth skin, straight nose, and pretty mouth. He knew Retter to be a plucky-type, and just a friend—but now! A new feeling for her began to grow inside him. Tom had to meet her!

"Come on, Retter. I want you to meet my brother, Tom. He just come back from New Orleans. He's talking to Dovey over there."

Retter's face showed surprise, shock, and then excitement as she realized just who this was—Tom Ammons! She would never forget him!

Catching Retter by the hand, Robert almost pulled her across the room to where Tom and Dovey still stood in conversation.

"Tom! Looky here! This is Dovey's sister, Retter."

Tom didn't look up immediately. He seemed to be engrossed in Dovey's conversation. Slowly, his gaze came up and then—with a jolt—Tom once again looked into the eyes of Retter. Their eyes held.

Retter was having trouble breathing; deep inside her chest her heart was pounding. This was the man who had promised a little girl that he'd come back and marry . . . such a long time ago. He looked different, so much older than she remembered. She couldn't speak, but neither did he.

As the two stared at each other, Retter lost track of everyone else around her. Something began to happen between the two.

Dovey could see this, and so could Robert. With a smile, Robert winked at Dovey. Serves her right, he thought.

Suddenly, a fiddler struck up the first dance. Grabbing Tom's arm, Dovey pulled him out onto the dance floor. He stumbled a little, his eyes still on Retter—lovely Retter in the red dress!

Not a word had been spoken between them.

With a sinking feeling in her stomach, Retter watched Dovey pull Tom away. He hadn't spoken to her at all! He didn't remember her! Tears filled her eyes, and turning abruptly, she ran from the schoolhouse. She had been right! Who would want the likes of her!

The darkness of the night reached out and swallowed her.

CHAPTER FOUR

Dovey's Mistake

Over Dovey's shoulder Tom watched Retter disappear through the door. His heart pounded. He shook his head—the music was too loud. It seemed that from out of nowhere had come a feeling that had been there all along. He could hear Dovey's voice vaguely, talking fast—her face swimming in front of him.

He spoke not a word to Dovey as he tried to shake this unusual feeling. Yet, the dark eyes of Retter kept flashing in front of him—no matter where he looked, he could see them. His mind began telling him that he was crazy—feeling this way, when he'd just met the girl. But he couldn't help himself. Gone was the feeling of playful flirtation he'd experienced with Dovey. He began to seriously wish he was free from this dance—he longed to hurry after Retter, and became more and more uncomfortable.

Dovey soon quit her chatter, and grew quiet and thoughtful also, but her eyes remained on Tom's face. She watched him glance more than once to the open doorway. Dovey couldn't fathom why Tom had lost interest in her. Why would he react the way he had upon seeing her baby sister? Retter was striking, in a funny kind of way, but she was much too young for this tall man.

Sighing, Dovey felt sad as she realized that whatever she and Tom might have had together was gone.

The dance ended. Tom looked down at Dovey to speak, but before he could say anything, Robert rushed up.

"Tom! Retter's mother asked one of us to git word to the girl's daddy about Retter leaving the schoolhouse. She's right worried about her!"

"I'll go, Robert. Why don't you stay with Dovey whilst I ride over to the Coggins' house." Tom started to move away as he spoke, then stopped and came back up to Dovey. Her white face stared at him.

"Dovey," began Tom, "I thank you fer the dance. I surely did have a hankering to show you a good time tonight. I hope you understand." Tom was ill at ease and shifted his weight from foot to foot.

Dovey smiled through tight lips. "Yes, I did enjoy our one dance, and I'll wait fer our next one. You hurry back now, you hear!"

Feeling cold and hot at the same time, Tom turned on his heel and walked over to Mrs. Coggins. Then, after a few minutes of conversation with her, he strode out the same door Retter had sped through, muttering to himself as he went, "Mabbe I kin catch up to her . . . "

Robert stood with Dovey watching Tom leave. The music began again, yet the two made no move to dance. Both seemed to be lost in their own thoughts.

Suddenly, a large shadow covered Dovey, startling her. Slowly she looked up into two staring dark eyes. The man was immense to Dovey, and since the oil light was to his back, she couldn't make out distinct features. When he spoke, his voice was gruff and emotionless.

"Dance?"

Dovey looked questioningly from him to Robert. The smaller man shrugged his shoulders and opened his eyes wide in another question. Not getting the reaction she wanted, Dovey's pride rose inside her, and anger shone in her eyes as they snapped at Robert. Then, turning to the stranger, there was a changed expression as she spoke—it was as if honey would melt on her tongue.

"Why, yes indeed, sir! I shore would like to dance with you. My! But yo're a big one, ain't you?"

Dovey's head was held high as her stubbornness shone through. Without another glance at Robert, she danced off, chattering away.

Robert looked after the couple, and then moved off the dance floor to a bench near the wall, close to the punch bowl. There was plenty of room on the bench, so he sat down and turned his gaze to the dancers. He watched the giant of a man, surprisingly light on his feet, dance with Dovey. From the expression on Dovey's face, Robert knew she was flirting again. He shook his head, and turned his eyes to glance around the room. He didn't see a soul he'd want to dance with. He felt drained—it seemed as if all the fun was gone from the evening.

Suddenly, there was a voice at his elbow, "Say, Robert Ammons, you wanta wet yore whistle?"

Robert turned to gaze at one of the Powell boys, who was looking at him with a crooked smile. Without hesitation, Robert rose, and ramming his hands in his pants pockets, he said firmly, "Joe! Jest lead the way!"

After her dance with the stranger, Dovey went from one partner to another. The disappointment of losing Tom still smoldered deep inside. It was seldom that she failed to get what she wanted, and tonight's failure hurt deeply. To hide this hurt, she had flirted even more than she'd intended, and with men she normally wouldn't have even noticed. One of these men was Joe Powell, who had led Robert off to receive his first drink of the night. Joe was usually a quiet backward boy, but after a few drinks, the vicious nature that hid deep inside him often easily came out, searching for a victim.

As the night wore on Joe decided that Dovey really wanted him, and he began to slowly, but surely, run all the other dancers away from her, until he had her all to himself. By the time Dovey had noticed what was happening, it was too late. She tried to pull away as the dance ended, but Joe only drew her closer. She could smell the strong liquor on the drunk man's breath as he leaned closer to her. They were standing close to the back door, with the flickering light too far away to help matters any. The darkness from the shadows of the dancers covered Joe's attempts at placing his hands in forbidden places. Dovey's small frame was no match for the long strong arms of the mountain man.

Trying desperately to get away from Joe, Dovey stomped him on his foot, and as he groaned and released his hold on her, she pushed away from him and darted out the back door. Using all her strength, she ran around the side of the building, and fell against the roughness of the bark on the logs, breathing deeply. Inside her stomach was a hard ball of fright.

Before she could catch her breath, there was a loud thrashing sound of running feet, and Joe was suddenly upon her. From the light of the moon, Dovey looked up and saw the anger in Joe's eyes. Her mind went blank as she stared at him.

"You little she-devil! Stomp my feet, will you!" Joe was beside himself as his voice grew louder. "I'll show you! You think yo're too good fer the likes of me! When I git through with you, no one will want you!"

As Dovey looked up into the wild man's face, fright turned into anger. She jumped away from the wall, pushing Joe off balance, and ran back the way she had come—back into the schoolhouse, yelling over her shoulder as she went, "You stupid no account jackass! Don't you ever touch me again!"

Behind her Dovey only heard one word, "Bitch!"

Inside, Dovey hurried over to where her mother sat, straightening her dress as she went. Her face was flushed, and her hair was beginning to fall in disarray around her face.

"Dovey! What on earth!" Her mother's surprised face matched her words.

"It's nothing, Momma! I wuz just dancing too hard. I'll jest sit here a spell, if'n you don't mind."

The calmness Dovey displayed was only on the surface. Inside, she was shaking. As she sat down beside her mother, she saw Joe come in, and watch her with cold hard anger. He made his way over until he stood at the end of the bench that Dovey and her mother occupied. Leaning back against the wall, he crossed his arms and waited.

Dovey's eyes searched the room, looking for Robert. He wasn't to be found. She began to think of the ride home through the tall dark pine trees, then looked at her mother, trying to decide what to do. From where she sat, she could see no one to whom she could turn.

Dovey began to reflect on her behavior during this night. She could see where she had made her mistake. If she got through this night she would know better next time.

Suddenly, Dovey felt the bench move underneath her. Glancing over toward the area where Joe had been standing, she saw him no longer standing, but sitting on the bench and inching his way toward her. He was grinning, showing discolored teeth, as he moved closer.

Fighting to keep her composure, Dovey swallowed, and gripped the edge of the bench. As far as Dovey could see, no one observed what was going on, and she was alone in her problem.

Joe was almost upon her as she opened her mouth to call her mother's name, when it happened.

One minute, Joe was breathing down her neck—the next, he was dangling from the huge hand of the young giant of a man Dovey had danced with earlier.

"This here jaybird bothering you, Miss?" came the gruff voice deep from within his bushy beard.

Dovey had never been so happy to see anyone in her whole life. Her head was bobbing affirmative so fast, more hair fell around her face.

"I'll take care of him fer you. Jest hold on fer a minute."

Joe's feet touched the floor only once or twice as the big man half-carried, half-dragged him out the back door.

Dovey watched with breathlessness and pounding heart, waiting for the man to come back inside. It was only minutes—then there he was—coming toward her.

This time the light was in her favor, and Dovey could observe the big man. She'd never seen anyone bigger, and the powerful way he walked intrigued her. All of a sudden, her heart was pounding again—but not from fear. She felt shy for the first time in her life. He stopped before her and held out his hand to her.

"Care to dance with me?"

Dovey never knew how she got to her feet, but she found herself minutes later in his arms and hardly breathing.

"My name's Henry—Henry Bridges. I'd like to come calling on you. Would you be agin it?" His voice seemed to engulf her.

"No, I would . . . wouldn't . . . " stammered Dovey. "I mean . . . I would be proud to have you come calling, Mr. Bridges."

The touch of the huge hands seemed to burn against her own.

"Henry . . . call me Henry. And don't worry about the feller I jest took outside. He won't bother you no more."

"What did you do to him . . . Henry?" questioned Dovey.

Henry laughed, creating a pleasant resounding noise in Dovey's ears, as her head rested against his chest. Drawing back a little, she looked up into the twinkling eyes of her new beau, and smiled questioningly.

"Wal, I jest squeezed him a little . . . and talked to him real serious with my fist! And he went off toward the river taking on something terrible."

Dovey laughed a little, and laid her head back on Henry's chest and sighed happily. Tom Ammons could run after Retter all he wanted, she thought—she had found her prince charming—right under her nose!

High above her, hidden from her view, the dark eyes of Henry Bridges had lost their laughter. It was as if a cloud had covered his momentary open expression. As the dance continued, the happy young girl was lost to the unexplainable change in this stranger that was her partner.

CHAPTER FIVE

The Promise

The light from the flickering fire cast shadows on Retter's sad face as she sat huddled against the cold wall of the cave. Around her shoulders was a tanned deerskin robe, which she gathered closer around her with her briar-scratched hands. The hem of her dress was covered in black burrs that had attached themselves during her wild dash from the dance at the schoolhouse. She sat staring into the fire, her thoughts on a night long ago—the night she first met Tom Ammons.

Across from Retter sat Charlie, gazing at her with concern, his white hair gleaming in the firelight. Tonight was the first time Charlie had ever seen Retter so sad and unhappy. The only way he could help her was to cover her cold arms with his deerhide, and wait for her to explain the reason for her unhappiness. So, he sat silent and uneasy.

The muffled cry of a mountain lion somewhere outside the cave could be heard, causing Retter to shiver. Charlie, turning his head slightly, listened to the sound. It was a sound of the night, talking to him.

Retter made no attempt to tell Charlie the reason for sudden entrance into his solitude. She couldn't really explain even to herself why she would react the way she had because of a man she hardly knew. There really was no sense in her feelings. She wondered why it meant so much to her that he would remember her. When she had found out that he was at the social, why did her heart carry on the way it had? She noticed the tall good-looking man standing with her sister, but hadn't recognized him to be Tom Ammons.

Then Robert had noticed her! From the look on his face, she'd been sure that he had liked the new Retter. That had pleased her. But, now, she was so unhappy! "Oh, Tom!" Retter thought, "why didn't you know me?"

Charlie rose quietly and walked with no sound over to the pile of wood stacked against the wall of the cave, and carried back a few small sticks of firewood. He slowly stacked the wood, criss-cross, onto the dying fire. The fire was placed close to the entrance, so the smoke would be drawn out the opening.

The wind had picked up, and could be heard whistling quietly. Popping, with sparks flying up, the dry wood caught fire, making the cave brighter momentarily.

The faraway look in Retter's eyes dimmed as she raised her face to look at her friend.

"Charlie, I'm so sad tonight," softly came Retter's voice. "I jest had to git away fer a spell. I'm much obliged fer yore welcome."

The Indian's eyes matched the sadness in his friend's eyes. "Retter hungry?" he asked.

"No, Charlie, thank you all the same."

She looked for a minute back into the fire, and then turned her face to Charlie, who had reseated himself on his bed of hides.

"Charlie, I have this here hurt inside my heart. It hurts so bad, I couldn't stay at the social tonight. This man I knew way back when I was a little thing, came home after a very long time. I know it seems far-fetched, but I waited all this time fer him to come back . . . and he never knew me a-tall. So, I run away up to yore cave. I wuz so cold, and I fell oncet or twicet. I wish he'd knowed me . . . " her voice trailed off as Retter gazed at Charlie through her tears.

The kindness in Charlie's face was evident as he leaned forward, saying, "Wind in trees cry! Big cat cry! Retter cry!"

Suddenly, the kindness was gone from Charlie's face; he

raised his fist in defiance as he spoke, his face deadly serious. "Charlie cut heart out white man!" he exclaimed.

For a moment, Retter stared at him. Then gasping, she said, "No, Charlie. Oh, no! You cain't do that! I'm fine! See, I'm smiling!" Straightening her shoulders nervously, Retter painted a false smile on her face. Then, rising to her feet, Retter drew the tanned deerhide close around her.

"I think I'll go home, Charlie. It's not such a big problem, anyway. Besides, I'm feeling loads better! I done fergot him already. Thank you fer the help."

With a blank look, Charlie watched her expression as she hurriedly prepared to leave.

"I'll bring this hide back tomorrow, Charlie. It's cold and dark outside. You mind walking a piece with me?"

Nodding, Charlie rose, and adjusting the knife in his belt, he followed Retter outside. With her back to Charlie, Retter never saw his amused smile.

The walk home had been silent. Retter was glad to see the light from the cabin as she approached. Telling Charlie good-night, she hurried into the welcome warmth of the kitchen, sighing in relief.

Her relief was short-lived, however.

There at the kitchen table sat Tom and her father, worried expressions on their faces.

Retter stopped short, her eyes wide, and slowly backed up against the door. She stood there, her hands behind her back, staring at the two men. The deerskin fell to the floor.

"Wal, Retter, jest where the dickin's you been?" the worried look of her father turned to anger. He stood up and leaned forward at the head of the table, his hands steadying him.

Tom sat still, gazing at Retter. She was a mess! Her hair was tangled and matted. Her arms and hands were scratched, and her dress was wrinkled and covered with burrs. Her pretty face was dirty, and there were tear trails in the dirt. As she stood there looking at first one and then the other, tears began to form again, and then slowly rolled down her cheeks.

Tom's heart went out to her! It was all he could do to keep from going to her and gathering her up in his arms.

"I'm sorry, Papa! I didn't know that I wuz a-worrying you." She spoke low and hesitantly, her eyes now downcast. She was so humiliated that Tom was seeing her in her present condition that she wanted to die right there in front of the two men.

"Wal, Retter, yore Ma's worried sick! She asked fer somebody to come looking fer you and to let me know you wuz gone from the schoolhouse. Tom here volunteered. We wuz jest set on going out to look fer you!"

As her father pushed back his chair, he was muttering, "Worry a person to death, these here young'uns!" Reaching for his coat, he continued, looking at Tom. "Tom, I'm much obliged fer all yore help tonight. Got one more favor to ask of you. Mind staying a bit with Retter whilst I go git the rest of my family?"

Tom cleared his throat as he answered, "No, sir. I'll keep a watch on her."

Retter's pride began to surface as she straightened up and spoke defiantly. "Papa! I kin take care of myself! I'm all growed now!"

"Retter, one more word from you, and you'll force me to take you out behind the smokehouse! Now be still!"

Her papa picked her up by her shoulders and set her to one side as he went out the door, kicking the deerhide aside. The door closed with a bang!

Tom and Retter were alone.

Slowly, she raised her head to where Tom sat. Their eyes met. Retter's emotions were so mixed up by now that she could hardly control herself. Her hands opened and closed nervously. Her first impulse was to run, but her feet seemed to be glued to the wooden floor.

As Tom looked at Retter, his heart was beating so hard he felt that she must hear it also! In all his twenty-nine years, he had never met anyone who affected him as much as this young darkhaired girl. He could see the rise and fall of her chest, and the desire to hold her close began to rise in him. Slowly, he started to compose himself, wanting to talk sensibly to her. He wanted to be very careful.

While Tom was readying himself, Retter's eyes grew wide with apprehension and fear.

"Retter, come sit here with me fer a spell." Tom spoke quietly as he gestured to a chair across from him.

Obediently, Retter moved to the chair he'd indicated. As she sat down, she rested her hands on the table, and then, with frightened eyes, she watched Tom's face.

"Retter, tonight I have a very serious thing to say. Seeing you, something good has come into my heart."

As Tom spoke, he reached over and picked up her hands and held them in his own. Retter stiffened a little with uncertainty, and trying to remove her hands, she said, "You've taken holt of my hands! What are you doing?"

Tom held her hands tighter, and started again. "Please, Retter, hold yore tongue a minute. I have something to say to you." Tom relaxed a little, and then smiled at the trembling girl, whose eyes grew wider as she stared at him.

"Retter, remember when I first met you? It wuz in this very room, nine years past. You were such a prettly little thing with big eyes." Tom's voice grew gentle and soft as he gazed at her.

Retter had forgotten everything by now except Tom. A deep warm feeling came stealing over her. She was beginning to think that he might feel as she did, and she didn't want to miss anything he said. Breathlessly, she waited for Tom to continue.

"There's fifteen years betwixt me and yoreself, Retter. And I'm here to tell you, I've been a wild one! But when I laid eyes on you tonight, I knew!" Tom's voice suddenly cracked with emotion, and he hung his head a moment. Then, raising his head and clearing his throat, he smiled again and continued softly. "I knew you were the one I wanted fer the rest of my life. How do you feel about that?"

With a wide smile, Retter said, "There never has been and never will be anybody fer me but Tom Ammons!"

With surprise, Tom straightened and stared at the young girl across from him. Then he rose with such force that the chair he was sitting in fell over in the floor.

Tom swallowed, then walked slowly around the table, and drew Retter into his arms and held her close. She was soft and warm.

Then, Tom tilted Retter's head back, and looked at her tear-stained, dirty face. He slowly leaned down and placed his lips on hers. His lips trembled with emotion as they seemed to sink into a deep well where there was no end.

Retter never knew how long the kiss lasted, but she would never forget it nor the feeling that grew in her soul.

With Retter's head pressed to his shoulder, and his big hand caressing her tangled hair, Tom had trouble believing that this was happening.

Suddenly, he swung Retter up in his arms, walked to her papa's chair at the head of the table and sat down, placing her on his lap. He held her to him as close as he could. She was so young, a rare treasure. Resting his chin against her shoulder, he said with emotion, "Retter, I told you a long time ago that I would come back someday. Do you remember?"

"Oh, yes, I remember!"

"You sat in my lap back then, too. I remember that I told you then I would come back and marry my little sweetheart." Tom paused, and then continued more softly, "Will you? Will you marry me someday, Retter?"

Snuggled up in his warm arms, her reply was muffled.

Tom tilted her head back again, so he could see her eyes, saying, "I cain't hear you, Retter."

"I SAID—it shore took you long enough to keep yore promise! I 'most got tired of waiting! My good years are a-wasting away!"

Her grin grew wider as Tom threw back his head and laughed loudly. He hugged her to himself fiercely.

Retter sighed with contentment and happiness, her heart resting on his, her arms around his neck, and her love in his pocket.

Outside the cabin, high in the North Carolina mountains, the wind in the trees cried. The big cat cried. But Retter Coggins didn't hear.

CHAPTER SIX

Charlie

The cat cried again. Charlie stopped to listen. It was closer this time.

The muscles in his arms grew tight as he readied himself to face this mountain lion. He waited and listened.

There began a prickly sensation at the base of his back. He knew there was a presence near him. Turning his head, he felt his long white hair pass over his shoulder, catching the gleam of the moon. His face now in the moonlight, the soft light caused the lines and creases of his skin to dissolve into a roadmap of age—but his eyes were alert and moved quickly to cover the surrounding area.

He could see nothing—and could hear nothing. He grew puzzled. There was something near him—but he didn't know what it was. He grew tense and mentally prepared himself for battle. Crouching, he withdrew the knife that had been sheathed to his side.

Then came a strange stillness. A light breeze began to blow, causing a rustling in the dried leaves. Slowly a light fog appeared out of nowhere. It drifted lightly before Charlie, the texture light and airy, looking as if it had been raked by the fingers of a giant hand. As leaves began falling here and there, Charlie stared—not believing what he was seeing. The fog began taking the shape of a man. Charlie had talked to spirits all his life, and now he believed that he was about to come face to face with one.

Straightening, Charlie still held his knife, but his hand

dropped to his side. The breeze died down—the night became still.

Charlie stared at the spirit before him, wonder consuming him as more and more details became clear.

The vision was that of an Indian chief in ceremonial dress. Hair from enemy scalps hung from his clothing, and his headdress of feathers touched the ground. In the dim light, Charlie made out a painted hand on the spirit's garment. He knew the significance of this—the spirit had killed an enemy with his hands. On his shoulder sat a great white bird.

The Indian spirit's stance was one of great pride—with his head held high and his eyes unwavering. In his hand was a staff, colorfully painted, with a knot of feathers dangling from the top. His eyes burned into Charlie.

Pulling himself up as tall as he could, Charlie waited to be addressed. He knew that this would be the moment of a great happening.

The face of the spirit slowly began to change. Under the prideful expression, a new look gradually became apparent. Deep sadness now touched Charlie. Raising the staff over his head, and throwing out his other arm, the vision sent the great white bird hovering over his head as he began to chant—it was the chant of death.

A stark chill went through Charlie as he realized what this signified.

Then as he watched, the wind began to blow through the tops of the tall pines among which he stood. The chant went up to meet the wind, and combined with it to create a sound that Charlie would never forget. It resounded in his ears.

Just when he felt he could no longer stand the mournful sound, the wind swept down to dissipate the smoke-like vision before him. The death chant was picked up and drawn upward, strewn through the treetops and scattered on the wind.

Almost before he realized it, Charlie was standing alone, his white hair sweeping out all around him. The cry of the wind was no longer joined by the cry of death.

David E Ammons

Crickets in the nearby grass began to sing, followed by a chorus from the throats of toads. Charlie's ears picked up the hoot of an owl on the limb just above him. From the distance came the cry of the cat.

As he gazed at the dark outline of the pines, Charlie now heard the sounds of life—the sounds that took the chill out of his bones.

Replacing the knife in the sheath strapped to his side, Charlie no longer feared the unknown—he had met the spirit of death—and had lived. But he now knew that his time was near at hand; the spirit of death would return.

The old man moved off, his footsteps making no sound on the forest floor. Even though the wind was cool against his face, Charlie felt warm inside. It was as if he'd won a great victory.

Winter came to the mountains of North Carolina, leaving blankets of snow everywhere. In among the pines, the snow glistened like sequined wedding lace. The trails of the forest were no longer identifiable—the only paths seen were the ones left by the footprints of the animal world.

From out of the mouth of Charlie's cave, a winy wisp of blue smoke made its way skyward. Inside, it was warm and comfortable.

Beside the popping fire Charlie sat, bent over, concentrating on the job at hand. His weathered hands worked leather straps in and out of the frame of a snowshoe.

He was used to being alone—the quietness of the cave soothed his thoughts—making way for memories. He smiled. Slowly the aged hands quit moving as the light of the dancing flames before him climbed into the darkened pools of Charlie's eyes. Then, the years fell away, and the flickering firelight became the campfire of long ago. He was in his village along the Tuckasegee River—rude log huts strewn in among a setting of woods, mountains, and river. He had become a child again.

From the outside walls of his family's cabin hung gourds

used for utensils, dried vegetables, and the skins of animals. The structure was windowless, and had only one entrance. Close by was a corncrib.

Along the banks of the river were rafts and canoes made from hollowed logs. And from the canoes protruded the spears the men used for fishing.

Children, the color of hazelnuts, ran here and there, followed by dogs of all kinds and sizes.

Over cookfires and over nearby stumps, where corn was pounded into meal, stood Indian women—their long hair held back by headbands made of feathers and skins.

Beside the living quarters were gardens planted by the women of the tribe, bearing corn, beans, squash, and tobacco.

In his dream, Charlie saw his father enter the village, carrying his kill for the day. His father would allow him to help skin the animal, talking to him in their native tongue, speaking the Kituhwa dialect.

He had always loved those times with his father, but when he reached the age of fourteen years, all life changed for Charlie. He was chosen to become a medicine man, and, therefore, he was turned over to the older shaman of the tribe. His upbringing was completed by these men. He became a "chosen one," and thus he was not allowed to associate with an ordinary child. Instead he went through endless hours of rigorous training and listened to countless stories of the past. Next began the secret and mysterious teachings on the use of herbs and bark, the rituals of cleaning, and the art of purification. These secrets were guarded with a silence that no outsider dared try to penetrate. In learning these things, Charlie excelled.

But the cost had been great for him. He had missed a part of his childhood, a loss that still hurt him. He had watched his Indian brothers making weapons for warfare, and he had longed to work with them. They had made war clubs from sycamore and bows from hickory—but what had intrigued him most of all were the eagle feathers used on the arrows. The eagle was sacred to the Cherokee—and his feathers were even more holy. The wand made from eagle feathers was a peace symbol. Only a professional "Eagle-Killer" could hunt the eagle—and then only with proper ceremony and preparation.

Still, the weapons made for the warriors and the chiefs of the tribe often led to nothing but tall tales; whereas the power and honor of being a medicine man were the greatest tribute a man of the Cherokee tribe could be given. A chief could come and go—but a medicine man would be a medicine man for all time. Charlie knew that he had been highly honored by his people.

As the fire in the cave burned brightly, the flames grew in Charlie's eyes like the Dance of the Eagle—brown bodies painted vivid colors, swaying and leaping to the beat of the drums.

Charlie stirred, shaking his head, and muttered to himself, "Old man cannot bring back old times . . . "

He stood up and walked over to his bed of hides and skins. Beside the bed stood a handmade spear, faded white eagle feathers dangling from the top—caressing the wall of the cave. Gazing down, he could see his bed of long ago—the bed his mother had made specially for him by dressing the edges with turkey feathers.

Lying down, he turned his gaze once again to the feathers of his spear. Then his eyes glazed over with the memory of his greatest triumph. Charlie could no longer see the flickering flames of his fire, and he forgot the loneliness of his small cave. He sank again inside his memory—until he was once again on the banks of the Tuckasegee—his eyes combing the rippling waters—his spear in his hand.

All around him, the mountains rose high and majestic—the shimmering pools of clear water alongside the canoe reflecting the rugged terrain. He jabbed at a streak of silver, and felt deep satisfaction as he brought a twitching, fighting trout out of the water.

Suddenly, the warmth of the sun overhead was covered by a shadow—a huge shadow that enveloped the length of the boat. As he looked above, the boy's eyes widened in fright and disbelief.

Hovering just over him was an unbelievable vision—a white eagle, at least seven feet from wingtip to wingtip. The long feathers in his wings were strong and stiff, spreading out like thin fingers, bent up at the tips by the upward pressure of the air. The long, curved talons on his feet seemed to be only inches from the Indian boy; the bird seemed to be staring straight at the fish on the tip of the spear. His beak was at least two inches long, and an inch deep. At this close range, the eagle looked fierce and proud—a symbol of power and freedom—as it hovered over the head of the startled boy.

Then—with hardly a noticeable movement, the bird dipped quickly toward the spear, his sharp talons digging into the scales of the fish.

Instinctively, Charlie pushed at the handle of the spear, pulling the fish away from the white eagle. Startled, the powerful bird ascended and then hovered above, seemingly undaunted by this first attempt. Only part of the trout remained.

The fish-eating bird began to circle the small boy in the canoe—his sweeping shadow playing hide and seek with his prey.

Below, the boy's mind tried to grasp just what was happening. He couldn't believe his own eyes—for never in his life had he ever seen a white eagle. This must be a special omen—an omen that could change his life. It had to be good medicine—but first, he had to get proof—proof of this white eagle. He had no desire to kill the bird—he wasn't a recognized eagle-killer—he was only a boy. All he needed was a feather or two. Maybe he could draw the bird closer.

Slowly, he raised the spear high over his head. Almost immediately, the handle shook in his hands as the rest of the fish was torn from the chiseled stone used as a spearhead. Then the giant bird was gone. It was as if he had been only a white cloud nestled in the blue of the sky.

Quickly, the boy's dark eyes searched the waters, and then his muscles flexed with smooth rhythm as the spearhead caught the flashing rays of the sun—then disappeared into the depths before him. And, just as quickly, another trout rose twisting in death on the point of the weapon, spinning droplets of cold water over the brown body of the boy. He laughed aloud—the thrill of success mirrored in his eyes.

His catch held aloft, the Indian boy watched the sky hopefully—his eyes darting from side to side—covering each direction.

Out of nowhere, he came—soaring gracefully down to the smallest of prey—the shining silver of the fish. Then the eagle was gone as silently as he had come.

The heart of the boy grew inside his chest, as a wondrous smile covered his face. His body trembled with the deep thrill of a powerful hunter—a hunter of the most sacred peace symbol of the Cherokee. To a young Charlie, the eagle became a white cloak of strong medicine sent from the Great Spirit.

Once again, the boy speared a fish and stretched it aloft for the talons of the eagle—holding his head back to watch the sky. He didn't have long to wait. The fierce-looking bird swooped down with hardly a sound, grasping his prey.

But this time, the boy was ready. As the eagle's claws pulled the meat from the spear, the youth lifted his weapon toward the body of the bird. He had no intention of harming the animal—all he wanted was a feather.

The point of the spear raked through the large tail that spread out like an opened hand. To the boy's amazement, three feathers dislodged and floated downward. The bird forgotten, Charlie's brown eyes fastened onto the drifting proof of the white eagle. He could see that the feathers were not falling into his canoe—they were floating down to the water that surrounded him. Quickly, he sank to the floor of the canoe and paddled with his hands, trying to position himself underneath his falling treasure.

He was still paddling as two of the large white feathers gently touched his face, settling into the boat. The other fell into the water beside him.

The reach of the small boy was not long enough, so he put all his strength into a last try. The next thing he knew, he was lying full-length in the water, his face stinging from the slap of the fall. Quickly, his strong arms churned, pulling him toward the floating feather.

High above the Indian boy, sharp eyes blinked. The seasoned hunter sat on the limb of a jack pine, watching the curious antics of the boy below. Then, as if in answer to a call, the eagle cocked his head toward the west—and quickly flew away.

By this time, Charlie had re-entered his canoe and had retrieved the beautifully shaped, wet tailfeather.

With all three feathers in his hands, he held them to his breast in silent gratitude. He knew that he would never forget this day. In his mind, he began to plan just how he would keep all eyes on him as he told his tale of the white eagle. This would be the day that little Cooweesucoowee had seen a white eagle, and had captured three tailfeathers to prove it. He would be known in his tribe—known as a powerful medicine man.

Bringing himself back to the present, the old man suddenly laughed aloud. Such a young boy he had been! At the time, he had not even known . . . that almost all eagles had white tailfeathers.

Still chuckling to himself, the wrinkled man turned his face from the light of the fire—and drifted off to sleep—up, up, past cloud after cloud—on the back of a soaring white eagle.

CHAPTER SEVEN

Raven Runningdeer

And Charlie slept. It was a deep sleep. The fire in the cave burned low.

Sometime in the night, Charlie woke to the stillness, to the emptiness of his surroundings. He slowly turned his head, seeing the low flames crawl over the blackened half-consumed logs.

Suddenly, his eyes grew large, and he stared in disbelief as he realized that there was someone—or something—in the cave with him.

Into the firelight she walked, tall and slender—dressed in buckskin. Her long black hair glimmered in the dim light. The dark-skinned beauty gazed at him with haunted eyes. Her hands seemed to reach out to him—then she was gone.

"Raven!"

Charlie's voice cracked with emotion as he raised himself on his elbow and reached out his hand to . . . emptiness.

He realized that he was again alone, and laid his head back on his robes of deerskin. His long hair lay about his head like clouds of silver.

He had seen his second vision—the vision of the only woman he'd ever wanted as a wife. Closing his eyes, he began to let thoughts enter his head that he had put out of his mind years ago. He drifted down inside his memories—back to that spring in the year of 1879. . . .

The Cherokee nation was well and beginning to prosper

again. It had been over thirty years since the removal of thousands of Cherokees, by the government, to the established Indian Territory in Oklahoma. The few who had escaped the removal had survived only by hiding out in the high mountains of North Carolina in the trackless wilds of the Great Smoky divide. These survivors had stayed on, defying every effort of the federal troopers to capture them. There had been little sustenance but toads, snakes, insects, berries, and the inner bark of trees. Many of the Indians had starved to death.

Yet, the Cherokee nation had lived and grown. The scattered and desperate refugees grew from a few hundred to over a thousand—grouped together mostly in an area later to be called the Qualla Boundary. In the year 1870, their chief was "Flying Squirrel," and Charlie was their medicine man.

Deep in his dream-like state, Charlie tensed as the memory of one special night came flooding back. Day was almost gone. Smoke from the many campfires filled the spring evening. Soft lavender clouds almost hid the setting sun from view. There was movement all around Charlie as he stood near Chief Flying Squirrel. The tribe was preparing for the first festival of the Cherokee year, the "First New Moon of Spring."

The flat ground on which they stood was to be the dance floor for the brown bodies in rhythmic motion. All around were high poles on which green branches of laurel were tied. The branches were to shade the sacred ground on which the ceremony would take place. Close by was the river, providing the water for the cold ceremonial plunges that the dancing braves would take into its deepest parts.

Suddenly feeling eyes on him, Charlie looked up to find the Chief's daughter standing near, respectfully keeping her distance—yet reaching out to him with her soft eyes.

Charlie's heart grew large, and filled him with a wondrous warmth. He marveled at this feeling! Such a feeling had not occurred until this beautiful dark-haired maiden had stood close to him. She wore a wrap-around skirt of deerskin, with red and yellow designs painted around the hem. Ornaments made from glass beads, and woven into a colorful design, hung from her neck. A red and yellow beadwork headband held her long black hair back, away from her face. Turkey feathers, held together by strips of bark, hung down from her waist. This was Raven Runningdeer, the only daughter of Chief Flying Squirrel—and the woman Charlie loved.

He had felt love for her as long as he could remember, but had kept his distance. He was a medicine man and could not openly court her—yet his yearning eyes had followed her every movement around the village. He had known that she had always looked back at him—sometimes with eyes that had puzzled him.

Now, as he returned the gaze of Raven, he began to discover a most disturbing fact. Suddenly, he knew that his feelings were shared by the young woman. A story was being unveiled before his eyes. Excitement began to fill his body—it was all he could do to stand his ground. His position with the tribe no longer seemed to matter.

All around them, preparations for the festival continued, as Charlie and Raven touched each other with only their eyes. Then, Charlie was called away—but left only after receiving a promise made by Raven as she nodded her head.

Later that night, as the chanted dance of the "First New Moon of Spring" filled the air, Charlie stood on the outskirts of the band of onlookers. His eyes searched for Raven.

All at once, she was there beside him. She touched his arm, motioning for him to follow her. Charlie followed, his heart singing.

Moments later, high above a secluded nook in the forest, a full moon smiled down on the medicine man and his love. Gentle moonbeams lighted the darkness, and hesitantly touched the forest floor. She drew her lover close—her fingers softly sensing the underlying passion racing through the muscles of the man reaching for her.

Then—under cover of the foliage—and without a sound, they had come together in the strongest bond of desire. The coolness of the still forest caressed their bodies as they fulfilled their innermost longings. Time, like a great winged bird,

David F. Ammons

hovered over them. In a few moments they experienced feelings neither one would ever forget.

Behind them, the chanting voices rose, as if keeping time with the movements of their bodies. Even the stars that filled the heavens seemed to dance to the sound of the drums. Then the pounding of his heart closed his ears to any sound except the soft moaning that whispered from her lips.

It was over all too soon, and Raven had vanished—still without a word—but leaving her red and yellow headband on the forest floor beside him. Charlie was left alone in the black of the forest—but he was left transported and transformed on the wings of ecstasy. He would never again be the same.

But with the morning sun, his ecstasy was torn from him, leaving him numb for a lifetime afterward. Raven had been taken from him abruptly by fate. At dawn, her marriage to a white man was announced by her father, Chief Flying Squirrel. Evidently, the marriage had been planned for some time, and was to be presented as a fitting conclusion to this first festival of the new year. Raven's knowing eyes had rested on Charlie—her unshed tears glistening in the mountain sun.

Within a week, she was gone—gazing with these same sorrowful eyes at Charlie as she rode by with her new husband.

As Charlie watched her go, his spirit filled with a bittersweet feeling. He could understand the reason for this marriage—and yet he didn't want to sanction it either. The white man had befriended the chief during the time of the removal years ago—taking his Indian friend and his family in and literally keeping them alive. He gave the hand of his only daughter as a token of friendship and honor. Charlie could not question the wisdom of the chief's decision.

Days went by—then days grew into months. With the snows of December came the news of a girl child born to Raven Runningdeer—a dark-skinned child who took after her Indian heritage.

And Charlie knew—the girl child was his.

Raven Runningdeer named her baby Anna.

Years passed. Charlie visited Raven and Anna only from afar. He watched—hidden in the foliage of the forest. Anna grew, and she was strong and lovely. Charlie was proud.

At age fifteen Anna married—her husband was another white man by the name of James Coggins. In the years that followed, all the children born to the Coggins family resembled their father, the white man.

In 1892, Raven Runningdeer was laid to rest on her husband's land—high in the mountains she loved. Charlie grieved at her graveside long after her family had gone.

Then, one year later, the last daughter of Anna Coggins was born. A tiny dark-skinned infant came crying into the world—a raven-haired remembrance of another time and place. Retter Coggins had been born.

By this time, Charlie had taught younger men of his tribe the ways of the medicine man, thus when Retter was born, Charlie left the tribe and moved into a cave high on a mountain overlooking the Coggins' land.

Then, Charlie watched and waited—and one day, as he had planned, Retter found him. His world was complete again. He was content to be her friend—but every time Charlie looked into Retter's eyes, he could see her—his Raven.

The fire popped. Daylight shone through the mouth of the cave. With the coming of dawn, Charlie awoke from his trance-like state, the thought of Raven so strong in his mind that he again called her name aloud.

"Raven!"

The only answer was the whisper of the wind.

The old man pulled himself up and wrapped a deerhide around his shoulders. Time would pass—spring would come, and he would see Retter again.

Retter, the granddaughter of Raven Runningdeer and Cooweesucoowee.

CHAPTER EIGHT

Spring—1909

"Wal, Retter, my birthday jest passed, and I'm all of thirty years old now." Tom was sitting in a homemade straight-back chair on the front porch of Retter's home. He was gazing at her as he sat leaning forward, both elbows on his knees, with his chin resting in the palms of his hands.

Retter was sitting on the edge of the porch, her legs dangling. The night air was warm, and the stars shone brightly in the heavens. Her heart was full of the beauty of the spring night.

The winter had been rough, but time had flown for Tom and Retter. The heavy blankets of snow had not kept Tom from visiting his new-found love. During these past six months, they had become comfortable with each other, and the warmth of their feelings had created a bond that held them close. Tom had been constantly amazed at the maturity Retter displayed. On her birthday, the first of the month, she'd only been fifteen, but to him she was a full grown woman.

"Retter, I think it's time fer me to talk to yore paw," Tom said, straightening up in the chair.

Instantly, Tom had Retter's attention. She whirled around, bringing her feet upon the porch, and stood to look closely at Tom, both hands on her hips.

"Tom yo're touched in the head, or something!" her eyes were wide with surprise.

"No, Retter. Listen to me a bit! I know we thought to wait until you were sixteen. But I'm thirty years old now, and I jest cain't wait much longer. I need you, Retter, more every day!"

His voice had gotten softer as he spoke, but great feeling showed on his face. He reached for her hand and drew her to him so she could sit on his lap.

Retter laid her cheek against his head and put both arms around his neck. She could feel the tremble of his body as she rested her warm hand on his bare arm. There were butterflies in her stomach as she thought of marriage. She'd never known a man such as Tom, and she couldn't have known the longing for her that Tom was feeling at this moment.

For more than six months now, Tom had sat near Retter, had watched her, and had dreamed of her. Something was welling up inside him, and he didn't know if he could control it much longer. His arms tightened around her. She had to be his—the sooner, the better!

"If you think it's time fer us to git hitched up, Tom, I reckon you'd better ask Papa, then," said Retter, as she stroked his dark wavy hair.

Tom reacted immediately to Retter's words. He scrambled up, setting her feet down carefully on the porch. He began to straighten his shirt, and then, hitching up his pants, he smiled nervously at Retter.

"Wal, time's a-wasting! Best not put off until tomorrow what I kin do today!"

With her hand over her mouth, she laughed at the sight of Tom, straightening his clothes and swallowing hard several times. They had never told anyone that they'd planned to marry someday. But Retter thought that her parents wouldn't be surprised. Her mom and dad had watched them covertly these many months.

Holding out his hand to her, Tom led her from the darkness of the porch into the flickering lamplight of the cabin.

Her mother was sitting on one side of the room, writing laboriously on a tablet. She didn't look up as they entered.

Her papa was cleaning his rifle as he sat on the edge of the bed against the far wall. His sharp eyes took them both in as soon as they stepped inside the room. Seeing the look on Tom's face, he hesitated in his cleaning, and waited.

Going directly over to where Jim was sitting, Tom stopped just in front of him. Clearing his throat, the young man began, "Jim, I want you to know that I think you have a wonderful daughter here. I thank you fer letting me come courting Retter these long months!"

Pausing, Tom looked around for Retter. She was just behind him, a little to the side. She smiled encouragingly at him. Looking back at Jim, he continued, "I love Retter more than anything—and I'm asking you fer her hand."

Tom breathed a sigh of relief that he had finally said what he had practiced saying a hundred times. But now there was tension in the air as he waited for Jim to answer. Perspiration showed on Tom's forehead, and the palms of his hands felt damp.

Jim let him wait. He looked Tom up and down—then he looked at Retter. She smiled brightly at him and nodded her head. Tom didn't see the smile, nor the nod.

Retter's mother had finally looked up when she'd heard the speech Tom had made. Her emotions were high, but out of respect for her husband, she had waited for him to speak.

Clearing his throat, Jim finally smiled suddenly and said, "It's of no surprise to me, son. Been seeing it coming fer quite a spell. Reckon it'll be best fer the two of you to tie the knot now, so I give you my blessing. But mind, now! You better not hurt my little girl, or I'll take this here rifle to you!"

Jim swung his rifle around and leveled it at Tom. From the look in his eyes, Tom knew he meant what he said. But that lasted only a second. Then, as Jim lowered the rifle and laughed, Tom relaxed and laughed nervously, too.

"Oh! My baby!" Retter's mother came running over and gathered her up in her arms.

Jim Coggins stood up and shook Tom's hand and then slapped him on the back.

"Wal, now! This here calls fer a swaller or two! Let's go out to the shed around back and have a swig of hard stuff!"

Looking apologetically at Retter, Tom was led from the room by her father.

Retter could hear her mother's voice, but the girl didn't hear what she was saying. Her thoughts were racing—on to the wedding night. The thought of that scared her to death!

"Ma," she began, "I'm scared! What of my first night? What do I do?"

Her mother drew back from her, holding her at arms' length, and gazed at her lovingly. Smiling, she said, "Retter don't fret none! It's the most natural thing ever's been. Tom's a gentle man, and he loves you, it's clear. Don't you worry none—jest be happy!"

"Oh, Ma! I do love you!" Retter threw her arms around her mother and buried her face in her shoulder. Tears of happiness flowed from both their eyes.

Out by the shed, Tom and Jim stood, silhouetted against the sky. Jim had given Tom a drink from a quart jar full of clear home-brewed liquor. Tom's throat still felt raw from the strong concoction that he had swallowed. It wasn't that he was no drinker—Lord knows he had had plenty in his lifetime. He just knew that Retter didn't approve.

Jim turned the jar up and had a second drink, and offered the jar again to Tom.

"Much obliged, but no thanks, Jim. I want to say goodnight to Retter after a bit, and she don't care much fer hard drink."

Jim laughed and put the jar back inside the shed.

"Don't let her lead you around by the nose, Tom!" Jim put his hand on Tom's shoulder. "Anyway, when's the big day? You set the date yit?"

"No, sir. But the sooner the better. I've a hankering to git it over with. I reckon I'll see if Retter's ready by next Sunday or so. What do you think, Jim?"

"Wal, I don't rightly know, Tom. All I know is that it'll take a spell fer me to git used to losing my youngest girl!"

"Jim, we'll jest be down to my paw's house. I have no place yit—but, I'll have a big piece of land from my paw one day. I have a good job down to the sawmill, too!" Tom seemed to be trying to reassure Jim of his position.

"I know, Tom. Calm down, son! Yo're talking too fast!" Jim laughed loudly and led the way back to the cabin.

As he entered the room, Tom's eyes sought Retter's, and he tilted his head toward the side door.

Seeing the sign from him, she beckoned him and said, "Ma, Tom and me will be outside a bit." Retter walked to the door and onto the porch before her mother or father had time to say anything. As Tom followed, the older man and woman looked at each other and smiled knowingly.

Outside on the porch again, Tom grabbed Retter to him, hunger for her swelling up inside him.

"Oh, Retter! I do need you! Think we could git married Sunday at church?" he asked.

"Tom, yo're a-busting my ribs!" Retter laughed softly. Then she placed both her hands on his face and looked up at him, love in her eyes, and said, "Yes, Sunday it is!"

With deep felt passion, Tom drew her to him and pressed his hungry lips to hers. The passion he felt was transferred to Retter, and she was swept up in the desire to hold herself as close to Tom as she could. They clung together, love and desire filling their souls.

Later that night as Retter watched Tom leave, she thought she was just about the happiest woman alive. Tomorrow she would go see her friend Charlie, and tell him her happy news!

The sun was setting in the west, fingers of gold and red painting the sky with color. The sweet smell of wild roses filled the air as Retter sat on the warm rock that overlooked the valley below. This was her favorite place to be alone. It was on top of the mountain near Charlie's cave.

The spruce trees by the rock on which she sat, were draped with grapevines, and at their base were wild rosebushes covered with pink and white blossoms.

The deep valley below was filled with pine, balsam, spruce and hemlock trees, all different shades of green—flowing here, yonder and about, then straight up to start another mountain in the distance. From where Retter sat, it looked like a never-ending patchwork quilt.

With twilight descending upon her, Retter could feel the warmth of the breeze against her face, causing her to realize that the tears that had welled up inside her eyes were flowing over, down onto her cheeks. The sadness in her heart had triggered the tears. Early this morning she had found her friend Charlie lying still on his bed of hides when she'd come to tell him her happy news. There had been death in his eyes as he tried to smile at her. Sitting there on the rock as the sun was going down, Retter could still hear his voice—she would never forget! She squeezed her eyes shut to clear her eyes of tears.

In the time she had with him, as he lay dying, Charlie had told her things about his life that he had never mentioned before. He kept repeating his Indian name, Cooweesucoowee. In white man's language it meant "large white bird." Charlie was proud of that name because he was a direct descendant of another man by the name of Cooweesucoowee. The white man had called him John Ross. This man had been his great-grandfather, an educated half-breed. John Ross's father had been white, but his mother had been full-blooded Cherokee.

Early in the 1800's he had left his white family and had joined the Cherokee tribe. But, when John Ross, in 1838, had led his people out of North Carolina and Tennessee, on the "trail of tears," not all of the Cherokee people had gone with him to Oklahoma. Charlie and his family had stayed in their homeland. They had peaceably lived off the land—farming, hunting and trapping, eating the nuts and berries of the forest. But now, Charlie had no family left to carry his name. He was dying, and the name "Cooweesucoowee" would be no more. As he spoke to Retter, she could see the sorrow in his eyes. The "Great Spirit" was calling him, and would leave no brave to follow the hunting trails in the shadowed forest. There would only be the sway of the pine trees in the wind as Cooweesucoowee went to meet the "Great Spirit."

As Charlie spoke, Retter began to cry. Her tears fell on Charlie's hand.

"Charlie, I don't want you to go! Please stay with me! I jest come up here to tell you about Tom and me gittin' married this Sunday. Please don't die, Charlie!"

Seeing her unhappiness, Charlie had spoken to Retter words that would be imprinted forever in her memory.

"Retter, hear Charlie speak. Will tell story of Raven Runningdeer." The old man spoke low and almost serenely, telling Retter of his one night alone with the woman he loved. It was the first time he had ever told of his secret.

As the story unfolded, Retter's eyes grew large with surprise and astonishment. She knew he told the truth; her heart felt the joy and the sadness of finding and losing someone that had always been a part of herself. Listening to Charlie, the young girl felt the pride of many generations rise within her—a pride that came from the direct gaze of one she could now call her grandfather.

As he spoke, Retter could see the sadness in Charlie's eyes float away with his words into the depth of the cave. His aged face took on an expectant expression, and he raised himself upon one elbow.

"Charlie must now go meet Raven—she calls." His voice faded, and his eyes now appeared to be glassy as he gazed out before him toward the mouth of the cave. But then, suddenly, he sat bolt upright, staring with wide eyes.

Retter turned with fright, but saw nothing.

"Spirit of death! He comes!"

The cave felt cold. Retter could still see no one, but she felt the presence of this unearthly being.

The dying man fell back onto his bed. Retter thought that he was dead, and fell forward against the quiet man, sobbing almost soundlessly.

Softly, Charlie's voice caressed the darkness of the cave, "Retter, my granddaughter, stand tall. You are of Indian blood! Wings of great white bird will hold you in its shadow. The Great

Spirit be with you." And, into her hand he pressed a faded red and yellow headband.

Retter, wiping her face with the back of her other hand, raised her head to hear his last whisper.

"Listen—hear the wind. . . . "

And Charlie, the Cherokee medicine man, died as he had lived—in peace and dignity.

That had been some hours ago. His body was still back there in his cave, lying on his deerskin bed. She had crossed his arms on his chest.

Suddenly standing, Retter threw her arms out wide, crying aloud, "Why, Lord? Why Charlie? He was so good and never did nobody no harm! Why couldn't I have the time to love him as my grandfather?"

Then, as if in answer to her cry, a sudden wind blew against her face. As Retter stood looking up, she could see the tall pine trees sway in the wind.

Brushing away the tears on her cheeks, she suddenly smiled. Charlie was with the Great Spirit now. But still, as she looked around her, she knew—she knew that his spirit was here, stalking the shadows of the forest—his footsteps making no sound on the fallen pine needles.

Looking down on the valley below, Retter stood tall and proud! In her veins ran the blood of the Cherokee Indian, a great tribe. Her grandmother had been Cherokee, Raven Runningdeer, and her grandfather, Cooweesucoowee, would be with her always.

And her new life with Tom would start soon—a new adventure! It was time to close the door on her old world.

The wind picked up again, whistling through the pines and the spruce. Retter looked behind her. There was no sign of anyone—but she knew he was there.

She listened. The wind whispered—Cooweesucoowee.

CHAPTER NINE

An End and a New Beginning

Today was the day! It didn't seem possible to Retter that the day had finally arrived. It all seemed unreal. The new dress she was slipping over her head was but a dream. She would have to wake soon!

Dovey was adjusting the dress around Retter, a sad smile on her face as she admired its texture. In her mind, she should have been getting married instead of Retter. She was the eldest! Instead she sighed with resignation. She had been seeing Henry Bridges since the social, but he hadn't spoken yet of marriage.

The two sisters were alone in the only bedroom in the Coggins' cabin. All the preparations for the wedding had been made. All that was left was the preparation of the bride—the very scared bride.

The dress was white broadcloth, with buttons down the front. It had a high neck and the waist fit snugly, giving her a graceful look. The long sleeves were fitted around the wrist, but were full and puffy at the shoulders. Around the high top of the neck, a small blue ribbon was tied in a bow.

Retter's hair was piled on top of her head in a loose bun, a few strands falling softly around her ivory face. Her eyes were wide as she stared at her reflection in the cracked mirror, and noticed the pink spots on her cheeks, and the trembling of her lips.

"Retter, you're beautiful!" Her mother had entered the room and was staring at her youngest daughter. There was pride in the mother's eyes and sadness in her heart.

Retter smiled timidly as she returned her mother's look. For some unknown reason, a calm suddenly settled over Retter. Her thoughts had come to a stand-still as she thought of Tom. All at once, it came to her! Why should she be scared? Tom was the most gentle man she had ever known. Even Charlie had told her that he was a good man. Her life was changing—but it was a good change. She was going to be the wife of Tom Ammons! The dream of a little girl was coming true.

Just then there was the sound of someone clearing his throat outside the door, and Retter heard her brother, John, say, "Retter, I have some flowers fer you. They're pink azaleas."

As John scuffled his feet, Retter hurried out to him, accepting the flowers and kissing him on the cheek. "Much obliged, John. I'm ready now that I have my flowers!"

Dovey, John, and Retter's mother then surrounded her, all hugging her and wishing her well. From over John's shoulder, Retter spied her father. He stood watching the small group, his face in the shadows of the hat pulled down over his face.

Breaking away, Retter hurried over to him and stood on tiptoe to hug him. Wrapped in his arms, she said softly, "Papa, I'll always love you."

There were tears in her father's eyes as he hugged Retter close. The little tomboy who had climbed up on his knee and gazed up at him with complete trust—who had ridden goats up and down the mountains—was the little girl he had watched develop into the tall lovely young lady that stood beside him. How he loved her!

He stepped back and gazed at her, saying, "Do yore papa proud, Retter! Don't go running when bad times hit—and stand with yore man no matter what comes! You hear me?"

"Yes, sir . . . I'm yore daughter—and a Coggins don't give up no how!" declared Retter as she stood proudly, her shoulders back.

"Good! Time's flitting away. Git yore things and let's go!"

Jim Coggins turned and went out the door, pulling his hat even farther down on his head.

A few minutes later, Retter sat on the back of the wagon as

it bounced and pitched, gazing back at the cabin she'd lived in for fifteen years. She'd never known another home. Tears filled her eyes as she tried to watch the cabin as long as she could—until it vanished around the bend in the dirt road. Emotion welled high in Retter's chest and the tears fell slowly into her lap as visions passed through her mind of past experiences lived in that old cabin. Happy Christmases—tug-of-war with her brothers and sisters over insignificant things—sitting with her papa in front of the warm fireplace, sweet pipe smoke filling the air—watching her momma take apple pies from the oven of the cookstove, and giving her the first bite! She would never again be a little girl, and how sad the feeling left her—it was the end of one part of her life.

As Retter bounced and swayed on the back of the wagon, the tears that fell cleansed her aching heart, and slowly, but surely, another part of her heart opened to welcome the new life that lay before her. Her life with Tom was almost here! Every bend in the road brought her closer to his arms and his love. Suddenly, through her tears, Retter began to see the green of the pine trees, smell the honeysuckle and azaleas blooming alongside the road as they passed. The soft shadows of the shady dirt road reached out and soothed her heart, turning the sadness into gladness. Turning abruptly in the wagon, Retter no longer looked back—she eagerly looked toward the upcoming turn of the road. Around that next bend lay her future!

Tom was pacing to and fro on the porch in back of the small church. He nervously fingered the change in his pockets as he paced. Today of all days, time seemed to be dragging.

Robert leaned against the door of the church and watched his brother. If he hadn't been so nervous himself, he would have laughed. His self-assured brother was finally shook up! Well, he really couldn't blame him—taking the welfare of another human being in your own hands was a big step.

"Robert, what time is it?" Tom had stopped pacing and was standing in front of him, anxiously awaiting his reply.

"Wal, Tom, you got only a half hour left of single life!" Robert grinned.

"Where is that girl? You don't think she ain't coming, do you?" Tom walked to the edge of the porch and, putting his hand over his eyes, gazed out to the winding dirt road that led to the church. In the distance he could now see a disturbance of the dust along the road. Suddenly, upon seeing the approach of his bride, he began to grow calmer, except for the quick beat of his heart in anticipation.

Robert came over and stood beside his brother, his arm over his shoulders. Glancing at Tom out of the corner of his eye, he could see that he need have no worries about him; he was going to be fine. Robert smiled.

The wagon pulled up with the Coggins family, Retter sat in the back of the wagon, and now rose with stiff legs. She barely felt them though, as she stood looking at Tom.

He came forward and swung her down onto the ground, and the two of them stood looking deep into each other's eyes. Each knew the love that swam in their eyes was real, and they didn't doubt each other at all. For them, there would be only romance and love, always.

Tom looked at the beauty of Retter, his gaze finding its way to her soft trembling lips. He leaned down and kissed her gently. Then cupping her face in his hand, he quietly said, "Retter, I do love you, and I'll be good to you."

Retter was softly smiling, but before she could speak, her father interrupted, "Tom! Retter! The preacher's already looking fer you!"

Tom took Retter's hand, and pulled it through his arm, laying his hand on hers as he walked his bride into the church.

There were few people in the small church. It was early yet, and the mountain folk had not arrived for Sunday services. The Ammons' and Coggins' families made up the majority of the onlookers.

Straight up to the preacher went Tom and Retter.

Preacher Samuel Milsap looked at the couple standing

before him. For some reason, he felt good about these two—they seemed to look right together, and he'd been the preacher in these parts long enough to know them well.

"Wal . . . Tom Ammons and Retter Coggins! Today's yore day! The good Lord hath blessed us with a beautiful day fer yore pledges to each other," he said as he shook Tom's hand. Then drawing Retter's hand into Tom's, he continued, his hand held high, "Blessed are all who enter the house of the Lord. Afore we go further this mornin', we'll go ta the Lord in prayer."

Retter listened intently to the prayer, squeezing Tom's hand. She prayed that her life with Tom would be filled with blessings and children! She did want lots of children.

The ceremony was short and beautiful. Almost before Retter could blink an eye, she was a married woman. After the last words were spoken, Tom gathered Retter up in his arms and kissed her with great feeling.

Afterward, with their family surrounding them and offering many congratulations, they looked at each other, saying not a word, holding hands. Retter's heart felt as if it would explode with happiness. Her throat was so choked up she couldn't talk. Tom squeezed her hand. She knew he was feeling the same way.

Tom and Retter drove away alone on his father's wagon. Everyone stood outside the church, waving the newlyweds out of sight. The sun shone brightly on the happy faces of the newest Ammons family as they drove along the dirt road. Retter could hear the singing of the birds, the breeze in the trees, and the waterfall below the church. The Tuckasegee River flowed alongside the road. As they looked at the river, the sun danced brightly on the rise and fall of the water over the rocks. The jewel-like sparkle was so bright it almost hurt Retter's eyes.

In the back of the wagon was a basket with a cloth over the top. Tom's mother had thoughtfully packed a lunch for them. It was a beautiful day!

Before long, Tom guided the horse up a newly cut dirt road that wound its way around, away from the river. The road had been cut deep into the side of a steep mountain. Up, up, they went—and around and around. The sound of the waterfall slowly grew softer, and then vanished. The branches of the huge trees on each side of the road mingled with each other, creating a cool cover over their heads. The shadows drew them close together on the wagon seat; trickles of spring water ran off the side of the mountain and overhanging cliffs; the spring water gathered at the bottom to become a trail of water across the dirt road; daisies and black-eyed susans grew abundantly along the side of the mountain, peeping their faces out from among the rocks.

From around Tom, Retter could see the other side of the road. It went straight down—just how far, she didn't know, but she drew in her breath a little as she turned her face to the front. Against her arm, she could feel Tom's body shake as he laughed softly.

Retter didn't know where they were going, and she began to feel a little sorry for the horse. Then, abruptly, they came to a level spot in the road and the wagon began to roll faster. Very softly came the rushing waters of another waterfall—the sound growing louder as they went on down the road. Almost at once, there was a valley before them—cleared, level land with a creek running through the middle.

"Are we there, Tom?" asked Retter softly.

"Wal, not quite there. This here spot is called "Grassy Creek Valley." Jest about a couple miles further up the road is the land I'm thinking about buying. Daddy's set on my taking the old home place—but it's only twelve acres. Anyways, Robert should get Daddy's land—he's taken care of Momma and Daddy all this time. And this hunk of land up here is nigh on to a hundred and eighty acres!"

Tom was excited about this, Retter could see. It was good to be a part of Tom's world now.

"Retter, some day we'll live up on that mountain in our own cabin with all our young'uns!" Tom laughed as he drew up on the reins of the horse, and said, "Whoa, now!"

Tom jumped down from the wagon seat and reached for Retter. He set her down on the shoulder of the road, and walked the horse and wagon over to the side. Unhitching the horse from the wagon, he led him over to drink slowly from the creek.

As Retter stood waiting for Tom, she noticed a spring close by. Taking a broad green grape leaf in her hand, she rinsed it off. Then cupping it, she caught the icy cold water in the leaf and drank deeply. It felt so good going down that she decided to have another.

"Retter!" called Tom from the wagon. "Retter! Here's our lunch Momma fixed. Come on! It sure does look good—fried chicken and biscuits!"

Skipping like a little girl, Retter hurried to Tom's side, then hand in hand they walked out into the open field that lay before them. Tom had a blanket over his shoulder that he spread out near the creek, close to a large rock.

They had a meal fit for a king that day, the sun smiling down on their happiness.

When their meal was over, they talked together of their future. Retter listened, with eyes that shone, to Tom's description of the cabin he would build. The cabin that would house their love and all their children.

There at the foot of the mountain, Tom and Retter dreamed of their lives together. With Tom's head in her lap and his long lanky frame spread out there on the blanket, Retter had never been so happy. Neither of them noticed the darkening of the sky as black clouds began to cover the sun.

Just then a sudden burst of wind announced the approaching thunderstorm. Quickly, Retter and Tom gathered up the basket and blanket and ran to the wagon. As Tom tried to catch the horse, Retter stood looking up the road that led to the top of the mountain. It was overgrown with grapevines and trees, and for a moment it looked foreboding! Something seemed to tell her to beware! She shook her head—all she could see was the heavy rain coming down in torrents.

Wrapping the blanket around her, she crawled under the wagon. A minute later, Tom crawled in beside her. She covered him with the blanket also, and together, in each other's arms, they prepared to wait out the storm. Thunder and lightning closed them in.

There in the rain, wrapped in a soggy blanket, Retter thought to herself, is this what our life will be like? Sunshine one minute—and rain the next?

Then, Tom's arms drew her closer to him, and the warmth of his body seemed to take her breath. She could feel the desire for her grow in him. His breath grew quicker, and he moaned softly. His hands, touching her gently, were trembling. Retter reached for him, and surrendered.

There, underneath the wagon at the foot of their mountain, in the pouring rain, Tom and Retter Ammons became as one.

CHAPTER TEN

Henry's Secret

After the wedding, Dovey, her heart full, had watched Retter ride away with Tom.

She was happy for her younger sister, but at the same time, she felt sadness, as she glanced around at the people that were now arriving for church. Some of them had witnessed the departure of Tom and Retter, and had found out about the wedding. Dovey felt that it wasn't her imagination that they were avoiding her. As she saw the covert glances, she assumed that they must be talking about her. At twenty-one years of age, Dovey knew they considered her an "old maid."

"Papa, kin I sit at the back today? I feel a little teary," Dovey said to her father as they once again entered the church.

"I reckon so, daughter." Jim Coggins patted Dovey on the arm and smiled; then he led his wife and John down closer to the front.

Dovey found a seat in the last pew, and leaned against the straight-backed bench. Immediately, her thoughts left the little church—and settled on Henry.

It was a puzzling relationship—this courtship of Henry and herself. Henry was big and powerful, and Dovey was small and dainty. The two of them made an odd-looking couple, so wherever they went together, heads would turn as they passed.

Except for the first time she'd met him and he had saved her from Joe Powell, Dovey had been uneasy with Henry. They had been dating for almost eight months now, and he had yet to make a pass at her. At first, she had thought he was just shy. But as time went on, she began to give up that assumption. There was something unusual about this giant who now claimed her as "his girl."

There was his jealousy, and his mysterious comings and goings—never letting her know where he lived, nor when he would be coming to see her. He had never mentioned marriage.

Well, after today, Dovey knew how much she wanted a husband and her own home. She had watched Retter and Tom—their happiness had been evident to all. It just didn't seem fair that her younger sister had found a husband before she had. A feeling of humiliation began to grow inside Dovey, until hot tears slid down her cheeks. Tonight she was going to talk to Henry—she was tired of playing the role of the quiet, patient woman. She had to know where she stood.

Even as Dovey made up her mind, another feeling began to grow—a strange uneasy fear. At times Dovey had sensed a darkness in Henry that seemed to be just underneath the surface, and it frightened her.

Dovey tossed her head—she didn't care anymore! She would talk to Henry tonight about their future.

Robert hitched up his pants and squared his shoulders. He stood in the growing shadows of the barn, listening to his father.

"Robert, Jim Coggins offered me the loan of one of his plow mules. Think you could walk over to the Coggins' stable and ride him back tonight? We need to git started early in the morning."

Robert leaned down and picked up two pails of milk; he was starting out the barn door as he answered his father.

"Shore, Daddy. Are we a-gonna start on that field Tom wanted to clear fer a stand of corn?"

Jim Ammons closed the barn door and began to walk beside Robert toward the house. "Yep. We'll git an early start in the morning, before sunup."

The two men walked up the steps and onto the porch, and

turned to look at the road that led away from the house toward Tuckasegee. From a distance came the clank of a wagon.

"Wal, here comes the newlyweds, Daddy!" There was a smile in Robert's voice as he gazed at the dim outline of a horse and wagon coming at a slow pace.

"Bet they got drenched in that downpour we had awhile ago. Poor kids!" The laughter in his voice belied Jim's touching words.

The wagon pulled up with Retter and Tom smiling happily at Robert and his father.

"Howdy, kids," said Jim Ammons.

"Howdy, Daddy—Robert. Right nice evening, ain't it?" Tom handed the reins to Retter and climbed down from the wagonseat. "Thanks fer the wagon, Daddy. We got caught in the rain, but it still wuz a good day." Tom smiled up at his wife.

Setting down the pails of milk, Robert hurried to help with the horse.

"Come on down, Retter—welcome home!" Tom's smile widened encouragingly at the now shy girl.

Retter's emotions were mixed. She was weary from the excitement of the day, and uneasy about entering a new home—living with new people. But she returned Tom's smile bravely and put her hands in his.

Jim watched from the porch; then, with a grin, he picked up the pails of milk and disappeared through the doorway.

"Daddy, I'll put the horse and wagon away and go on over to Mr. Coggins' to get that mule," called Robert after his father. "I'll be back directly."

Robert watched as Tom put his arm around Retter and led her into the Ammons' cabin. Life at home was going to be different now that a girl would be staying here again. He was looking forward to it. He had missed his sisters.

The path that led over the mountain was well worn. Tom had used it often while he was courting Retter. The sun was almost gone as Robert set out on his journey. The evening air was cool—just the way Robert liked it. He took deep breaths as he climbed.

The night grew darker, but he could see well. His long legs covered the ground at a steady pace. It took close to an hour before Robert was nearing the top of the trail above the Coggins' cabin. From just atop the crest of the trail, he gazed down on the lights of Jim Coggins' home.

Robert hitched up his pants and squared his shoulders—then set off down the path.

He was nearing the barn when he heard a loud voice. He stopped, curious and a little uneasy, as he tried to see in the growing dimness. Once again, the loud voice was carried to him on the breeze.

Robert followed the angry tones to reach the half-opened barn door. From where he stood, he unabashedly listened to the argument that was going on within the barn.

"Dovey, jest what has got yore dander up?" the voice was gruff and demanding.

"Henry Bridges! You tell me jest what are your intentions! All these months we been seeing each other, and you ain't said nary a word about your intentions!"

Robert leaned closer, and peered around the opening. A lantern hung high on a rafter, casting soft shadows on the figures below.

Henry towered over the small Dovey, but the woman stood her ground, her hands on her hips. Even though her back was to Robert, he could tell from her stance that she was angry.

"Henry! Will you answer me! Do you care fer me a-tall?" Dovey's voice filled the corners of the loft.

The big man didn't answer. His now stony face was illuminated by the lantern light—only his eyes were shadowed in darkness. But what Robert noticed, above all, was his expression. Although his bushy beard covered the lower part of his face, Robert could see that his lips were clamped together in restraint.

Dovey began to walk back and forth in front of Henry. She rubbed her hands together tightly as she paced. Words began to flow, almost keeping cadence with her steps.

"Henry, you have come here courtin' me. You've stayed awhile—then left. Sometimes you'd fetch me a flower, but most times, jest yerself. You ain't ever stayed too long, and you ain't ever talked about yore kinfolk. I know nothing about you at all—nothing AT ALL! Don't you want me to meet yore ma? Where do yore kinfolk live? You do have a ma, don't you?" The angry woman stopped her pacing and faced Henry again.

The silence in the barn deepened. Even Robert grew uncomfortable in his spot hidden from view.

"Henry, I only got one more question fer you." Dovey's anger was controlled as she paused. Robert knew this question was important because he saw the rise and fall of Dovey's shoulders, as she took a deep breath and then exhaled.

"Are you ever gonna ask me to marry you?"

Robert blinked his eyes in surprise. Even from where he stood, he could feel the pain in Dovey's voice. He could imagine the courage it took for this prideful young girl to ask this question. Robert's heart felt a warmth for her—then he switched his attention to the big man before her.

Henry had yet to say a word.

"Will you say SOMETHING!" The anger was back as Dovey stomped her foot in exasperation.

"I cain't marry you, Dovey." His voice low, Henry's lips barely moved.

For a moment, Dovey stood still. Then she cocked her head and threw out her arms. "WHY?"

In Dovey's voice, Robert thought he heard panic. He moved closer, straining to hear Henry's voice.

"I jest cain't, Dovey! Cain't we jest leave it the way it is?"

"Henry, listen to me! I'm longing fer my own young'uns. I want my own place. Retter's only fifteen, and she's already got her own man!" Dovey paused, then turned away from Henry, facing, without seeing, the man who was eavesdropping in the dark of the doorway. There were tears on the girl's cheeks, anger and hurt criss-crossed her face in quick succession. Robert's own eyes softened in sympathy.

"I cain't marry you, Dovey. Believe me, I would if I could."

"Why not?" she demanded.

For a moment, Henry didn't speak—then he took a step toward her, halfway holding out his hand.

"Cuz—cuz I'm already married," he said quietly.

There was heavy silence as the shocked Dovey gathered each hand together in a tight fist.

"Henry," she began finally, her voice strained, "Henry, why have you done this to me?"

"Please, Dovey—my wife don't know about you—she's over to Balsam Grove. I come over here to work, and I seen you at the dance. It jest come over me that I jest had to have you!" The big man moved closer to Dovey, his look darkening.

From where he stood, Robert could see that Dovey was unaware of Henry's advance toward her. She was working hard at trying to control her emotions though she could do nothing about the tears that continued to flow.

"Dovey, I have to have you—if only once. I been biding my time—waiting fer the right time and place. I reckon this is it."

With these words, Henry was upon the surprised Dovey before she could resist. His huge hands pressed her arms to her sides as he picked her up and brought her closer to him; then his heavy arms encircled her.

"Don't fight, Dovey, and it won't take long." Henry tore at the top of her dress with one hand as he held her with the other.

Robert was through the door and upon the two before either one saw him. He hadn't stopped to think what he was doing—all he could see was that Dovey needed help.

"YOU GIT YORE HANDS OFF HER!"

With these words, Robert grabbed at the hand that held Dovey. His fingers caught Henry's thumb, and he pulled back with all his strength.

Pain shot across the big man's face as his knees bent slightly. "Awggg . . . let go!" he yelled.

Dovey sank underneath the huge man's arms and ducked

back out of the way. She pushed herself close to the wall of the stable nearby, staring in terror.

Even Robert was surprised at his momentary control of his opponent. He applied more pressure to the thumb, and without thinking, swung with his left fist and hit Henry hard in the face.

The impact broke Robert's hold on Henry's thumb, and instantly Henry was upon him. The blow to the face hadn't even slowed him down.

Robert was no small man, but he was certainly no match for Henry. This big man grabbed Robert's shirt at the neck, and he began to beat Robert unmercifully on the head.

The sudden onslaught by Henry had frightened Robert's instincts for self-preservation, and for a minute, he lost his urge to fight back. Henry twisted Robert's shirt, continuing to batter him. As if he was detached from himself, Robert could see the high color of Henry's face spread into his eyes. Now, Robert felt as if he were falling away from himself; the pain seemingly in someone else. From somewhere far away, he could hear a voice screaming.

Suddenly, the hand that held his shirt turned loose, and he crumpled to the hard-packed dirt floor. There was a deep harsh cry, and then, blackness came.

When he came to, Robert's head was lying in Dovey's lap. He touched his face, and cried out.

"You be careful now, Robert; yore face looks like a newly dug tater patch. I never seen such a mess!"

"What . . . what happened? Where did he go—did I win?" Robert tried to laugh but failed.

"Upon my word, did you win! No, Robert, you shore enough didn't win." Dovey patted his shoulder and smoothed his shirt, grinning nervously.

"Did he jest give up then—thinking I was dead or something?"

"No, he's laying right over there, blowed-out like a candle. I hit him over the head with the back of a pitchfork. I must of busted his head good, cuz he ain't moved since! How do you feel?"

Robert drew his breath in sharply and let it out slowly in a small whistle. His eyes traveled over her face to meet her eyes. Deep inside, Robert could see her unmasked concern. This discovery warmed him.

"I'm feeling right good—like I been kicked by a mule!"

"You poor thing! I'd better git you up to the house, so we kin fix yore busted face up."

Dovey had started to move when Robert stopped her. "Wait a minute . . . jest a minute. I got something to say."

"Wal, hurry up. I'd like to see if yore worth doctoring or not."

"Dovey, you ain't Henry's girl no more, are you?"

"I should say not!" Dovey almost shouted.

Robert reached for one of her hands, and held it. "To skip the long and the short of it, kin I come calling on you then? My intentions are good!"

"Robert Ammons! You heard everything! You heard it all!" Her face turned bright red, and she dropped her chin to her chest, avoiding his eyes.

"Course, I heard it all. Where do you think I got the idea. Dovey! Look at me—in the eye. I won't lie to you—I don't love you . . . I don't think. But who knows what kin happen. There's a warm something growing here . . . " He placed her hand on his heart. "Do you think you could feel something fer me?"

"I already do. Didn't I bang Henry on the head!"

"Wal, then, we kin have a go at it, cain't we? Never kin tell, mabbe we done found something! What do you say—wanta try it?"

Dovey reached out and with her petticoat dabbed at the blood on his mouth. She smiled at him.

"You know, jest awhile ago, I would never have said this, but now I kin. I like surprises—and yore one surprise I really like!"

CHAPTER ELEVEN

The Ole Biddies

Retter sat in front of the popping fire, her knitting in her lap. Her head was tilted to one side, listening. She thought that she had heard Tom's footsteps outside the door. But the door didn't open. There was only the sound of burning wood in the fireplace.

Laying her hands on her rounded stomach, Retter leaned back in her rocker and looked with vacant eyes into the fire—her thoughts going back over the past five months of her marriage. It had been the happiest time of her life. Tom had gone out of his way to please her, and she had responded with more affection than either of them had known before. Even though the years between them were great, Retter knew that she had found the right man.

Since their marriage in June, they had lived with Tom's mother and father at the old home place. The cabin was very small, so Robert and Tom had fixed up the loft in the old barn so that Robert could have a room of his own. The Ammons family had been taken with Retter, even if at times she was a little spitfire! Retter hadn't wasted any time showing Tom's family that she was a hard worker. When she had worked as hard and as long as any other member of the family, admiration began to show in the eyes of the entire Ammons clan. This feeling grew even more when they found out, after three months of marriage, that Retter was pregnant. As near as she could tell, Retter believed she must have gotten pregnant on her wedding day—in the pouring rain. It had always been a superstition that if it rained on your wedding day, you would cry a lot in your married life. But Retter believed that on her wedding day, it wasn't she who had cried, but the sky! The sky had cried tears of joy and cleansed for her the path of happiness ahead. And when she'd found out about the baby, she was sure of it! She wanted lots of children.

Sitting there in her rocker, Retter drew her shawl closer around her shoulders, not realizing that the fire was dying down.

As Robert came into the living room from the kitchen, he stood for a moment gazing at her. His childhood friend had become a beloved sister now, and the affection he showed was deeply felt. Seeing the fire was slowly going out, he went over to the woodbox near the hearth and threw a couple of logs on the glowing coals. Almost immediately the fire relit, and flames jumped high and flickered, dancing around and about the dry wood.

Coming out of her deep thoughts, Retter smiled lazily at Robert, saying, "Robert, I git so sleepy here lately—and when I'm not sleepy, I'm daydreaming!" Retter shook her head at her own situation, laughing softly.

"Wal, now, Retter . . . in yore case I reckon it's okay, being yore in the family way and all!" Robert sat down on the hearth as he spoke and leaned back on the woodbox, sitting Indian-style.

"I wonder what Papa wanted Tom fer today? He's been gone fer nigh on to six hours. It seemed important, so I been sorta fretting over it some," Retter said as she leaned forward in the rocker, looking earnestly at Robert. "Do you know, Robert?"

Robert shifted nervously as he tried to think of a way to get Retter away from this conversation. He didn't want to tell her what Tom had said before he'd left. In fact, the whole Ammons family had stayed in the kitchen, creating work for themselves, so as to keep away from Retter. They didn't want her to see their uneasiness.

Shaking his head, Robert spoke, "No, Retter. I have no idea

at all. Say! Since I been courtin' yore sister, I been wondering something! Mabbe you kin tell me how to git on the better side of her."

Smiling, Retter unwittingly fell into his change of conversation. "You shore do ask hard questions, Robert. Dovey is a hard woman to figure out—even if she is my sister. She's more of a homebody than me, and she kin cook and sew just as good as Ma. She shore kin change, though. One minute, she's bossy and sassy—the next minute, she's done gone out of the house with some sorta quiet spell on her."

Robert had begun this conversation for one reason, but as Retter had spoken, he had gotten interested in what she was saying. Dovey had him puzzled, and maybe talking to Retter about her would enlighten him.

"Retter, yo're like a sister to me—always has been like that, ain't it? But I shore do feel differently about Dovey. I don't want to be her brother!"

Retter laughed and leaned back in the rocker once again. "You men are something, Robert. It's so easy to figure us out. All you gotta do is make a woman feel like she's the onliest woman in the world, and she'll fall fer you! Course, our feelings kin git hurt something fierce, sometimes, when you least expect it, so you've got to have patience. But, what is most important, is not to let her have her own way all the time, cuz a woman don't really want to be the boss."

Robert stared at this young girl in the rocker. "Retter, where did you learn all this—yo're not near as old as me, and yit . . . " He shook his head in amazement.

The girl pushed her foot against the floor, causing the rocker to move back and forth. Retter's laughter mingled with the crackling fire. "My ma told me!"

Just then, Robert's mother called for him from the kitchen. "Robert! Kin you help me a bit?"

Standing, Robert grinned at Retter, and said, "Guess they cain't get along without me!" Robert moved off toward the kitchen.

When he had left, Retter got up from the rocker, laid her

knitting down, and went over to the door. Drawing the shawl still closer around her, she opened the door to look down the road. Maybe Tom would be coming!

A gush of icy wind hit her in the face, sending strands of dark hair fluttering around her head. Shivering, Retter stared outside. Snow covered everything she could see. The boughs of the pines hung low, burdened with the weight of the glistening snow. Even the fence-row that ran alongside the road was almost completely covered. The sky overhead was heavily clouded with gray, but in the western sky, red and gold streaked the gray with the colors of the setting sun. Twilight was almost here, and still no Tom!

Closing the door, Retter shivered again. Slowly she walked to the fireplace, and stood in front of it, her hands linked behind her back. As she stood in that position, her rounded stomach grew warm from the heat. Worry lines edged the shadows of her face.

Retter then moved back to the rocker, picked up her knitting, and sat down once again. She leaned back, her gaze following the gray wisp of smoke that swiftly rose—chased by orange flames—disappearing into the dark depths of the chimney.

The lines of worry slowly eased as the warmth of the fire relaxed her body. The room behind Retter was dusty with the softening of day as she laid her head back on the rocker and closed her eyes. The light from the fire nudged her gently, but soon she was fast asleep.

It was some time later when the door to the living room was flung open, the cold wind gushing in. Tom tromped in; his mustache was frost white, and his hat, pulled down over his eyes, covered most of his face. He closed the door and stood there, shaking his tall frame to get the light covering of snow to fall onto the wooden floor. The heavy coat made him look bulky and much larger than he was. He took his hat off and hit it against his leg, letting the waking Retter see the smile on his face.

"Hello, sweetheart! Are you okay?"

"Oh, Tom! I'm so glad to see you!" Retter got up and hurried toward him, relief flooding over her.

Tom caught her in his arms and hugged her close. Even at four and a half months pregnant, she was still so light it surprised him.

Suddenly there was a muffled noise from inside his coat. As she gave him a puzzled look, Tom stood Retter back from himself. "Tom," she said, "Tom! What's in yore coat? Cain't be yore belly groaning—it's too high up!"

Grinning broadly, he reached one big hand inside the lining of his coat and drew out a small ball of white fur. Two tiny black eyes looked back at Retter as she stared.

"This here puppy is yore's, Retter. It's a girl puppy sent from yore pa!" Tom said as he rested the small ball in Retter's hands. Out of the corner of her eye, she saw the look Tom cautiously gave his family as he looked over her head to where they stood behind her. She made a mental note to ask questions later. Right now Retter was too happy with the puppy! She held it to her face, whispering softly as the puppy licked her cheek. In the winter months, there was no going outside for very long in the cold to see the animals around the farm. Now, she had something to care for; it would fill a void in her life she hadn't even known she had. Her papa still understood her even though they hadn't seen each other in months.

The family gathered around and talked baby-talk to the puppy, laughing at one another. Tom took his coat off and hung it near the door, and going over to the fireplace, he stood with his back to the rest of the family. He held out his hands to the warmth of the flickering flames, absently rubbed them together, and then once again he held them out, flexing his fingers. Staring at the leaping flames, Tom seemed to be in a different world.

Retter watched, but said not a word. Leading the family back to the kitchen, she asked Robert to give the puppy some milk while she talked to Tom for a minute.

Coming up behind him, she softly said, "Tom, you better tell me now."

Turning slightly, Tom looked at her for a minute, and then sighing, he said, "Wal, there ain't much to tell. But I'll tell it.

Yore pa sent word fer me to come to face the rest of yore family. Seems they're his aunts or great aunts—or some such thing. I guess they'd been having words with yore daddy about him letting me marry you. I'm not fit fer you, and I'm too old fer you, too—fact is, I never should've even courted you! I spent most of four hours listening to all my faults!" Tom's face was grim as he looked back into the fire.

Retter had sat back down in the rocker, and from where she sat she could see only Tom's back in the shadows. The firelight outlined his frame, and the glow seemed to make him immense. Retter thought, as she looked at him, that she was glad she wasn't his enemy. Without saying a word, she waited for him to continue.

Suddenly he turned, and moving over to her, he dropped down on one knee beside her, saying earnestly, "Retter, I would never hurt you in any way, you know that!"

Tenderness showed in his eyes as he looked into her soft pretty face. She laid her hand over his on the arm of the rocker, and smiled.

"Yes, I know, Tom."

Standing up again, he began to walk slowly to and fro before the fireplace, his hands behind his back talking quietly. "And I told them all that, too! They wouldn't even listen to me . . . those old biddies!"

Retter giggled out loud at the outburst, and averted her head.

Stopping his pacing, Tom turned to her and finally smiled broadly, saying, "Wal, yore paw told them a thing or two! He gave them what fer, he did! He said that he liked me, Retter! I was his friend, and he done gave me permission to marry up with you. Besides, he says, too late now—Retter's with child!"

Slapping his knee, Tom laughed loudly. "You should've seen them—his aunts, I mean. Their mouths and eyes were both round as eggs! Wal, anyway, after they left, yore paw and me laughed a lot, and he gave me yore puppy fer you. But jest afore I left, he got real serious agin, and told me I'd better take care of you, or I'll know something!"

Leaning with his elbow on the mantlepiece, Tom grinned at Retter. She grinned back at him.

Softly, Tom said, "I promised to take care of you, Retter, afore we got married, and I'm a man of my word! A man's only as good as his word!"

Retter got up from the rocker, walked over to Tom and put both arms around him. Then he wrapped her up in his embrace. They were standing there together when Robert came into the room with the puppy, and then quietly turned and went back out again.

CHAPTER TWELVE

The Firstborn

The cold dark winter swirled around the old home place, leaving in its wake mounds of snow and ice. Christmas came, then the new year. Just when it seemed to Retter that it would never be warm again, she opened the door one morning to see the first redbreasted robin hop past—then stop, cock its head at her, and seem to say, "Welcome, spring!"

Retter had gotten so big she could hardly walk straight. Sitting wasn't so bad, but getting up was another story. Most of the time she had to have help.

It was the middle of March, 1910. Retter was due any day. For many weeks now she had unhappily decided that she was permanently pregnant! This ninth month seemed to be more than she could handle. She would cry at just about anything. Even Tom was keeping his distance. All Retter could think of was how could she have wanted a lot of children! She must have been crazy!

Late in the day, Retter grew even more uncomfortable—as pains started in her lower back. She didn't tell anyone—she just accepted the additional burden. At supper she refused to join the family, still saying nothing.

For some reason, Retter's thoughts turned to Charlie. That morning when she had awakened, she had opened her eyes to the shape of the old Indian in the corner of the room.

"Charlie," she had cried out—but there had been no answer. When she had finally pulled herself up and focused her eyes, she had found that her Indian had been her husband's coat hanging on a nail.

Still, all through the day, he had been there—hidden deep within herself. She had felt a slight pressure on her body, as if Charlie had placed his deerskin hide around her shoulders for warmth. Somehow, Charlie's presence calmed her emotions.

Tom's mother began to watch Retter, her eyes narrowing with speculation. Calling Robert into the kitchen, she sent him out the back way, instructing him to bring back Retter's mother. Preparations were begun for the birthing without Retter's knowledge.

Tom had gone out to purchase seeds for the cornfield he was going to plant soon. He arrived just as Robert pulled up with Retter's mother. He almost went into shock! Robert cautioned him to take care not to upset Retter.

They entered the cabin together. Retter had already been laid down in the back room. Tom's mother seemed to have things under control as she greeted Retter's mother, and the two disappeared into the back room, leaving the men to look at one another. A fuzzy, white, half-grown puppy stationed herself by the door, lying with her head on her paws.

Hours passed. It grew dark. Robert lit the oil lamp. Smoke from cigarettes hung heavily in the dimly lit room.

"I need a drink!" Tom's voice was hoarse as he spoke.

"I think we could all stand a swaller!" said Jim Ammons, unexpectedly.

Tom and Robert laughed in relief.

"There's a jar of blackberry wine in the shed. I'll git it," said Robert. He left the room.

Tom sat down at a table next to a window. He leaned over and opened it, breathing deeply from the cool night air. Propping his elbows on the window sill, he stretched out and looked at the sky full of twinkling lights. Softly, he prayed, "Dear God, please take care of my little family. Help Retter, Lord."

Midnight came. One o'clock came. Only Tom was still awake, his head on his arms as he lay at the table.

All of a sudden, sounds came from the back room. Soft crying, then moaning, then . . . yelling!

"Oh, my God!" Tom uttered a moan to himself as he jumped up, waking his father and brother. "It's coming!"

Tom's mother ran through, with no thought of the men as she passed. Intense worry was written all over her face. She came running back with a kettle of boiling water.

The periods of yelling came closer together now. Sweat broke out on Tom's face. How could he stand this any longer?

And just then—the cry of a baby!

The screaming had ceased; only the cry of the baby could be heard—then silence.

Tom's eyes were fixed on the bedroom door! It opened, and his mother came out, a big smile on her face, a bundle of white in her arms.

Slowly, Tom stumbled over to her and looked down at his firstborn. With a question in his eyes, he looked at his mother. The baby curled tiny red fingers around his own finger.

"It's a boy, Tom!"

"And Retter, is she all right?" asked Tom softly.

"Yes, she's fine. It's a good birthing. Retter screamed loud and helped herself, like the fighter she is! You should be proud of them both, Tom!"

"Kin I see her?"

"Only fer a minute—she's tired, Tom."

Looking down at the worn Retter, Tom felt more love for her than he had ever felt before. She was his—and they had produced a miracle—together!

"Tom," Retter's voice was weak as she spoke, "Tom, we have a boy. Are you happy?"

Tom leaned down and kissed Retter gently.

"I'm proud of both of you."

Retter's eyes were happy, but they began to close as she spoke. "Give him a name, Tom." Her voice trailed off.

Tom turned and reached for his son. His mother smiled as she handed him over. Retter's mother stood over to one side, also smiling.

Tom looked down at his son, something growing deep inside. Love as he'd never known spread up through him. Then, in concentration, he gazed first at one mother, then at the other.

"Something from our side could be . . . Luey. And something from Retter's side could be—yore maiden name, Mrs. Coggins . . . Bryson." Pausing, Tom smiled broadly and then said, "Retter! Meet Luey Bryson Ammons! Our firstborn—born March 16, 1910!"

Retter didn't hear. She was asleep—a ghost of a smile on her face. She was dreaming of standing on a mountaintop with the wind blowing in her hair. She wasn't alone. In the shadows of the pines behind her stood Charlie, her shield of protection. In her dream, Retter saw Charlie hold up ten fingers, and smile.

What did it mean?

CHAPTER THIRTEEN

An Act of Anger

The first few weeks after the birth of the baby seemed to Retter like a dream. For some reason, after the initial happy reaction, depression had set in, and the pain she felt as her body healed didn't help her mental attitude. Mrs. Ammons had heated water for soaking, and it was helping the healing process, but it didn't help Retter's depression. Because of her attitude, the people around her soon began to leave her alone again, which only made her feel worse. She felt no one cared.

Tom was still involved in clearing off the patch of new ground for his cornfield. When he wasn't at the sawmill, he was at his field, so he was gone most of the day. In the evening, he was so tired, he'd eat supper and soon be fast asleep.

Mrs. Ammons had been used to cleaning her home every day, so actually she needed no additional help in caring for the family. The baby cried very seldom and slept most of the day. This all left Retter with a lot of time on her hands, but nothing to do. She'd always been active as a girl, so she grew more and more depressed in her idleness. Even the air surrounding the young woman seemed to be explosive.

The day of reckoning dawned with a lovely sunrise. Retter watched from her bedroom window as the sun came up. Vivid reds, golds, and oranges spread over the tops of the lofty pines. Morning tiptoed into the room with rays of sparkling sunlight.

Retter had just finished nursing her son, and he was sleeping in the cradle Tom had made for him. Tom had left before the sun came up to help with the chores and then to go over to his cornfield.

Retter's chin rested in the palms of her hands as she propped her elbows on the wooden window ledge. She had always loved the sunrise. The painting of the sky was never the same, but it had always, in the past, created the same feeling in her—quiet, inner peace. Today this feeling didn't come. There was no peace inside her—only frustration!

Just then, Mrs. Ammons walked into the room. She hadn't knocked, even though the door had been shut. Anger welled up inside Retter. She'd begun to understand her frustration. She had no privacy at all, and she was still treated like a child!

Retter watched as Mrs. Ammons went over to the cradle and looked lovingly down at the baby.

"Luey's the best little thing," said Mrs. Ammons. "Never cries, and he's so easy to care fer. Did you feed him yit, chile?"

"Yes, I did!" said Retter, the tone in her voice cold.

Mrs. Ammons eyed Retter with uneasiness written on her face. The birthing was four weeks ago, and Retter should have gotten over this depression, thought Mrs. Ammons. I'll have to speak to Tom about this.

As Mrs. Ammons left the room, Retter looked outside again. She couldn't see where Tom was working. Maybe if she could know exactly where he spent most of his days now, she might feel a little better, so she decided that later she would walk over to the piece of ground Tom was working.

For the time being, she thought, she would gather up Tom's clothes and do a little washing. Just this thought made her feel better.

As she walked around the bed, she stopped by the cradle and looked at her son. Such a pretty little baby—and Mrs. Ammons insisted on calling him "Luey." Well, she was going to call him "Bryson," and that was that! Retter pulled the covers up over his shoulders, then turning, she went out to get the tub ready for washing.

She looked into the kitchen as she passed. There was no one there. The only sound in the open kitchen was the buzzing of the flies as they swarmed around the honey jar on the table.

Going on through the small hallway, she went out the open front door.

The sunlight was in Retter's eyes for a minute, so she stopped to adjust to the light. Finally, she looked over to the corner of the cabin to where the old black washtub sat. The washtub was already full of water, and had a fire built underneath. There stood Mrs. Ammons, shaking out a pair of pants that Retter knew were Tom's. Mrs. Ammons dropped them into the water, and she pushed them under, punching hard with a stick.

Anger woke inside Retter. She tried to control it, but from the stormy look in her flashing hazel eyes, anyone could readily see she was upset.

"Mrs. Ammons, I come out here to wash Tom's pants!" said Retter, her voice rising as she spoke.

"Now, Retter. That's okay. I'm usta taking care of Tom, so it's no trouble at all. You jest go take care of Luey. I kin do this." Mrs. Ammons again punched down the clothes with a stick.

As Retter stared at the older woman's back, she began to shake. There had to be something she could do. She didn't think she could stand this much longer.

Another thought struck her.

"Mrs. Ammons," she said, beginning to turn to go back into the house, "mabbe I kin do the churning."

"No, chile. I'll do that later. Ain't you a bit tired?" Her voice trailed off as she turned and found that Retter was no longer there. Mrs. Ammons looked all around her, but did not see Retter. Shrugging her shoulders, she turned back to her wash.

Inside the cabin, Retter was bundling the baby in a light blanket. She folded a couple of diapers, and having no way to carry them and the baby, too, she stuffed them into the top of her dress, down into her bosom. There was a determined look on her face, and so much anger stored up inside that she believed it would overflow any minute. She'd decided that since she could do nothing here, she'd go watch Tom work, or maybe even help a little. Anything to get rid of the terrible feeling that was eating at her so.

With Bryson wrapped up in the blanket, Retter came out the door and stood for a moment watching Mrs. Ammons. She'd have to pass her to follow the path that Tom took every day. Holding her head up high, Retter marched past Mrs. Ammons, not even looking at her.

"Retter! Where are you going?" called Mrs. Ammons as she walked past her. "You ain't taking Luey nowhere, are you?"

"I'm going to see Tom—and my baby is to be called BRYSON!" yelled Retter, as she stopped and looked back at the older woman. Retter's eyes looked dark and foreboding. Then abruptly, she turned, and anger pushed her down the path.

Mrs. Ammons' mouth was hanging open from surprise as she watched Retter leave. She couldn't understand just what was wrong with that girl!

As Retter hurried along the path, she was talking out loud, "Cain't do nothing! NOTHING! Jest care fer my baby, and my baby's too little to do anything at all! I want my own place. THAT'S IT! I want my own place! I gotta talk to Tom."

Mumbling to herself, she moved as fast as she could, holding Bryson close to her.

The path ahead was rocky, but clear of brush. Suddenly, the trail divided. Retter stopped and surveyed her problem. It looked as if each was well marked. Since both paths went downhill, the rains had washed small gullies out of the middle of each of them. For a minute Retter was undecided which way to go; then she decided to take the left trail. It looked as if it went downhill farther on. Tom's patch of ground had to be relatively level to grow good corn, so the left path must be the one. Tom shouldn't be too far away.

At the bottom of the incline the trail veered to the left, and the terrain grew more rocky, with the pines growing more dense. Almost before she realized it, Retter found herself in very unfamiliar surroundings. She had grown up in a forest, but in her haste and anger, she'd somehow made a bad choice of the direction she wanted to go. Fear for her child's safety began to replace the anger she'd felt before. The dark shadows all around seemed to grow bigger, as she stopped and gazed at the trees that now were all around her. Wild grape and muscadine vines covered the bushes close by the edge of the washed-out trail, giving them weird shapes in the shadows. The rustling sounds in the underbrush seemed to grow louder. She turned around a couple of times as her heart began to race. Fear gripped her. Wildly, her eyes began to dart here and there, looking for the way she'd come. In her haste, she'd lost her sense of judgment and now felt helplessly lost.

Then she spied a large rock close to the path, near an old pine. Looking over her shoulder, she slowly made her way to the rock and sat down, leaning slightly to rest her back on the trunk of the tree. She felt something soft give a little as she leaned against the bark. She pulled away and touched her back over the top of her left shoulder. Her fingers came away sticky with pine resin. A disgusted sigh escaped her lips as she spoke aloud, "If I was a cussing woman, I'd turn these woods blue with it!"

Hearing her own voice in the stillness that enveloped her, reminded her that she was alone except for her baby. As she sat there, she worked at controlling her emotions, so she could rationally figure out a solution.

"Wal," she again spoke aloud, "since I first come downhill, and then went back uphill, then I suppose I should go back downhill and then uphill agin. Yep! That's it! Now, which way is that?"

The jigsaw pieces of her puzzle seemed to be playing hide-and-seek with her imagination. Thus she closed her eyes and tried to calm herself.

Suddenly, the cracking of a twig close by caused her eyes to fly open. There, about twenty feet from her was a big black bear! It stood on all four legs, its nose in the air, sniffing the breeze. She could see its bright eyes and smell its strong odor. Flies swarmed around its bushy black coat. Retter froze.

Then over to the right side of Retter, the rustling of the underbrush grew louder—and all at once, out came a little black bear cub, so fat he wobbled. He rambled along, rolling his head from side to side, paying no attention at all to the frozen Retter. Right up to his mother he trotted, and she lowered her nose to him and playfully pushed him on up the trail—then ambled off, not once looking back.

Breathing a sigh of relief, Retter relaxed her hold on Bryson, and started to get up from the rock. Then she noticed a small feather floating lazily in the air and finally alighting delicately on the pine-needled forest floor. It was the color of the feathers Charlie always had strapped to his walking stick. She looked over her shoulder. There was no one. But, in her mind, Retter suddenly remembered something Charlie had told her long ago. "Anger is like rushing stream—always leads to hidden rapids!"

Looking around her again, Retter hurriedly chose the way she wanted to go and almost ran down the rocky trail. When the path led around to the right, she knew she was correct. She hurried on toward the opening in the forest she could see ahead. Upon reaching the fork where the trails came together again, Retter followed the trail she had not taken before. This had to be the way. She had to see Tom!

Within minutes, the forest around Retter opened up and there, before her glad eyes, was Tom—plowing. He was too far away yet for her to call to him, so she sat down on a stump of an oak and waited. Before long, Tom spotted her, and laying the reins on the handle of his plow, he loosened the bridle on the horse, and walked toward her. Nearing the stump where she sat, he wiped his wet forehead on the arm of his shirt.

"Hello, there! Are you doing okay today, Retter?"

Just hearing his voice brought a warm pleasant feeling to her body. She was so happy to see him.

He kissed her softly, and dropped down on the ground beside her, placing a blade of grass in his mouth. His eyes were on her questioningly.

She spoke so fast that her words were falling all over one another. She told him of her unhappiness at home, and of her anger. Then she told him of getting lost, and of the bear and her cub.

After she had finished her story, she waited for Tom to speak. The tale of the bear had shaken him, but he could see that all was fine now. He eyed Retter for a few minutes and then spoke softly. "I knowed something wuz wrong these past weeks. I oughta had spent more time with you. I'm sorry fer it, Retter."

As Retter reached out her hand to him, smiling, the baby began to squirm in her arms. She squeezed Tom's hand, and then releasing it, she uncovered her breast for Bryson to nurse. She held the baby's head close, and he happily began to suckle.

Tom watched with love, softly smiling. All was quiet except for the smacking sound of the baby.

Tom broke the silence, saying, "Retter, I've been thinking about that there place on the mountain over near Grassy Creek. I think Robert'll help me git that land. I'll work on it. Soon as I kin, I'll git you yore own place. I promise!"

Retter smiled a dazzling smile at him. She'd had so many bad feelings go through her today that she was thankful for this feeling of joy. Looking up, she could see the sky was bright blue, with white clouds scattered all around. Retter was happy, sitting there on the stump, nursing her baby, Tom lying on the grass beside her. She would have her own place soon—up on the mountain.

The smell of the freshly plowed earth tickled her nose, and she laughed. High in the sky, the sun smiled down on her.

CHAPTER FOURTEEN

April Taken Unawares

"The spring social at the schoolhouse is next week, Dovey. You wanta go with me?"

It was late in the day. Robert sat on the Coggins' porch, a dishpan of early peas in his lap. He had paused in his shelling to speak to the girl who sat close by.

Her quick hands continuing to shell, Dovey glanced up at the mild-mannered man she had grown to lean on.

"I'd be right proud to go with you, Robert." She let her hands drop to lie in her pan of peas, and gazed out at the ring of gold atop the darkening horizon. "You know," she continued, "it'll be good to see everybody and to dance a bit, won't it?"

"Yep! Shore will. Onliest thing is, I don't think I'll like all them backwoods boys looking at you! Might git my dander up!" Robert's voice had grown harder as his big fingers fumbled to break a small peapod.

"Ah, now, Robert. Them boys and their looks don't amount to a hill of beans! When they see how I look at you, there'll be no question as to who I care fer." Dovey leaned over and patted Robert's hand, smiling into his eyes.

A warmth shot through Robert at the touch of her hand, and he swallowed hard. His eyes took in her small olive face, and a hunger filled his body. How he wanted her!

But Dovey, not seeing his look, settled back into her chair, and continued with her task. Her thoughts had moved forward to the question of what she would wear for the social. She didn't see the evident longing on Robert's face.

Sighing, Robert dropped into reflection—growing as quiet as his companion. These past months of courting Dovey had filled a void in his life. He felt as if he'd matured much more than his years. Dovey cared for him, he knew this; her words had revealed her affection. But when he had tried to carry the relationship further, she had held him off—quietly reassuring him that in time she would demonstrate her deep feeling for him.

Robert suspected that this attitude in Dovey came from the experience she'd had with Henry. Something had happened inside the girl that night in the barn, but Robert couldn't put his finger on the problem. A spark had gone from the light in her eyes. And a veil had covered the shine—as if a guard had been posted in her heart.

A feeling of despair moved up into Robert. He suddenly stood up, and turning, set the pan of peas down in the chair.

"Dovey, it's almost dark, and I have to help Tom in the morning. I'd best go."

The surprised girl stared up at Robert. Slowly, she, too, rose and left her pan of peas in her chair. She laid her hand on the perplexed man's arm.

"If you hafta go, you hafta go. I'm much obliged fer the help you've allowed me today—picking peas and all."

"It weren't nothing," he said. His hand went to her face, his fingers touching the softness of her cheek.

She stood still—gazing, still in surprise, into his eyes. Her lips parted.

Suddenly, Robert raised his other hand to her other cheek, and firmly held her face still. "Dovey, I told you some time back that I didn't know if I loved you or not. Wal, I know now—I love you." He paused, but only for a second, and then continued. "I cain't come back to see you afore the dance on Friday next week. I want you to think on marrying me. We'll talk about it then . . . and remember, I love you, Dovey. I love you!"

He leaned down quickly and kissed her hard on the lips—then he was gone—leaving a trembling woman on the porch in the twilight.

Dovey stared after him, frustration filling her. Her first instinct was to call after him—but she hesitated. Instead, she only watched him go, struggling with her feelings.

The touch of his kiss lingered. She raised one hand, covering her mouth—then slowly brought her fingers down until just their tips felt the burn of her lips.

It felt good—his kiss. She relaxed and let the feeling spread. Her heart began to beat faster, her breath came quicker—until her ears hurt with the pounding of the feeling that now raced through her body.

"Oh, Robert," she breathed finally. "Oh, Robert—I love you, too!"

But he wasn't there to hear.

As the week passed, Robert slowly became so irritable that even Retter felt the blister of his tongue. The family, as a whole, wondered about his sanity. He seemed to be somewhere else in spirit when he was with them in body.

When it started affecting his appetite, his mother knew something significant was bothering him. One morning, after breakfast, she asked him to help her with the dishes. Sullenly, he positioned himself beside her as she poured hot water from the black iron pot into the dishpan.

Steam rose, bathing the smoothness of Robert's face. He didn't move away—only stared, his gaze fastened to the spinning water, watching the swirls settle.

"Robert, you and me are gonna talk!" began his mother as she adeptly cut a few flakes of soap into the hot water. She didn't look at him.

"What is it you wanta talk about?" answered her son, his gaze still on the water that now was becoming cloudy with the melting soap.

"About what's ailing you, Son, that's what! Lessus hear it, boy!"

"It ain't nothing Momma—nothing at all."

"Don't you lie to me! There ain't nothing that gits me riled faster'n a lie!" Her hands hit the hot water so sharply that

Robert's shirt and her apron were covered with wet splashes of cloudy water. She still hadn't looked at him.

His mouth open, Robert stared at his mother. Her gray-streaked hair was pulled back from her face, and fastened in a bun with hairpins at the neck. Her stocky figure was filled with anger.

"Momma, why are you mad at me? I ain't done nothing!" Robert felt like a little boy, and he didn't like it. Anger began to rise in him.

"A long time ago, I taught you to talk to me or to your daddy about anything that ails you, and now's one of them times. I want you to tell me jest what is causing you to act like . . . like a horse with a boil on his tail!"

The anger left Robert as laughter poured out of him. The words he had just heard were so far removed from his mother's nature that there was no way he could stay angry. She had used her husband's words to describe her own feelings. Robert laughed so hard that his mother finally broke down and smiled.

The barrier had been broken. Robert could now talk—and he did.

He told his mother about what he had said to Dovey. His deep feelings for her had grown so fast that he couldn't go on being near her without showing his love.

Now that he had finally told Dovey how he felt, he was afraid of what her response would be.

"Yo're so afraid, you ain't fit to live with, son!" his mother snapped, but she was smiling. There was relief in her eyes as she turned to him, wiping her wet hands on her apron. "Lessus sit down at the table, have another cup of coffee, and talk a bit."

Robert sat down, and turned to watch his mother get the cups, then pour the coffee. As she stirred the cream into her cup, she paused in reflection. Then, raising her eyes to his, she said, "Son, you love this girl, don't you?"

"I shore do, Momma. I don't know where it come from, but I shore do!"

"She ain't seen anyone but you fer quite a spell, so she thinks highly of you, too, I'll bet. But that's not the point.

What's important is that you do yore best in helping yoreself." She took a sip of coffee.

"I don't rightly know what you mean, Momma." Robert had yet to touch his coffee. His eyes hadn't left his mother.

"What I mean is, don't let this feeling of defeat eat you up afore the fight has even been fought. Yo're comin' around, hittin' out at the people who love you, because yo're afraid that yo're not worth lovin'. The folks in this house love you, or at least, they used to!" His mother chuckled, and placed her wrinkled hand on his shirtsleeve. "Son, the Lord helps them who help themselves. Tomorrow is Friday—and the social. When you see Dovey, don't you show her a shell of a man. Yo're a good man! Yo're a strong man because yo're gentle and kind. Both you boys turned out that way. I only hope and pray that yore brother Frank is as good as you and Tom." The little woman's eyes grew sad for a moment, then her attention snapped back to Robert. "You hear me, boy! Whatever this girl's answer to you is, it doesn't change what you are. But, if her heart's not longing fer you, there's something wrong with her!"

Robert smiled at his mother's words, but he almost trembled to think that Friday was so close. He had listened intently to his mother, and he knew that if Dovey's answer was no, it would be long before he'd get over it.

"Momma, yore words are good words. I'll think on it."

Although he spoke little, his mother smiled. She noticed that the look on his face had softened, as if a burden had been lifted from him. She felt he was now in a better frame of mind to face his tomorrow—the tomorrow that could change his life.

The path over the mountain had never been so long—nor so hard to climb. The violets he had picked along the way grew clammy in his hand; he switched the bunch to the other hand.

Before he knew it, he was looking down at the cabin. He gazed at the shadowed dwelling, not really seeing the old weathered building. In his mind was a picture of his love—but she was hazed, as if in a ghost-like dream.

Then, as was his custom, he squared his shoulders, hitched

up his pants, took a deep breath, and walked on—with the last of his courage.

He saw her from afar—she was waiting for him on the porch. Anxiously, he fixed his attention on her face. Even as he got closer, he couldn't see her expression. She seemed to be looking down at her hands in her lap. He hurried.

He could see her clearly now; she suddenly looked up, to see him almost upon her.

Her face lit up with happiness, and she threw out her arms, running down the steps and into his embrace. "Oh, Robert, I will marry you. I've missed you so much. Please don't leave me alone so long agin—ever!"

Her arms went around his neck, and she kissed him, baring her deepest desires for this gentle man.

He sank into a still, deep place—a shimmering pool of feeling.

The fiddler was playing the last song. The slow music had almost all the participants out on the dance floor. Romance had filled the evening, for it had turned into a night of celebration. Tom Ammons had announced the forthcoming marriage of his brother Robert to Dovey Coggins.

Retter had never seen her sister, or her brother-in-law as happy as they were tonight. In turn, she responded with her own happiness by moving closer to Tom. This last dance of the evening had everyone longing to be alone, each with his own lover.

As Retter pressed in toward Tom, her eyes closed for a moment. It was just then that a sudden chill crept up her spine. Her eyes flew open—to see a large shadow by the hallway entrance. She shook her head, and blinked her eyes, looking again at the darkened doorway.

There was nobody.

Had she imagined it? She must have, she thought—it was just like an image of Charlie she had once seen. With a shake of her head, she dismissed the shadow from her mind.

When the dance ended, the couples began to say their

goodnights, lingering only to tell Robert and Dovey, once again, how happy they were for them.

By the time Robert had walked Dovey out by the hitching rail, most of the mountain people had gone.

Dovey's father had insisted that Robert drive Dovey to the social in his wagon, and had provided his best mule for the occasion.

"Robert," Dovey said quietly beside him, "something's wrong. Daddy's mule ain't tied to the rail."

Tom and Retter stopped behind Robert and Dovey, and the four stared at the wagon that stood alone. Tom held his lantern high, the light casting swinging shadows.

"Robert, you check over by the creek, and I'll walk around back. Maybe some kids turned him loose," said Tom as he hurried away.

Robert said not a word, but rushed off into the darkness toward the creek that ran alongside the schoolhouse.

Dovey and Retter looked at each other. Then Retter said, "Dovey, I'm gonna look over on the other side, near the outhouse. You stay here—and don't get close to that drinking trough. There's water splashed out all over."

"Wait . . . Retter!" Dovey began, but the younger girl had vanished also.

It was some minutes later before Robert came back leading the mule. Tom and Retter both emerged from the shadows as Robert brought the animal up to the wagon.

"I found him down by the creek. Shore is strange to me. Must be the full of the moon. Where's Dovey?"

Retter stopped still, and looked around the lantern-lit clearing. "She's not here? DOVEY! DOVEY!" Retter's voice had grown suddenly shrill as she repeatedly turned around, calling out in all directions, "DOVEY! DOVEY!"

The night was still. Even the tree frogs and crickets were silent.

Tom set the lantern down near the water trough, and

cupping his hands around his mouth, he joined Retter as they both called Dovey's name.

"Tom! Looky here!" Robert was stooping beside the oil light, one knee resting on the muddy ground.

Tom and Retter were beside Robert in seconds, and all three gazed at fresh footprints—water still oozing into the muddy imprints.

"What do you make of it, Robert?" Tom said, his finger tracing the large outline.

"Them big footprints cain't be nobody else's but Henry Bridges!" Robert stood suddenly, hitting one fist against the palm of his other hand. The sound echoed in the dark cathedral of the pines. "Tom, Henry's done made off with Dovey!"

CHAPTER FIFTEEN

Underwater Bridge

All around was the damp smell of rich earth and resined pines. Dovey's cheeks were stiff with the salt of her dried tears, and her arms hurt from the bruise of Henry's hold.

The horse, carrying a double load, moved slowly—ever upward. There was no trail before them, only the dark denseness of the upper forest. Night was now their companion.

Henry leaned forward, pushing the pine boughs and the oak branches away from his captive, but the sting from the pine needles still cut across Dovey's face and arms. She cried out, her tears beginning again.

"We'll be out of this stretch of woods soon—out onto the granite cliffs," Henry muttered, leaning closer, his breath touching her ear.

Dovey shuddered involuntarily, pulling her shoulders up closer to her face. Her hands were tied to the saddle horn, and she had long since lost the feeling in her fingers.

Henry had come upon her while she waited for the others at the schoolhouse. He had come from behind, covering her mouth with his hand, lifting her as if she weighed nothing. With the ease of a seasoned mountain man, he had stolen her away—leaving no sound in the evening haze.

When they had reached his hidden mount, she had cried and begged him to let her go. In silence, he had lifted her to the saddle, tied her hands, and mounted behind her. Her cries had gone unheeded.

After the initial struggle with this powerful man, Dovey

had tried to calm her rising terror, and to collect her thoughts. It was hard for her to imagine that Henry really wanted to hurt her. They had courted for months, and he had been nothing but a gentleman—except for the night in the barn! She'd forgotten how frightening his attack on her had been.

Henry had lived so much of his life in the backwoods, alone, that he had felt uncomfortable in any crowd. At least, that was what Dovey had always believed—until now! She understood one thing though—he was at home here in the forest. He knew exactly where he was going—trail or no trail. The question now was, what would he do once he got there?

As this thought settled in her mind, she felt her heart tremble with new fear. She had to get away—somehow!

"Oh, Lord, help me!" she prayed.

Suddenly, the horse stumbled, throwing the man and woman forward. As the animal righted itself, a loosened rock clattered its way down the steep incline. The weight of the big man behind her had crushed her wrists against the saddlehorn.

"Ohh, Henry," she cried, pain in her words. "Please loosen these ropes about my hands. I ain't feeling them at all."

"Jest as soon as I take them ropes off you, you'll try to git away. Them ropes stay!"

"Henry, what are you going to do with me! I ain't done you no wrong! Anyways, Robert'll find you—and Tom's with him! Ain't no telling what'll happen to you if he ketches you! Tom carries a gun!"

"Shut up!" Henry's voice carried malice.

"Henry, YORE CRAZY!" The frightened woman screamed to the tops of the lofty pines, as she once again struggled helplessly in Henry's hold.

The strong man laughed strangely as he listened to the echoes of the frightened girl's screams—then he pulled her tight against him as the labored horse continued through the damp night.

Biting her lip, Dovey closed her eyes, trying to fill her mind with the image of Robert. If only she could see him in her thoughts, she believed that the sense of him would strengthen her. She concentrated.

Slowly, she pieced together the features of the man she loved. His eyes were searching, delving down into the blackness in the well of her mind. She knew he would come for her. She had to believe that! She relaxed and let her body move with the forward motion of the horse.

Time climbed beside them—its presence joining the movement of the overcast sky. Ahead was the dark of the unknown.

In the background of her meditation, she became aware of a new sound. It began as if from nothing, yet constantly grew—soft at first, then becoming a loud, steady, rushing noise.

Drops of water opened Dovey's eyes, the cool touch jarring her out of her reverie. With her eyes open now, she was surprised to find that the noise she'd manufactured in her mind, was not a product of her imagination at all. The sound engulfed her, the roar deafening.

Dovey looked up—the clouds shifting at that moment, allowing her to see what lay before them. The man and woman on the horse were on the edge of a cliff—and from above them, coming as if from the heavens, a high waterfall plunged to the earth, dancing in billows of white foam below them. Clouds once again covered the moon.

Dovey's pink party dress was soon soaked, the heaviness of the broadcloth pulling at her shoulders. Her teeth began to clatter, as her body shook with the coldness of the dark night.

Henry pulled a slicker out of his saddlebag, and covered them—drawing Dovey still closer to himself. He clapped his hand over her bosom, and squeezed—his fingers pushing around the buttons of her blouse.

At the touch of his fingers, Dovey cringed—her body stiffening at the unfamiliar intimacy. She tugged at her ropes, and moaned deep in her throat.

The big hand tore at the buttons, laying open the bodice of the dress. Henry began to fondle one breast, then the other—his breathing growing hard against her back.

In silence, the young girl cried in her shame. The roar of the waterfall drowned her heart's scream.

Henry turned the head of the horse, and the pain began to descend onto the ravine of blackness. Down deep into the spray of the falls rode the prisoner, Henry, and the horse.

"Tom, these tracks show only one horse—they're riding double!" Robert was once again kneeling in the lantern light, his searching eyes reading the trail before them.

"Jest means that they'll move slower than us. Henry won't expect us to be right on him. He don't think we'd leave Retter alone to come after him. Good thing she ain't afraid of the dark and kin ride like a man."

Robert stood, and turned to remount Jim Coggins' mule. "Yeah, and he must've thought this ole mule wouldn't stop by the creek to graze. Where'd you send Retter—to our place, or on to the Coggins'?"

"I reckon she's at our place by now. Daddy'll git everybody together. But we've got to ketch up to Henry soon—afore the rains come." Tom leaned forward, the slickness of his horse giving him more freedom of movement than he wanted. His hand fisted in the horse's mane. "From the way I see it, their trail leads off into the high country, straight up into the backwoods. Must not be using a main trail. What's off in that direction, Robert? Lessus think about this afore we rush off with our heads half-cocked."

"Ain't nothing up there in them mountains but the granite cliffs and Whitewater Falls!"

"Wal, where do you think he'll come out? Try to think like him!"

Robert's legs hugged the chesty mule, as he handed the lantern back to his brother. "Onliest way out of there is down below the falls—hard way down, though—wet and slippery!" Robert's stomach felt like he'd swallowed a rock. His face was grim.

"Okay, then," said Tom, "we cain't foller him in this dark up that mountain, so we'll cut around and come up aside the river. By then, it'll be daylight. He'll have to come out sometime, the son of a bitch!" Tom's acid tone was drowned in a rush of hoofbeats as the brothers soon lost themselves in the blackness.

The pain in Dovey's head pounded. Her teeth had been clenched so long that when she finally eased her mouth open, the relief of her tensions was like a release from bondage.

After they had begun their descent, Henry's interest in her body had been transferred to the safety of the trip down. It had seemed to Dovey that it had taken hours for her and Henry to edge their way downward on the slope beside the waterfall. Never before had she been so scared. But the horse had been surefooted, and had not slipped once.

Now, along the river, the banks were unevenly tiered with rocks, tree roots, and stands of dense brush.

The night wasn't as dark as before. Dovey looked up to see the eastern sky growing gray with the first light of dawn. She turned her gaze down to her wrists. There was a dull-colored wetness staining the ropes that bound her.

Tears clouded her eyes, and she once again tasted the salt of her fear. Henry hadn't gone to all this trouble without something evil in mind—now Dovey knew this. From this standpoint, there was no escape. She had been taken too far, too fast, in too dark a night, ever to be found. Henry had taken her away from home, probably never to return her again. Despair filled the young woman. Home had never looked as good as it did now. Her whole body had become one deep longing for home.

Henry had guided his horse around to what looked like a seldom-used trail alongside the river. Beds of browned pine needles covered the now widening pathway; overhead stood tall white pine and beech; dampness hung in the air; earth smell enveloped the frightened girl.

Through her tears, Dovey saw only a green-brown hazy wall of laurel and pine—a grapevine veil disappearing somewhere above. She felt her hands being loosened—the sudden pain of circulation jarring her sharply. She pulled her hands close to her body, rubbing them to feel the pain. Her fingers grew sticky with her own blood.

"Dovey!" Henry was standing beside her. He reached upward, catching her underneath her arms, and lifted her down. "Come on with me! We got things to do!"

Dovey's feet didn't work. Exhaustion and fear filled her, and the girl suddenly collapsed—to lie shaking beside the horse. Her mind was no longer clear—she seemed to be falling somewhere between the real and the unreal world.

She felt herself being pulled, decaying leaves and pine needles cushioning her body. In the air above her was the sound of Henry's cursing as he dragged her close to the exposed roots of a pine. She felt the tug as he pulled at her dress. The wet broadcloth was stubborn, causing more curse words in the coming morn.

Once again, Dovey felt the roughness of his hands as he touched her bare bosom. Both hands anchored themselves into her bodice, and suddenly, the dress came apart.

Dovey eyes flew open—and she could see the crazed glaze in the eyes above her. No longer did he even resemble the man she had courted for so long. Desperation pushed through her body, suddenly giving strength to every limb. She pulled her legs quickly up to her chest, and kicked out at the giant of a man.

Surprise was on her side, and the sudden onslought caught Henry off guard. But only for a moment. He had been pushed backward, but he caught himself, and dropped to lay flat in front of the spirited girl. Then he laughed and crushed his lips to hers. Dovey tasted her own blood.

Henry began to fumble at his belt, pulling himself up, propping his body with his knees. In his haste, he had removed both hands from Dovey.

The now determined girl forgot the aches and pains of the long horse ride, and quickly scrambled out from under the man.

But he grabbed the hem of the torn dress, issuing a sound that resembled the growl of a mad dog, jerking her back toward him. In seconds, he was up and holding her at arms length. "I like it when you fight, girl!" Henry threw back his head and laughed loudly.

From where it came, Dovey never knew, but suddenly a new feeling surged through her. Anger as she had never before known it exploded within her. Instead of running away, she went toward him—all thought gone from her mind. She felt only a surging anger blinding her to all consequences.

The sudden rush she made at Henry put him off balance. His laughter caught in his throat. As he stumbled, he cursed and hit Dovey across the face with the back of his hand.

Almost losing consciousness, Dovey flew through the air and landed on a pile of soggy leaves and moss. The wet coolness quickly brought back all her senses, and she rolled over and away from where she had landed.

Her first impulse had been correct, for only seconds later Henry landed in the same spot. To Dovey, his heavy body hitting the wet leaves sounded almost like another slap in the face.

The girl scrambled up, pulling at what was left of her dress until it came off in her hand. Standing only in her long half-slip, she pulled the garment up over her breasts, covering herself, but at the same time, giving herself freedom from the heavy broadcloth gown. She saw Henry struggling to raise himself. Quickly, she ran behind a stand of young oaks, her eyes darting here and there, searching for weapon of some sort. She stooped to pick up a stick near her feet. Rotten, it fell apart in her hands. The ground was slippery—it was hard for her to stand. All elements seemed to oppose her, which only deepened her anger. She wanted to scream.

Suddenly, he was in front of her—only a few feet away. His eyes were horribly small now, almost closed in their single violent intent. Dovey knew now that he meant to have his way with her and then kill her. This man was evil.

She retreated until her back touched the limbs of a cluster of old oaks. Her arms behind her, she pushed against the stiff branches.

Henry came slowly, his arms reaching out, shortening any escape route for the small woman. She became aware of a stench of rotten wood on his wet clothing.

Then, almost as if it had been planned, her right hand brushed the rough bark of a heavy limb. At her touch, the branch loosened, and suddenly it filled her hand. There was no more time to think—no where to run.

As the big man bore down upon her, she grasped the limb as tight as she could, raised her arms above her head, and she swung with all her body and soul at the ugly face of her attacker.

The rotten wood burst in his eyes—decayed matter covering his head. Both hands flying to his face, the crazed man screamed into the dense leaf-cover above.

Dovey immediately knew that it was time to run. She whirled around the clump of trees and ran down to the bank of the river. Along the edge, the water looked shallow. Without another thought, she ran through the water, her feet sliding in and out of the silvery liquid.

A ray of sun shot through the overhang of leaves alongside the river. As she rounded a curve in the bank, she noticed from the corner of her eye a dark ridge of scaly rock running across the river just beneath the surface of the water. Taking a quick glance behind her, she swallowed the fear that rose like bile in her throat, and ran with full force across the underwater bridge—to vanish in the laurel jungle on the other side.

CHAPTER SIXTEEN

In Retter's Shadow

In among the dense leaves Dovey hid herself, to wait and watch. She forced her breath to come slowly—to help calm her heartbeat. In her stillness, she realized, with a shiver, that she was cold and wet. She wrapped her bare arms closely around her body, glancing covertly about her. The spring morning grew suddenly cool in the depth of this valley close to the river.

Then she heard him—running in the water, rounding the bend—splashing toward her hiding place. Her breath almost stopped.

His gaze combed both sides of the river. Even though hidden, Dovey felt the heat of his frustration and anger as his look seemed to slide right through the leaf cover and touch her. But his stride didn't slacken and soon his running had carried him out of sight.

Her gaze jumped to the path she had taken across the river. The sun had moved higher, leaving only shadows in its wake. The underwater bridge had vanished—for the time being. Dovey felt her arms grow limp as her fears faded. She would be safe for a little while.

Suddenly the woman in hiding realized that water had oozed into her shoes. A chill swept through her body, causing the hair on her arms to stand on end. Her teeth chattered.

She moaned and began to move away from the soft ground beside the water. Careful to walk slowly so as not to attract attention, she began her search for a spot of warm sunlight.

"Just in case Robert and Tom are still following us," Dovey

thought, "I'd better stay close to the river so they can find me."

Henry had gone down the river, but soon he would have to come back for his horse. Dovey reasoned that she should also follow the river—but she would have to climb a little higher so she could see both banks. She didn't want to run into the man on his way back.

Climbing and walking helped take her mind off what could very well happen to her if Henry found her again. Reaching a knoll above the river, she noticed an animal trail that ran along under the tall pine trees, far enough away from the river to make her feel safe, yet close enough to allow her to see the banks on either side. She set out walking with long steps.

But soon Dovey found that the trail made by the small animals of the forest had been made only for the animals themselves. Briars and scrub growth blocked her path. Sometimes she could barely fit herself through openings in the branches.

Hunger pains began gnawing at her. But she found spring water bubbling out of the mountainside and stopped to drink. This helped settle the hollow feeling in her stomach.

Sunlight now found its way through the leaves, speckling the forest floor beneath her. Her chills were soon gone—but her bare arms now showed deep scratches from the sharp-thorned briars she'd worked her way through. She had felt the pain, and deep inside, had cried over the scarring of her skin. But, once again, she had thought that it would be as nothing compared to what would happen if Henry found her.

Time passed slowly as the now almost exhausted woman picked her way through the woods—yet still kept an eye turned toward the river.

First, she heard the sounds of the forest stop. The birds quit chirping—the tree frogs stopped croaking. For a moment all she could hear was the rush of water as it passed over the river rocks, making little waterfalls.

Dovey stopped and listened intently.

Then she heard the murmur of voices . . . and approaching hooves hitting rocks.

Leaning against a pine, she strained to see around the bend in the river below. Whoever was coming, was already close upon her. From her vantage point, Dovey could see well.

Suddenly, catching a movement from the corner of her eye, the woman in hiding glanced over at the bank on the other side. A lone man had moved out from the foliage and stood looking at the river below.

It was Henry.

Once again Dovey froze, pressing herself as close to the pine as she could. The rough bark almost scratched her face, and the smell of resin bit into her nostrils.

Robert's voice floated up to Dovey.

"We're getting close—another half hour and we'll be right at the falls. Best be on our guard, Tom."

The sound relieved and scared her at the same time. But she couldn't take her eyes off Henry. He made no effort to hide himself. Yet he had no visible weapon, either. He stood calm and waiting on the bluff above the gorge.

Two riders came around the bend below. Dovey finally tore her gaze from the big man standing across from her and looked at the unsuspecting brothers.

Their faces grim, the men showed the fatigue of the night's ride. They didn't look up, pacing their horses slowly near the water's edge.

Dovey didn't know what to do—she wanted to scream—but she didn't want the men below to be hurt by the man above them. She moved slightly, leaning out to see the riders more clearly.

The horses were carrying them away.

Dovey glanced over at Henry. His eyes seemed to jump the gorge and burn into her gaze. He had seen her.

Resolved to do something—anything—she turned to run the way she had come, yelling as loudly as she could, "Robert! Tom! I'm here!"

Her scream erupted into the damp air just as Henry began his move—he had disappeared into the brush of the gorge. She knew he was heading toward her.

Below, the riders had heard the cry, for she caught the quick sound of horses running through water. But she couldn't count on Robert and Tom reaching her in time. The thought of Henry's hands on her again frightened her so badly that all she could think of was running away.

Suddenly, hands were upon her—lifting her—holding her tight. She fought, her arms and legs flying out—cries coming through clenched teeth.

"LET . . . ME . . . GO! LET . . . ME . . . GO!"

"Dovey, it's me—Robert! Calm down—it's me."

She turned wild, frightened eyes on the man who was trying to help her—but just as she did, Henry loomed up out of the brush. Dovey stared in horror as he came upon the unseeing Robert.

Before she could say anything, Henry had pulled Robert and herself to the ground. As Henry clamped an arm under Robert's chin, Robert released his hold on Dovey.

The pain of landing had taken her breath away, but she regained her reflexes fast, and jumped up. She backed away slightly, and stared at the face of Henry. His eyes showed no emotion, and his face was a study of a peculiar deathly calm.

"Henry!" Dovey cried, "Let him go!"

At his lack of response, Dovey forgot about herself. Once again, she went at the big man who had been strong enough to pull two people off a loping horse. She pushed him, she kicked him, she bit him.

Brushing her away as if she were only a fly, Henry only tightened his hold on Robert.

But then, the sound of a gunshot ripped the air. Dovey's attention flew toward a third man who had come upon the scene. As Tom pulled the trigger of his rifle again, smoke drifted from the barrel of the gun in his hand.

Again the report ripped the air.

Henry dropped Robert, turned like a wounded animal and headed into the heavy forest, away from the bullets aimed at him. Tom followed him, leaning low against his horse's mane.

Dovey hurried over to Robert. The dazed man had one hand on his neck; he was using the other to push himself up from where he had fallen.

"Robert, are you all right? Are you hurt?" Dovey touched his arm, her gaze soft on him.

"I'm . . . fine. How about you?" Robert had got to his feet and now stood gazing down at her. "Where's your dress!" he suddenly demanded, his voice louder.

Dovey stared wide-eyed—then snapped, "I took it off—it was wet and torn. Anyway, I could run faster without it!"

Robert's look softened so fast that he almost looked as if he were ready to cry. "I'm sorry," he said quickly. "I was just so worried."

In two steps, he was there beside her, holding her tight—she felt his body close against hers. She pressed herself closer.

She was silent so long that Robert suddenly asked softly, "What are you thinking, Dovey?"

"I'm worried, Robert," she answered. "I'm beginning to think like Retter!"

CHAPTER SEVENTEEN

Bryson's Brother

Tom sat in the middle of the floor looking at his handiwork. Sweat was slowly rolling down the side of his face. His hat was pushed back on his head, and the tips of his dark wet hair curled around the brim. His clothes and hands were covered with creek mud. He was tired, however, the expression on his face only portrayed happiness. Tom had just placed the last river rock into the fireplace of his new home. His smile spread as he surveyed the room.

The walls, ceiling, and floors were all wooden boards he had procured from the sawmill where he worked. The fireplace and hearth were made from river rock he had hauled up from the Tuckasegee River down in the valley. The fireplace covered one whole wall, with shelves built on either side along the adjoining walls. Almost directly across from each other on either wall were two doors. The door to the left faced the road that led up to the cabin. The one on the right opened onto a small wooden porch.

The door to the bedroom was at Tom's back. It was a small room, with narrow stairs against one wall. These led to the attic. There was only one window in this room, on the back wall.

The windows throughout the house were without glass. Since glass was an expensive luxury, the windows were covered with slats nailed together on a brace. There were supports underneath and overtop the window openings, allowing the cover to slide back and forth.

In the front room there was also only one window—one that looked out to the east.

The only room in the three-room cabin to have two windows was the kitchen. Retter had insisted on that! She had also wanted a porch between the living room and the kitchen—on which to sit in the evenings after supper.

The trials Tom had gone through these long months had been worth it! The cabin was finished! He and Retter had been married almost three years to the day, and their home was finally done.

Tom's thoughts went back over the long months. At first he had had no help from Robert with his plans for a home up on this mountain. Henry's escape had left turmoil inside both families—the Ammons' and the Coggins'. The search for Henry had taken days and although there had been a few clues, the end result had been no concrete evidence of the whereabouts of the deranged man. Dovey had taken to her bed after her ordeal. And then, even Retter had been distracted as she had taken over the care of her sister.

Even after interest had finally been turned toward the building of Tom and Retter's cabin, there had been more problems—the struggle to procure the money for the purchase of the land—then cutting through the trees, up and down the mountainous terrain—and then having the lumber hauled in by wagon loads.

Finally, Robert and his father had gone out of their way to help with what little money they had, but mostly they had given their backbreaking labor. Tom had saved some money from his New Orleans days, but then, even with the money his father had advanced him, he still hadn't had enough money to complete the purchase of the land. But Robert had come up with the last bit he needed, and Tom had bought the whole parcel of land up on this mountain—one hundred and eighty-six acres. Tom thought how fortunate he was to have family that pitched in and helped one another when help was needed.

In return for all his help, Tom had told Robert he could have his share of their daddy's land. After their marriage, Robert and Dovey had been living at the Coggins' cabin. They were to move in with the older Ammons' as soon as Tom and Retter moved out.

David F. Ammons

Tom took a deep breath, and then released it in the form of a deep contented sigh. Providing a home for his small family was deeply satisfying. And his family was growing—Retter was due anytime now with their second baby. Bryson was two years old as of last week, and he was such a rascal! As big as she was, Retter still ran after him—continually correcting him.

Rising from the floor, Tom quickly walked to the door and went outside to clean off his clothes. The caked mud clung to him. Hearing voices, Tom looked up to see his father and brother approaching.

"Tom, are you ready fer a bait of cold biscuits and ham?" called Robert as they drew near. "I allowed you'd be pretty hungry by now."

"Yep! You shore allowed right! I'm so hungry I could eat a bear," said Tom, rubbing his hands together and grinning. "I jest laid the last rock in the fireplace. We're done!"

With broad grins, the three men jovially pounded each other on the back and congratulated one another. Such a great relief they felt! Other things were to be done, but at the moment, the most important milestone had been completed.

Standing back, Jim Ammons looked up at the darkening clouds and shook his head, saying, "We'd best be finishing up, boys. Looks like it's coming a gully-washer!"

Together, the men went into the house, found their lard can of cold biscuits and ham, and sat down on the floor in the empty room near the fireplace, between the two open doorways.

Through the door to the east, they watched the clouds roll, tumble, and grow blacker. The wind had picked up and seemed to be pushing the dark clouds faster and faster to cover the entire sky. It grew darker outside, and the rustling of the leaves in the trees announced the oncoming storm.

Suddenly, the rains came. Not slowly, but all at once. It seemed as if the sky had opened up and buckets of water were overturned.

Tom got up, went over to the door and, leaning against the door brace, watched the rain hit the ground outside. It had been dry for a long time, and in clear areas where the rain struck the bare ground, the dust danced all around—almost like steam rising. It rained so hard and so fast it wasn't long before streams formed and the rainwater ran freely downhill.

Between the cabin and the hill on the south side, Tom and his father had built a rock wall. This wall ran from the other side of the back porch all the way around to the woodpile on the east side.

Water ran off the wall down onto the walkway, alongside the chimney and underneath the cabin, flowing then over what was to be the front yard, down into the creek below the cabin.

Standing there watching the rainwater, Tom was lost in thought. He could see the rain falling on a wagon that had covered two happy people in love. The thought of Retter as she had been then made a warm feeling rise in him, bringing a smile. She had been so young and lovely, so naive and hungry for his arms. She had been so open and then trusting, she had given herself to him. He would always be thankful that he had found her, and she had wanted him.

Then, as suddenly as the rain had come, it was gone. There was a soft clean-smelling breeze that made its way through the doorway and into the cabin. The rain had washed the day and now was ready for the night.

Tom longed to see Retter. For some reason, he grew impatient, wanting to gather his tools up and get on down the mountain, over to his father's house. With long steps, he began to hurry around the room, putting his tools in a burlap bag.

His father and brother, seeing his haste, began to help him. Before long, they were on their way down the mountain. The rain had really been a "gully-washer." The road had already been washed out in places. The waterfall down below them was loud in their ears as they walked, Tom carrying the sack over his shoulder. To Tom, it seemed as if a huge hand were at his back, pushing him.

"Tom, I gen'ly walk down this here mountain—not run! I've a hankering to slow the pace down a mite!" said Jim as he put his hand to his aching side.

"Ah, Paw! I'm sorrier than I kin say. Don't know what's come over me! It's a far piece to the house from here. I reckon I'd best slow down. I fergit about yer back." Tom continued to apologize to his father until Jim grew impatient with him.

"Tom, it ain't no never mind! Pretty soon we'll be acrost the crik, and it won't take no time at all afore we'll be home. Jest slow up yore talking, too! What's ailing you, son?" said Jim.

"Don't know, Paw—but I feel like I oughta be at the house. You reckon Retter's in a family way?"

"Oh, lawdy me! Move on, son. Move on!"

An hour later they arrived at the small cabin. Night had already fallen.

The crying of a newborn baby greeted the Ammons men as they entered the cabin. Looking at one another, amazement showed on their faces. Nature had taken its course, and had almost announced it to the father as he was hurrying home.

The room was dimly lit by the light from two oil lamps. The smell of freshly brewed coffee filled the air.

Tom's mother came through the door from the kitchen. She had heard the arrival of the men. Her face was wreathed in a smile, and her first words answered all their unspoken questions.

"Everything's jest fine! Retter's resting—and you have another son, Tom."

Tom's eyes were wide as he spoke, "Another son! Paw, Robert! You hear that! Another . . . "

As Tom had spoken, he had suddenly spied Bryson peering out from behind a chair near the fireplace. His face was solemn and still. He was staring at his father.

"Bryson, come out from behind that there chair and come to yore paw," said Tom, kneeling down, one knee on the floor.

Bryson came running, and threw his arms around his father, a muffled sob escaping his lips.

"What're you fretting fer, son?" Tom urged him to talk.

"Daddy, Mommy hurt . . . Mommy . . . cie," he said, as he pointed his fat finger toward the back room, then glanced at his grandma.

Over the top of Bryson's head, Tom looked at his mother. She shrugged her shoulders and went into the bedroom.

Shaking his head, Jim led Robert out of the room toward the kitchen, heading for the coffee, leaving Tom alone with Bryson.

Picking Bryson up in his arms, Tom hugged him close. Then, walking over to the rocker that Retter always used with Bryson, he sat down. Setting the child on his lap, he gently laid Bryson's head against his chest. As Tom started to rock, he began to speak softly, "Bryson, Daddy will tell you a story. Remember on cold wintry days when yo're all alone—with nobody to play with? Remember Momma telling you that someday you would have someone all yore own fer a playmate? Wal, today, yore Momma went to a lot of pain to git you that there very thing—a little brother. There in the back room—there be yore very own brother. 'Course he's only a wee thing yit. It'll be a spell afore you kin play with him—but Momma did it! And she's fine. She's jest tired now. She took on so cuz it did hurt her some—but Son, anything worth having hasta hurt some! Want to go see them now?"

Bryson looked at his father, big tears rolling out of his eyes. Sniffing, he wiped his nose and his eyes with the sleeve of his frayed shirt. He seemed to be turning over in his mind what his dad had said to him.

Then, sitting up straight in Tom's lap, he spoke, "Tee Mommy?"

"You shore kin! Lessee Momma first."

Tom picked the little boy up and, carrying him in his arms, he took Bryson into the dimly lit bedroom.

Retter, with her long dark hair spread out on the pillow, lay with her eyes closed. She didn't hear her husband and son enter the room. Her newborn baby was lying in her arms, now asleep.

Father and son looked at the two lying there. The only sound in the room was the ticking of the old clock on the table near the bed. Beside the clock was a picture of the Ammons family taken last year when the other children had all come out from Washington to visit. They seemed to be watching Retter and her new son also. Mrs. Ammons sat in a darkened corner of the room.

Suddenly, the silence was broken by a tiny voice, "Daddy, Mommy not hurt . . . Mommy seep. Tee baby? Tee?" Bryson straightened his back and drew himself up to his fullest height. "Daddy, brover mine!"

With laughter rising right out of his heart, Tom squeezed his son as pride filled him.

In the days and years to come Bryson would indeed take care of his new brother, James Edward Ammons, born March 25, 1912.

THE AMMONS FAMILY
Standing: Cora, Jim, Tom, Robert, Lillit, Frank
Sitting: Mrs. Amons, Retter with Bryson

CHAPTER EIGHTEEN

Another Side

The soft breeze caressed Retter's face as she sat on her porch high on the mountain. It was twilight. The chickens were going to roost, clucking as they passed Retter on their way to the hen house. The mountains that surrounded the cabin loomed up in front of her, outlined against the lighter sky, giving her a sense of warm coziness. This was her favorite time of day. It was her relaxing time, and it was usually shared by Tom. Tonight, however, Tom wasn't here. He'd gone to town much earlier for supplies and as yet hadn't returned. Tom should have been back an hour ago, but Retter refused to be worried as yet. He'd been late before.

Retter's hair was let down from her usual loose bun on the back of her head, and with it draped over one shoulder, she was brushing the long shimmering strands. In all her eighteen years, Retter's hair had never been cut—it was so long she could sit on it. As she brushed her hair, she watched the sunset, and smiled as she thought how time seemed to have flown these past three months since little Jim had been born. They had finally gotten moved into their new cabin only a week before. Tom had done everything Retter had wanted—her happiness now seemed complete.

As Retter sat there, she began to hear the sounds of the night, softly at first, and then louder. There were the male toads puffing out their throats to utter loud flutelike mating calls, and the answer of the soft-voiced females. And in among the toads' mating calls was the song of the tree crickets. These familiar sounds were relaxing and comforting to Retter. As long as she could remember, she had sat with her papa on their porch at home and listened to the "critters o' the night."

Just then Bryson came out of the lamp-lit kitchen carrying a small burlap bag, holding it open and close to his nose.

"Momma! Wocks!" he said. Then, laying the sack in Retter's lap, he shoved one chubby hand into the sack, and brought forth a handful of small brown nuts. "Tee, Momma! Wocks!"

Laughing, Retter caught his hand, and putting it back into the bag, she said, "No, Bryson. It's not rocks—these are chinquapins. They're little brown nuts that taste sweeter'n spring-fresh rosenears. Jest put 'um back into the poke and lessus git ready fer bed."

Retter stood up, and dropping the sack of chinquapins into the chair, she led Bryson into the cabin to dress him for bed.

Bryson slept in the back bedroom. Since it was so small, it contained only a bed with a straw tick mattress and a crude wooden chest.

"Momma, I kin do it!" said Bryson as he began to unbutton his worn shirt. The shirt was too small for him already, with the sleeves so short that the cuffs could not be buttoned.

As Retter watched her son, she sighed softly, wishing she could afford to get the material to make him a new shirt. Leaning over, she took the shirt that the grinning Bryson triumphantly handed her, saying, "Tee, Momma!"

"Yes, Bryson, yo're such a big boy now. Momma's little helper!" Retter said as she knelt and hugged him close to her.

Bryson laughed and put his hands into her long hair that spread out on the floor behind her. "Momma purty," he said.

"Thank you, son," Retter answered as she hugged him tighter. Then she stood up and went over to the chest. From the top drawer she drew out his nightshirt and laid it on the bed. Sitting on the edge of the straw mattress, she beckoned for Bryson to come to her. Slowly she began to remove his pants. "He's so small," Retter thought as she slipped the nightshirt over his head. Most of the time she forgot how small he was because he was such a bright boy. He seemed old beyond his years. He had begun to talk much faster than other children his age, and he understood things easily.

Retter stood as Bryson climbed upon his bed, the straw cracking and swishing. As she pulled the small quilt up over him, she asked, "You want the window open?"

"Yes, peas," answered Bryson, adjusting the cover over him.

Retter slid the wooden slat that covered the window to one side, allowing the warm June air to float into the room. Then leaning over, she kissed Bryson on the cheek and swept his hair back from his forehead. "Goodnight, my little man," she said.

"Night, Momma," was the sleepy reply.

As Retter passed through the front room on her way back to her chair on the porch, she paused beside the cradle that sat beside her bed. Jim was sleeping peacefully, both arms raised over his head, lying on the quilt Retter used for a mattress. Smiling softly, Retter hoped he would be as fast to learn as Bryson. She blew out the lamp.

The stars were shining brightly in the darkened sky as Retter walked out onto the porch again. Her hair, that hung all around her, moved lightly as the warm breeze greeted her. Moving to her chair, Retter picked up the burlap bag of chinquapins and stood gazing at it. The sight of the nuts had brought back memories of the first time she'd been introduced to them. Sitting down in her chair, Retter allowed her mind to go back to one day in September, a few years ago. She must have been ten years old. That was the year she'd met Charlie, her Cherokee friend—and her grandfather. He'd been teaching her all about the forest and the different types of herbs for healing the sick and injured.

In September, the days are hot and the nights are cold, and this specific day had been no exception. Retter had been with Charlie all afternoon, climbing hill after hill, searching for just the right root or plant. This day Charlie had gathered sumac leaves, dandelion roots, and wild plum bark. It was late in the day, and the air began to feel cool on Retter's arms. "Charlie, are we going far? It's cold!" Retter's arms were crossed in front of her as she hugged herself for warmth.

"Come, Retter, Charlie cover arms," Charlie said. He laid down the sack he was carrying, and taking the small blanket he had draped over his shoulder, he put it around Retter.

The warmth of Charlie's body still clung to the blanket, making Retter comfortable immediately. Gratefully, she smiled at him as she pulled it closer around her. She wasn't ready to start for home yet, so she watched Charlie intently. "Charlie, kin I go on with you?"

Charlie gazed at Retter for a minute; then holding up one finger, he nodded.

Smiling broadly, Retter followed him up a path almost hidden by fallen leaves. By the time they reached the top of the grade, Retter was out of breath and eager to rest. It was still daylight, but the shadows were long.

"Retter see big tree?" As he spoke, Charlie was indicating a large tree with spreading branches. "Retter listen. Chestnut tree be big tree. Wood last long in fire. Bark make good "tanning" to skins. Leaves good! Make skin tough. Leaves heal broke skin. Chestnut good to eat. Good tree!"

This was a long speech for Charlie. Retter was much impressed. Charlie continued on up the mountain, motioning for Retter to follow. "Charlie show Retter one more tree."

Before long, they reached a knoll where there was a grove of the same kind of tree in a smaller version. The small leafy tree was almost as tall as Charlie, with toothed glossy green leaves. In among the leaves were prickly burrs.

Charlie watched Retter's observations closely. "Retter see?" he asked. Then he broke off the stem that held one of the prickly burrs. Carefully placing one thumb on either side of the burr, he pressed, pulling apart the shell to produce a small brown soft-shelled nut. Smiling at Retter, Charlie said, "Chinquapin." He held out the nut to Retter, saying, "Eat."

Retter cracked the soft shell with her teeth, and a white-yellowish nut fell out onto her palm. She put the nut into her mouth and chewed slowly. Then smiling at Charlie, she said, "Sweet! It's good, Charlie."

"Chinquapin is Cherokee tree. Good tree! Tree be son of chestnut tree. Shell nuts and eat."

Before long Charlie had a handful of nuts, and Retter ate them as fast as Charlie gave them to her.

"Retter eat 'nuff. Make belly sore." Charlie laughed as he gathered leaves from the branches of the little tree. Then, as Retter began to help him, she noticed it was getting darker.

"Charlie, we'd better go on home. From here it's a fer piece."

"Charlie take Retter home," he said as he filled his deerskin bag with the leaves they had just picked. Then with Charlie leading the way, the two went down the mountain just as the sun was setting. Retter was not the least bit frightened of the dark as she followed Charlie. As they passed the tall chestnut tree, Charlie paused and turned to Retter, placing his hand on the trunk of the tree. From somewhere behind her, a light seemed to shine on Charlie's face as he spoke, "Retter not forget—Great Spirit lives in chestnut tree. Someday Retter have big trouble in life. Take leaves, soak in water, Great Spirit help Retter. Charlie see."

Then, turning abruptly, he continued on down the mountain with the little girl following at his heels.

Standing on the porch, Retter could still see the back of her friend as she had followed him. Tears welled up in her eyes as she shook her head, coming back to the present. She missed this Indian that was her grandfather.

Suddenly, Retter heard a faint sound coming from the road that led up to the cabin. Tilting her head, she strained her ears to hear the slight sound. Listening intently, she heard it grow louder.

Looking around her, she felt fear steal over her. Where was Tom? What should she do?

Going into the cabin, she took down Tom's rifle from over the mantle of the fireplace, and then walked to the open doorway to the front yard. She could see a light in the distance, bobbing and jerking. Carefully listening, Retter suddenly realized that what she was hearing was someone singing. She couldn't make out the words, but it was singing, she was sure. She was also sure that it was a man's voice. What she was suddenly looking at was a man coming up the road with a lantern, and it wasn't Tom. The voice was not at all like Tom's.

Retter held tightly to the rifle, then moving out of the entrance, she closed the door. Light from the full moon outside shone through the open window.

The fear in Retter grew stronger, her body tense and shaken. She would protect her babies—no matter what!

The singing grew louder, and now she could tell by the sound of the voice that the man was drunk. All at once, the singing stopped. Then there was a loud crash, and the light from the lantern went out! From her position by the open window, Retter listened to slurred curse words, and then the sound of footsteps staggering right up to the door.

Retter cocked the rifle and with shaking hands, held it up before her, aiming it at the closed door. To get to the door, two steps had to be climbed. These steps were hard for the drunken man to make, so more cursing could be heard through the door. The wooden lever used as a door handle lifted.

Suddenly, there stood Tom, drunk and grinning crookedly at Retter. "'Lo, Etter, don' shooo!" Then he threw back his head and laughed loudly.

As Retter slowly lowered the rifle, the baby awoke and started to cry. From within the bedroom behind her, she could hear Bryson calling her.

Anger began at the bottom of her churning stomach and grew to fill her hotly as she glared at Tom. "Tom, yo're stinking drunk!"

Tom still grinned at her with what seemed like a glassy fixed stare. Then slowly, he pitched forward into the room, falling flat on his face with a loud bang! He didn't move.

Retter stood still for a moment, staring at her soft-spoken mild-mannered husband lying on the floor. She could smell the strong stench of liquor—it sickened her. Going over to the lamp, she struck a match and lit the wick, the light filling the room with shadows. Disgust written over her face, Retter walked over to Tom, and pushed him with the toe of her shoe. She couldn't move him. With her hands on her hips, she stared down at her husband. She had never seen him drunk before, and it not only angered her, but disgusted her.

With the sounds of the children in back of her, Retter spoke aloud, "Tom Ammons, if you think yo're sick now, jest you wait till you wake up!"

Turning on her heel, she went to her children, leaving Tom on the floor. Tom had found his bed for the night.

The crying stopped. The light went out. The only sounds to be heard in the cabin on top of the mountain were the snoring of the drunken man on the floor . . . and the cracked muffled sobs of an unhappy young woman alone in her bed.

CHAPTER NINETEEN

Making Up

The pain in Tom's head woke him the next morning. The pain was so fierce that it even hurt for him to open his eyes. The warmth of the morning sun shining through the open window felt good against his back so he thought that if he could just move, his head might not hurt so much. But moving made everything worse. He'd really tied one on this time, he thought, as he gathered his nerve to try to get up. Moving again, he moaned aloud.

Bryson had been sitting on his stool near the fireplace, watching his father. Seeing him move, and then moan, Bryson jumped up and ran over to Tom.

"Daddy wake up?" Bryson leaned down and gazed at his daddy's face. He could see only the movement of the eyelids. He ran out, calling his momma. The floor moved underneath his footsteps, and each movement jarred Tom's sore body. He moaned once again.

Then, with great effort, Tom straightened to a sitting position, holding his aching head with both hands, his eyes closed. There was a bitter taste in his mouth. His tongue felt as if it were too big. He dropped his jaw and moved his tongue from side to side, pushing out the sides of his cheeks. Even that hurt his head. The smell around him sickened him.

Footsteps on the porch outside and then inside the room had an immediate effect on Tom. He knew Retter was there, and he dreaded looking up at her. Well, it had to be done! He opened one eye—just in time to duck! Swish! The straw broom just missed him . . . and here it came again!

"Retter! Please! I'm feeling awful poorly." Tom scrambled to his feet, the roaring in his head so bad that he thought it would explode.

"Tom Ammons! Yo're bound to feel worse'n that when I git finished with you! Yo're shenanigans askeered me to death last night!" As she spoke, Retter swung the broom again, this time hitting him on the shoulder. Her mouth never stopped. "Never seen the likes of you, Tom! I'm so put out with you! Why did you do it? Why . . . ?"

Suddenly, Retter backed off from Tom as he was protecting himself with his arms up over his head. Tears were streaming down her face. Turning, she ran out of the room toward the kitchen. The door to the kitchen slammed shut, and the latch dropped into place.

In the sudden quiet of the room, Tom stood looking after Retter. She was right, he felt worse now than he'd ever felt. Obviously, he'd hurt her tremendously by celebrating in town yesterday. He stumbled over to the fireplace, and laying his arms on the mantle, he rested his head on his arms. He would try to explain later. Now, his main objective was to cure his headache. What he needed was a good cool dip in the creek. Better yet, he'd get some soap and walk down to the waterfall and let the cool water run over his aching head. Dejectedly, he turned and went into the bedroom to get the towel and soap. In a closet underneath the stairway that led to the attic, he also found his only other change of clothes. Throwing his clothes and towel over his shoulder, he went through the front room and out the door that opened onto the front yard. The bright sun hit him square in the eyes as he descended the steps to the yard. Grimacing, he walked very slowly down the path that led to the waterfall below the cabin. His shoulders sagged.

In the kitchen, Bryson sat quietly on the bench by the table. His frightened eyes followed his mother's figure as she moved quickly back and forth between the table and the stove, slinging pots and pans. She'd wiped the tears from her eyes, but she was still angry at herself for crying. She had wanted to hurt Tom! He was just like all the rest of the men after all. Go to town and come back stinking drunk! But, maybe there was hope for him after all—usually the rest were gone all night!

Slowly, Retter began to calm down, and she sank into a chair at the end of the table, near Jim. She'd positioned his cradle next to the table, so she could watch him while cooking. Her eyes fell on Bryson. Suddenly, she realized how he must feel. He was very still and looked so small.

"Bryson, come sit here with me," Retter said as she beckoned to him.

Relief written on his small face, Bryson climbed down and ran to his mother. She hugged him.

"Don't be askeered, Bryson. Everything's okay," she said. Then, she held him out and smiled at him. "Why don't you go out to the henhouse and see if the hens have laid an egg or two."

This brought a smile back to Bryson's face. He ran to get an empty lard bucket from the smaller table in the corner. Retter unlatched the kitchen door and let Bryson out. Then she walked out onto the porch, and leaning over slightly, she peeped into the front room. Tom wasn't there. She went all through the house; Tom was nowhere to be found. For a moment, she was afraid he had left her. Then she reasoned that he loved the children, so he would be back. Slowly, she returned to the kitchen, deep in thought.

For the life of her, she couldn't figure out how men could love those corn squeezings so well. Maybe they needed to release the feelings of responsibility that are always on their minds; this excuse for drinking was as good as any. Retter stopped and stamped her foot! It's just a crutch! That's all! And she didn't like weak men! She began to get angry all over again. She had responsibility herself—and she didn't resort to drink! She wasn't weak!

Shaking her head to clear it of the unanswerable questions,

Retter walked over to the kitchen table and began to mix flapjacks.

When Tom arrived from his cool bath, he looked like his old self. His headache wasn't entirely gone, but the cool water had helped. Laying his old clothes down on the back porch, he quietly walked to the kitchen door, and stood watching Retter at the wood stove.

She was still angry, he could see by the way her lips were clamped together. She was so pretty with her dark hair pulled up into the soft bun on the back of her head, loose strands flying around her face as she worked. The long blue and white gingham dress she wore was covered by a plain white apron. Her arms, that at the moment held a bowl of batter, were tan and slender. Tom's eyes lingered on her bare tanned arms. Love for her welled up inside him. She was the mother of his two boys, and how he loved her! He would have to be very careful with the explanation of his undoing.

"Uh, Retter," he began quietly. "I'm sorry fer my drinking yesterday."

Startled at his unexpected presence, she turned around and stared at him, her eyes wide with vexation. She said nothing.

"See, Retter, this is how it happened. Elic Watson wuz down to Nicklesen's and we got to jawing about old times—and I got to telling him about my new cabin and all . . . so, we decided to celebrate my new cabin and my new son alls to one time. It done went a mite too fer, I reckon. You know, Elic always seems to have a bottle somewheres. Retter, I'm sorry fer my wrongdoing."

Tom had lived long enough to know that his pride didn't mean anything to him if it meant not having his Retter. Besides, none of his friends could see him at this moment, anyway.

His eyes followed Retter as she walked slowly to the table and set the bowl down. Her face was down, so he couldn't see her expression. The pounding of his heart began to sound inside his head.

"Retter! Please say something!" he burst out.

Deliberately walking slowly toward him, she stopped just in front of Jim's cradle. With a straight face, she said, "Wal, seeing as you had a reason fer celebrating, I kin understand. But askeering me the way you done, I cain't see! It's in the "dark of the moon" and things unnatural happen in the darkness of the nights."

At first, Tom had nodded his head during the short speech Retter had made. Then, during the last part, he had smiled slightly. He knew Retter believed in old wives' tales and superstitions.

"'Sides," she continued, "I have a better way of celebrating than gitting drunk, Tom Ammons! Shore would hold a heap much more better feeling than that stinky ole stuff—if you know what I mean?" Retter was finally smiling broadly at Tom. She held her arms out to him, her eyes twinkling.

Laughing, Tom grabbed her to him and held her close. His heart was beating even harder than before, and he could feel Retter's heartbeat match his, beat for beat. Hungrily, his lips sought hers. Their kiss was long and moving. The desire for forgiveness had been satisfied. Now, the desire for the nearness of his wife seemed to consume him. He wanted her—in fact, it was as if he'd never had her before. Retter clung to him, her need matching his.

Suddenly, there was a tugging at Retter's dress. Pulling away from Tom's embrace, she looked down at Bryson's concerned face.

"Momma! Momma?" he said.

"It's okay, Bryson. Momma and Daddy's jest making up."

Retter adjusted her dress and pushed at her hair, looking coyly up into Tom's slightly disappointed face. Then with her head high, she turned on her heel to go back across the floor, saying over her shoulder, "Anyways, if it had been me celebrating at Nickelsen's, I'd have had a 'dope' and a 'moon pie!'"

Tom began to laugh and then couldn't stop. Retter laughed too, and finally Bryson joined in, not knowing why he was laughing. The warmth of laughter resounded within the walls of the little kitchen.

That evening, Retter was hurrying to complete the cleanup of the kitchen. Tom had watched her all day—had touched her in soft places—and had whispered sweet words in her ear. Emotions were high in each, as the close of the day was almost upon them. Tom had already rocked Jim to sleep and was at the moment tucking Bryson in.

Going to the open window, Retter threw the dirty dish-water out. She stood there a moment, looking out at the night. The toads and crickets were singing. Looking up at the dark sky, Retter suddenly straightened and turned her head to one side, as if listening to something. Her forehead wrinkled as she strained to hear.

As Tom came into the room, he felt a cool shiver go through his body when he saw his wife. He watched quietly as the light from the lamp flickered, making their shadows dance on the walls.

Shaking her head, Retter turned and looked at Tom. "A strange thing jest happened, Tom," Retter said as she looked at him. "I feel that there's a change coming fer us."

Tom stared at her. "Change? What kind of change?"

"Wal, it had somethin' to do with yore job. Are you low on lumber down to the sawmill?"

"Come to think of it—yes, we are." Tom continued to stare at Retter. "Retter, you skeer me sometimes!"

Retter laughed as she untied her apron and drew it up over her head. Crossing the floor, she hung it up on a nail near the door. Then, gliding up to Tom, she put both arms around him and hugged him close. "I love you, Tom Ammons," she said, "no matter what job you have. And there's never gonna be anyone else fer me but you!"

Tom gazed down into two liquid pools of love. Sweeping her up into his arms, he walked over to the lamp and blew it out. Retter began kissing his neck a little as he went through the door and pulled it shut with one hand. Outside on the porch, they looked up into the sky again. The dampness of the night reached out, laying cold fingers on Tom's face. He shivered. Retter began nibbling at his ear and caressing his hair with one hand. She seemed light as a feather to him, and he loved the feeling she was giving him. He could feel it grow from the bottom of his feet to the top of his head.

"Retter," he muttered, "yo're a little vixen!"

Retter only moaned into his ear.

With long steps, he crossed the porch, going into the front room and across the floor to their bed. The swishing, cracking sound of the strawtick mattress was like music to him as he placed Retter on the homemade quilt. Dropping to his knees, he laid his head on her bosom, his ear to her heart. Excitement grew in him as the warmth of her body tingled his skin, and the rise and fall of her chest quickened. He didn't want it to end, this shaking sensation she created in him.

"Tom," came her soft whisper, "I'm waiting."

CHAPTER TWENTY

Footsteps in the Shadows

Retter's premonition was correct—there was a new job for Tom. Before the summer was over, he had become foreman of a lumber crew.

Life for Retter changed. Tom was gone from home longer because of the travel to and from his job locations, so Retter began to do more and more of the chores involved in running the household and the work outside. The garden had to be hoed and weeded, and the vegetables gathered and canned.

She loved flowers, so she planted gladiolus, dahlias, bluebells, irises, and roses all around their cabin. And just below the window of her kitchen, she planted a patch of giant hollyhocks, so she could look out at the surrounding mountains through the flowers.

A year went by. A year full of work and happiness for the little Ammons family.

By the time winter, 1913, came to the mountains, Retter was heavy with child again. When the cold weather turned the full trees into stark limbs upraised in loneliness, it began to snow. White blankets covered the mountains. Charlie had always told Retter that with the wonder of snow came peacefulness. Snow was a gift from the Great Spirit—given to bring people closer together under white blankets of love.

To Retter, this was true, because Tom was home more often in the wintertime, since the crews couldn't get through the snowdrifts to the job sites. The cabin at night would be full of love and contentment for the family. Tom would read stories to the boys, and even sometimes act them out. At other times in the evenings, the fire would be stoked up brightly, and Tom would get the board out and play checkers with Retter and his sons. They never tired of the game.

Then spring came. The lumber crews went out, taking Tom from his family once again. They missed him greatly. Their small world seemed lonesome and not quite so much fun.

In March, a new little brother arrived—Albert Abraham Ammons. With his birth, Retter began to believe she was outnumbered! How she had wanted a girl! Then she had looked into Albert's big blue eyes, and realized how lucky she was to have three big healthy boys, all born in the month of March, two years apart.

As Albert grew, it was clear to all that his personality was different from that of his brothers. He was quiet and observant—not at all like Bryson and Jim, who were loud and demanding. As the months passed, Albert's little frame seemed not to grow at all, but his bright eyes flashed almost as often as his grin. Retter would sit by the cradle and just look at him. Such a tiny baby . . . and yet . . . there was something almost eerie about the feeling she got from him. For a long time, Retter couldn't figure out just what it was. And then—one day it came to her! She could see Charlie in Albert's baby eyes! After that, somehow Retter knew that Albert would always be with her to help her and take care of her. It was something that Retter just accepted, but then forgot, tucking it away in some far corner of her memory.

Winter came again to the mountains. Cords of wood had been cut and stacked alongside the cabin. All the signs of winter were saying that it was going to be a bad one this year. The woolly worms were big and bushy; the oak trees had had abundant acorns; and the squirrels had gathered and stored them all. It was the winter of 1914.

Retter stood at the front door of the cabin, looking down the road, hoping to see Tom coming up over the rise. Night was almost here, and if Tom didn't get home soon, he would be climbing the mountain in the dark. Supper was almost ready, and Bryson and Jim were clamoring for something to eat. She had stalled them off, getting them to play in the kitchen.

Tonight Retter was having vegetable and beef stew for supper. The smell of the simmering dish filled the room. In the warmer on top of the stove was a large cake of cornbread. This was one of Tom's favorite meals, stew and cornbread.

Going over to the small table in the corner, Retter knelt, and from a burlap bag underneath the table, she took a couple of onions. Then, going over to the table, she picked up her paring knife and began to peel off the mushy outside of the onion.

Just then, Retter heard a muffled sound outside the door, and stopped for a moment to listen.

Tom suddenly came through the kitchen door, smiling broadly, saying, "Yummm! I shore do smell somethin' good!"

His face was red from the cold, and he smelled of the forest. Off came his heavy coat, his scarf, and hat. He laid them on the chair by the door, just as two of his sons attacked. He was almost knocked over in their zeal. It was such a nice feeling for Retter, seeing the boys together with their daddy.

Retter felt a tugging at her dress, and looked down as Albert tried to pull himself up by holding onto her skirts. Smiling, Retter stooped, and picking him up, she carried him over to Tom.

As Tom reached for Albert, he leaned over and kissed Retter, saying, "Hullo, sweetheart, you look a little tired tonight."

She brushed back her hair from her face, and smiled, shaking her head. "Yes, jest a bit, though. It's mostly cuz I'm more bored than tired. I need something new to do, I reckon," she said as she turned to set the table for supper.

Tom pulled out a chair by the table and sat down, holding Albert in his lap, the older boys going back to their stick game.

"Wal, I think I got jest the thing fer you, Retter," said Tom. "If yo're up to it!" He laughed as Retter swung around, giving him all her attention.

"Wal, go on, Tom Ammons. Lessus hear it!" Retter stood eyeing him, with a spoon in one hand and a bowl in the other.

"Yesterday the cook over to the lumber camp quit, and I have to hire a new one. You want the job?" Tom watched to see how Retter would react. "The job site's close—over near Possum Holler."

For a few minutes, Retter said nothing. She finished setting the table and then began spooning the stew into the bowls. Tom sat silently and watched his thoughtful wife.

"Where would I leave my young'uns, Tom, whilst I'm cooking?" she said as she finished filling the last bowl.

"You kin take the kids with you. The kitchen's powerful big, and I'll make a pallet on the floor fer the baby. You jest hafta cook one meal around noon. You could leave the house about nine—it'll take about an hour to walk it. Then, you could git back afore two. It's jest fer about two weeks, and it's our last job fer the winter. Besides, I could see my family a bit more than I have of late."

Tom wanted her to take the job, Retter could see. He had really put some thought into it. His eyes were still following her. She thought she might as well take it . . . at least she'd get out of the house for awhile before the heavy snows came.

"Okay, Tom. Reckon I'll do it!"

"Good! Good! You start tomorrow!" Tom, smiling broadly, leaned back in his chair and held Albert up over his head, holding him nose to nose, talking gibberish to him.

Almost under his breath, in between his playful sounds, Retter suddenly heard Tom say, "Henry's been found."

Retter stood still in surprise, her hand on the handle of the stove warmer, looking back at her husband. "Where!" was all she could say.

Tom brought the baby down into his lap, his full attention on Retter. "Seems he's been trapping back over on Roan Mountain in Tennessee. His wife's brothers finally caught up to him. Them Cherokees fixed it so he won't bother any woman again—if you know what I mean."

"No—what did they do?"

"Well . . . they cut it off." Tom grinned at Retter's quick blush.

"Oh," she said, and put the cornbread on the table.

The walk to the lumber camp started out pleasantly. The crisp air was invigorating to Retter. Albert, being so small, wasn't too hard to manage at first, but he seemed to get heavier and heavier. Bryson and Jim walked in front of her. Soon, however, Jim's legs got tired, and Retter picked him up and carried him on one hip, with Albert on the other. Before long she had to stop and rest.

As she sat on a rock, looking back over the path she'd just walked, she noticed the closeness of the brush. The path was almost overgrown. Leaves covered the ground, and here and there little streams of spring water crossed the path, working their way down to the creek below. Moss covered most of the rocks. This must be a real shady path when the leaves are on the trees, thought Retter.

"Bryson, you git Jim down from that there log! Yo're both gonna be falling off, and throwing a fit!" called Retter as she stood up. "Lessus take our leave now and git on down to the lumber camp."

Just as she started to move she felt a little uneasy. She stood still a minute and listened. She could hear nothing but the rushing of the creek below. She took another step, shifting Albert to the other hip, readjusting her coat—and the uneasy feeling came over her again. Looking over her shoulder, she called to the boys to run ahead of her, and she briskly walked on down the path. She was listening intently as she moved. There was a soft rustling of the leaves to one side of her. She stopped. The rustling stopped. Around her nothing moved. Suddenly, there was a squirrel above her, jumping from limb to limb. Breathing a sigh of relief, and shaking her head at her uneasiness, Retter hurried on down the path—not feeling the intentness of the eyes that followed her.

It was a little after ten when Retter and her boys arrived at the lumber camp. Tom had kept an eye open for them, and hurried to meet them when they came trudging out of the woods. Taking Albert from Retter, he hoisted him up on his shoulder, asking Retter how their walk had been.

She mentioned her uneasiness and then laughingly told him of the squirrel. They continued their conversation, forgetting about the incident.

Cooking the noon meal for lumberjacks was no little thing. These men worked hard and ate heartily. Retter was a good cook, but the first day, she didn't cook quite enough. Tomorrow she would know better.

After the meal, Retter was worn out. She sat with a cup of coffee by the fireplace, before getting the boys ready for their walk home. It was close to two when the little caravan left the clearing. Tom watched them go, proud of his wife's cooking and of his sons' behavior. Then turning, he swung his axe over his shoulder and hurried on over to the job site.

Retter was walking fast as she came upon the rock where she had rested earlier that morning. She passed it on by, the boys still not tired. But as Retter walked, she began to get a quivery feeling in the middle of her back. This time she knew that eyes were on her! She could feel them. Glancing over her shoulder, she could see nothing behind her. Slowly she began to observe each side of the trail, her eyes carefully covering the area around her. Still she could see nothing. Then—there came the rustling sound again. Retter drew Albert closer, and walked faster.

"Momma, why are we walking so fast? We're plumb tuckered out," said Bryson as he and Jim tried to keep up with their mother.

"Come on now, boys. It's jest a little ferther. We kin make it." Retter knew she couldn't stop and rest.

Without further incident, they reached home all worn out. Retter hurried into the cabin, her relief so great that she almost fell into her chair by the kitchen stove. It was almost a half hour before any of them moved, they were so tired. Then, Retter got up and started preparing supper, determined to tell Tom about the fear she had experienced. But the more she thought about it, the more she could see that it was only a feeling. She hadn't actually seen anything. Nothing had happened. So, by the time Tom got home, Retter didn't even mention her fear.

The next day, however, she decided, after much deliberation, that she'd better have something to protect them—just in case. But what would she take with her? She sat at the kitchen table and thought about it. Her eyes fell on the paring knife lying near her cup of coffee. A knife it would be, but not this knife! Years ago, Charlie had given her a blade in a leather covering. It wasn't a big knife, but it was exactly what she needed. After rummaging around, Retter finally came up with it. Since it was too big for her coat pocket, she put it in her apron pocket. At least it gave her a feeling of protection. She felt Charlie would approve.

As Retter and the boys passed over the leaf-covered trail later that morning, there was no uneasy feeling. Only the darkening of the cloud-covered sky. The wind had picked up, whistling through the bare trees and swishing the pines. Looking around her, she found no reason for fear, except that it looked like the first snowstorm of the year was on its way.

Lunch took Retter longer on this day. She cooked more food than the day before, so it took her longer to clean up afterward. By the time she had finished and was ready to begin the trip home, it was almost dark, and the snow had finally arrived. Already the ground was covered, and flakes were still coming down. Bundling up the boys, Retter decided she'd better do as she had done yesterday—not stop for anything until she got home.

Albert was so tiny yet that, as Retter looked at him, she decided to protect him even further from the cold. She unbuttoned her coat and the front of her loose fitting dress, nestled Albert next to her bosom, and rebuttoned her dress and coat around him. Surprisingly, this was very comfortable for both of them.

Well, she was ready. Tom had hurried off after lunch to try and get as much done as possible before the storm, so he could finish earlier and go on home. He told Retter that if he did indeed finish early, he'd be right behind her.

She would have liked to have had a lantern to carry with them, but she needed both hands to hold Albert and maybe Jim also a little later on.

The snow let up a little as they left the lumber camp. Already there was about an inch on the ground. There was no wind blowing. It was quiet and still as mother and sons trudged over the snow-covered path.

Almost immediately Retter knew they weren't alone. This time she could hear footsteps up above the trail, in the shadows. When she stopped, the footsteps stopped. When she started, they started. This went on for a quarter of an hour. Retter believed that she could hear heavy breathing, or did she imagine it?

The day got darker, the snow began to fall again, and the wind began to blow against Retter's back. The pat . . . pat . . . pat . . . up above her continued.

"Bryson, hurry on there, son. This storm is bearing down on us."

Jim had come back to his mother and was holding onto her dress, his tired legs going as fast as they could. They were about three-fourths of the way home when Retter realized that the sound of the footsteps was gone. Apprehension grew in her because this could mean only one of two things: that *it* had left, or that *it* had gone on ahead of them.

At the next bend in the trail, there was a large oak tree with a limb that protruded out over the path. It was here that the half-grown, half-starved black panther waited for Retter and her children. His crazed hungry eyes gleamed as he pawed the limb of the tree, his claws digging into the bark. He had watched these people for two days now, and he knew that they would put up little fight. They weren't as big as the others that had invaded his woods. Soon, they would be here. Saliva dripped from his

David F. Ammons

open mouth—his large black tail swished slowly from side to side. He waited.

Retter could see through the softly falling snow that the last bend of the trail was ahead. Suddenly, a limb fell across their path, startling them. Bryson ran behind his mother. Slowly, Retter surveyed the area. She looked long and hard. Something seemed to be telling her that there was trouble ahead. The falling limb was just that, though—a fallen limb. Evidently the wind had blown a branch down. Moving her coat back, Retter reached into her apron pocket and removed the knife from the leather holder. For a moment, she thought about leaving the boys where they were while she investigated, but she gave up the notion. She wasn't leaving them anywhere!

"Bryson, hold Jim's hand and walk behind me," she said softly.

Then slowly, Retter moved forward, the knife in her hand. As she approached the big dark tree, Retter suddenly saw the gleaming eyes of the panther. His powerful shoulder muscles rippled as he poised himself on the limb—she knew he was waiting for his opportunity to pounce.

Retter was almost underneath the limb when he leaped!

"RUN, BRYSON! BACK THE WAY WE COME! RUN, I SAY!"

The boys ran.

In the fraction of a second, as the panther leaped, Retter brought the knife up to meet the cat, the knife edge flickering. Too late the black panther saw his mistake. His chest was torn open by the weight of his own body as he met the upraised knife.

Retter and Albert fell beneath the cat, the warmth of his blood covering them. There had been no sound from the animal, so for a moment, Retter lay still underneath him. The cat didn't move again.

With power she didn't know she had, Retter pushed the dead cat off her and her son. The white snow around them became stained with blood. Retter stared hard at the cat—her hands began to shake, and then she began to cry.

Albert said not a word; he simply clung to his mother. Neither of them was hurt.

At that moment, Retter heard a cry behind her. It was Tom! Scrambling to her feet, she turned. But before she could answer his call, he was there, his face pale and stricken. Bryson and Jim were with him. They had met him coming.

"RETTER! RETTER!" Tom cried, "Are you ALL RIGHT?" He ran up to her, taking in what had happened in one glance. He held her by her shoulders, looking her up and down. "Did he scratch you at all? Little Albert's okay? Are you all right?"

"Tom Ammons, will you hesh up! I'm fine!" Retter finally had gotten her voice back. "I'm jest covered with this here "painter's" blood. I have to git it off me!"

Kneeling, Retter picked up a handful of snow and began rubbing her face.

Tom looked over her shoulder at the dead cat, and shuddered. The softly falling snow was covering the black panther. Tom thought about what might have happened, and shaking his head, he turned to Retter, saying, "Retter, why did you have the knife with you?"

"I wuz afraid—I could feel eyes on my back before. So I found the knife Charlie gave me," she said, wiping her face on the tail of her dress.

Tom reached down, and pulling Retter and Albert up to him, he held them close. Bryson and Jim pushed up close to them. Then, with his arms around Retter, Tom turned to lead them down the path, Bryson's hand in his—Jim's hand in his mother's.

The little family soon disappeared through the swirling snow. The panther had already begun to stiffen with death.

A shadow fell across the snow-covered cat—and high in the swaying pines, with the snow falling softly, the wind whispered . . . Cooweesucoowee.

CHAPTER TWENTY-ONE

The Old Mica Mine

Snow fell! Every hill and valley was covered by new blankets of white, broken only by small streams that wound their way down to the Tuckasegee River. Here and there, small animals would venture out to find water and as much vegetation as possible.

Christmas came and went, and the small family began looking forward to spring. Tom would plan and replan his garden, going through the seed catalogs—choosing just the right kind of seed to plant.

Spring was upon them almost before they knew it. Planting time arrived. Tom and Retter sowed their garden of vegetables, making sure to observe the time of the moon. In the "dark o' the moon," they planted all the vegetables that grew underground. And in the "light o' the moon," they sowed all the vegetables that grew above the ground. After the first whippoorwill sang, they planted their beans.

With the planting all done, Tom went back again full-time with the lumber crew, while Retter filled her days working and playing with her three boys. Tom and Retter rarely had time alone, and when they did, they were both too tired to appreciate each other. The days began to run together, and before long, it was July.

One morning, when Retter rose to prepare Tom's breakfast, she stood on the porch watching the sun come up over the mountains. All around her were quiet shadows and the stillness that comes just before dawn. There was a soft warm breeze blowing—bringing with it the smell of her roses. Smiling softly, Retter leaned against the porch post. The breeze plucked at the hem of her dress and played with her hair. A pleasant feeling of anticipation came over her. Today was special. She and Tom were to have the day to themselves.

Tom had been commissioned to explore the possibilities for a new job site over near Caney Fork. Last night Tom had asked Retter to go with him. The happiness he had brought to her eyes was genuine. Just the thought of spending a whole day with Tom excited Retter. While Tom checked the woods, she could gather herbs for her poultices. Just to be free of the children for a day was a blessing. She really needed this day.

Tom had come to the door behind her, and was gazing at her as she stood silhouetted against the sunrise. His love for her had been covered with everyday chores and daily routine. Standing there, he felt his emotions begin to pull themselves together and work their way up—to emerge strong and susceptible to her every movement. His wife was young, lovely, and desirable. The soft features of her body drew him from the doorway to walk quietly up behind her and place his arms around her.

Feeling the warmth of Tom's arms, Retter leaned softly back against his chest, sighing contentedly.

"Retter," Tom whispered in her ear. "It's early yit . . . want to go back to bed?" His hands began caressing her.

Retter laughed softly, laying her hand on his. She could feel the tightness of his body as she melted even closer to him. She knew he wanted her.

"The bed's still warm, Retter."

She could feel the warmth of Tom's breath on her neck as he bent to place his lips on her smooth skin. Tingles of delight ran up and down her spine as the thought of the pleasures that awaited her flooded her heart. Turning, Retter's arms went around Tom's neck as his lips met hers.

"Momma, kin I have some milk?" A small voice came from the doorway. Tom and Retter turned at the same moment to see Jim standing there, barefooted, in his nightshirt. He was rubbing his sleep-filled eyes with his small fists.

"Damn!" muttered Tom, disappointment all over his face.

Just as disappointed, Retter stood on tiptoe and kissed his cheek. Then, looking at him with love on her face, she said quietly, "Later." Then she smiled.

Tom began to laugh and hugged her. Then, together they went into the kitchen, with sleepy-eyed Jim following.

Later that day, Retter waved good-bye to the boys and her mother as she and Tom pulled away in the wagon drawn by two horses. The huge wagon, owned by the lumbermill, was used by Tom when he scouted new areas for his boss. It was big and cumbersome, so Retter and Tom bounced around on the seat as they rattled down the graveled road, through Tuckasegee and northwest, on toward Cullowhee. The day was hot and dry in the valley. Caney Fork was beyond Tuckasegee and a good drive for them. As they entered the dirt road that led up to Caney Fork, it began winding its way through the mountains. The coolness of the shade of the huge spruce and hemlocks greeted the hot and dusty couple.

Retter had packed a lunch of cold biscuits and ham and had brought empty buckets, just in case she found blueberries. The burlap bag underneath the basket of food was for her herbs. She had come prepared to be active today.

It wasn't long, however, before the dust was stirred up on the narrow road, and hung all around them like a low cloud. The bonnet Retter wore covering her hair was her only shield from the dust. As they went farther back into the forest and higher up on the mountain, springs of icy water sprang up on all sides, running across the road, ending the dust that caked their throats.

Retter and Tom seldom spoke as they bounced to and fro on the wagon seat. There were almost no cabins alongside the road, and of the few cabins they did see, the people were not known to them; the mountain folk stared at them as they passed.

Retter's back was starting to ache with dull pains that grew steadily with the sway of the wagon. Just when she'd decided that she'd just have to speak to Tom about resting, he drew back on the reins and pulled up on level ground.

All around them were dense woods with sunlight peeking through the leaves, looking like strands of gold. The air around them smelled of wet pine needles and musty earth.

Jumping down from the wagon seat, Tom stretched a little and turned to Retter. With a thankful heart, she let herself be helped down. It felt so good to just stand.

With her hands on her hips, she bent backward a little, and then slowly walked over to the edge of the road and looked down through the sloping terrain below her. It wasn't too steep, and the underbrush looked promising. The dampness of the area seemed just right for the crowfoot she needed to gather.

"Tom, are you gonna stay around here a bit?" asked Retter, turning back to watch him loosen the halter on the horse's mouth.

"Yes, I am. Gotta go up over this here ridge and check the markings of the line. I should be back in about half an hour."

As Tom set off up the mountainside, he called back, "Don't go too far, Retter."

Getting her burlap bag from the wagon, Retter chose the easiest and clearest spot to climb down from the edge of the road. The ground underneath her feet was soft and slippery with wet pine needles. Carefully, she picked her way until she reached the tall trees just below her. There in the soft shadows underneath the brush, she found the small plants she called "crowfoot." The plant had five rounded petals with a gleaming, satiny surface. The leaves were deeply cut into three parts that looked somewhat like the feet of the crow.

Before long, the bag was half full, and the industrious Retter had traveled farther down the incline than she had intended. Then she suddenly smelled mint. Nearby, close to an old stump, she saw the plant in question. The sun shone through the trees onto the clump of mint. Without noticing the irregular contour of the ground, Retter hurried forward toward the stump.

All at once, her foot went down into a partially covered hole, and she lost her balance, falling forward. She cried out as she rolled downward through the leaves and pine needles. As bits of sharp rock dug into her body, she could hear nothing except a roaring in her ears.

With a solid thud, Retter's rolling body was stopped by a tree trunk, and with the jerk of her neck, she heard a small cracking sound. There was immense pain in her left arm, that lodged between the tree and her body. Opening her eyes wide, Retter slowly gazed about her in fear, trying to get the bearings on her immediate surroundings. Overtop was the dark green cover of densely grown vines, mingled with the limbs of trees. Bushes seemed to cover the whole area to one side of her, and protruding out from among the bushes were huge boulders. Underneath her, she felt not pine needles, but slivers of shiny soft rock. Shaking her head, she looked closer at the material in which she lay—it was mica.

Closing her eyes, she moaned, and then reopening them, she tried to sit up. She was sore in almost every part of her body, and she was sure that her left arm was dislocated. There seemed to be no broken skin. She rose to a sitting position and held her arm out in front of her. Small pieces of mica had attached themselves to her bare, scratched skin.

Looking up at the hill she had just rolled down, it scared her again to think of the fall she'd just taken. And near her right leg, the ground fell steeply off into a creek bed below. Ugh! That would have meant more damage than she had already suffered.

Standing slowly, Retter turned to look in back of her—and then she saw it. The gaping black hole that stared back at her! She had rolled right up to the entrance of an old mine shaft. The brush and boulders on one side covered it from the eyes of anyone who was standing above. With the light shining through the leaves, hitting the mica here and there, the ground all around shone like cut diamonds.

Suddenly, a weird feeling descended upon Retter. For some reason, she felt as if it were meant for her to fall and find this mine. Fear left her as she moved closer to the entrance. Her observations of the opening told Retter that this was an old mica mine. She had seen others before, and was familiar with the mineral. The rock itself could be split into thin sheets and was almost clear of color. It was soft and easy to break, so the shiny entrance of the mine was not unusual.

Pushing on through the brush and drawing her sore body closer yet to the entrance, Retter could see inside now, and adjusting her eyes, she saw that sometime, long ago, there had been a fire built just inside the entrance. The half-burned logs were still in position.

Her arm throbbed, and since she was so sore, she decided to wait a little before climbing back up the mountain. Tom wouldn't be there yet, anyway.

She ventured farther into the old mica mine, holding her left arm close to her body, her hands trembling. She'd just wait here awhile, and then begin her climb.

As she sat there, she gazed around. Years ago someone had stayed here, she could tell. Suddenly, her eyes came upon a stack of bones—all different shapes. With her eyes wide with apprehension, fear rose again. She moved quickly to stand and leave the mine—but her sudden movement brought a growling from behind the jagged rock that hung out from the wall. Looking closely, Retter could see two red eyes in the darkness. She gasped and sank back down on the dirt floor. The eyes watched her closely.

After the initial shock, Retter fearfully began to calculate just what to do. Since she didn't know what this animal was, she thought she'd better wait, and then try to slip out later. She watched the animal carefully—waiting.

But the thing in the corner wasn't going to just stay in one place and watch her. It slowly stood up . . . blinked its eyes . . . and began to move toward her.

As she saw it more clearly, she breathed a sigh of relief. It was a dog! A big, brown dog with sad-looking eyes. He came closer, dragging one leg, and began sniffing at her. He growled low in his throat. He was such a sad-looking sort, Retter thought. She very carefully held out her right hand to the dog and said, "Here, doggy, come here," and she clucked her tongue.

He stopped and hung his head low, his eyes not leaving Retter's face. Slowly, he edged closer to Retter's hand, still dragging one rear leg. He was so skinny that the ribs of his chest protruded. The odor that clung to the skinny dog brought a wrinkle to Retter's nose as he stopped just within reach of her outstretched hand.

Retter was so engrossed in this ugly dog that she had forgotten the pain in her left arm.

She let him smell her hand, and suddenly, he licked it—and whined a little.

Retter's heart went out to the half-starved dog. Since her little white dog had been killed last year by a coon, Retter had missed having a dog. Yes, indeed, she decided, she needed a dog.

He sank down on the ground beside her, and Retter began rubbing its head. He inched still closer to her until his head was lying in her lap. She could hardly stand the terrible odor, but love had already blossomed between the two. The odor didn't matter.

From outside the mine, Retter suddenly heard Tom's voice calling her. She answered.

Before long Tom was there, standing in the entrance of the mine, his face in the shadows. "Retter, what the dickins is that? It stinks to high heavens!"

Smiling, Retter said, "Tom, this here's my new dog. I'm gonna call him 'Mica.' Please help him. His paw's hurt."

Later that night, the newest member of the Ammons family lay stretched out, clean and well fed, at Retter's feet on the porch. He looked and smelled like a different dog.

Retter's arm was in a homemade sling, and Tom was getting the boys ready for bed. Retter was determined that her arm wasn't going to stand in the way of her being with Tom tonight.

Her right hand dropped to Mica's head, and she absently patted his sandy coat. She didn't see the love in the eyes of the dog as he looked up at her.

At that moment, Retter couldn't have known that Mica had been sent to her—to save her life.

CHAPTER TWENTY-TWO

A Hero

Nine months later, on March 21, 1916, a fourth son was born to Retter and Tom Ammons. Since Albert had been given the middle name of a president, Abraham, Tom decided to name his fourth son after a president also—Thomas Washington Ammons. Retter was happy with this name, especially since their son would have Tom's name also.

Retter was now twenty-two years old, and had four children. Bryson was a big help to Retter, being the oldest of the four. Since he was six years old, he had been taught to watch over his brothers and help Retter with the chores around the house.

Tom, a strong man, worked very hard for his family. But his family was growing, so he decided to keep his eyes open for a better job—one that paid more money. At the same time, he began planning the development of his farm, so as to grow everything they needed to eat. As soon as he completed the barn he was building, his father was going to give him a cow that was with calf. He had decided to put the barn between the house and the spring. It would be a two-stall barn, and Tom had already finished the first stall.

Over near the spring, on the hill adjacent, Tom had built a beehive. The hive had several drawer-like sections, with a removeable drawer in which the swarm could be transferred. On one of his hunting trips, he had found wild honeybees in an old tree trunk. They had been very overcrowded, so Tom had kept a close eye on them, so as to get them when they began to swarm.

It would be soon, he knew, so he was prepared. He had made a bee veil and had bought a bee smoker with a small bellows and a nozzle. This would blow out smoke and calm the bees when he captured them.

To Tom, bees were fascinating. Since his youth, he had tried to find out everything he could about them. This was one of the reasons he had made the sacrifices to purchase the set of encyclopedias that lined one of the shelves in the front room. It was through reading about the small insect that he had begun to learn the great many advantages of maintaining a beehive. The bees produced mouth-watering honey; the wax, made as a by-product, could be used to make candles for the mountain home; and the bees would pollinate the corn.

In his studies, Tom had read about the three different classes of honeybee. There was the queen, which laid the eggs. Then there were the workers, which gathered food and cared for the young—these were undeveloped females. And last, there were the drones, that fertilized the queen.

Actually the honeybee colony is a family home, where the workers care for and feed the helpless young; they collect and store the honey and do all the housekeeping in the hive. The workers also guard the entrance against all their foes and would die before allowing enemies to enter.

The queen bee is the force that holds the colony together. She does nothing but lay eggs, and if she ever leaves the hive for any reason, the bees become lost and disorganized. The queen is fertilized by the large male drones, who die immediately after the mating. As a result of just one mating with only one drone, the queen can lay eggs the rest of her life, which can be as long as five years.

In time the honeybee colony becomes overpopulated, and a form of emigration, called swarming, takes place. The old queen, taking many of the workers, leaves the hive and seeks a new home. This is what Tom was anxiously awaiting. He wanted the new home to be his beehive.

Daily, Tom went by the old tree and watched with increasing excitement as the signs of overcrowding became more and

David F. Ammons

more apparent. He checked his equipment constantly to make sure it was kept in an inconspicuous spot. As a last thought, he wrapped an old coat around the bee smoker and a saw, then placed this bundle in the drawer section he intended to take with him when it came time for the bees to swarm.

On his way home from work one day, Tom discovered that the swarm was in the development stage. Thousands of wild bees had already come out of the tree trunk and had gathered above on a small limb of the old pine. They were crowded together on the branch, in among the green needles, so closely knit that they looked like a hornet's nest. The sound they made was loud and almost scary—but to Tom, it was beautiful.

He ran to the cabin as quickly as he could, picked up the drawer and the bundle, and ran back. Out of breath, he stopped below the pine, and breathed, slowly, in and out, until he felt calm enough to put the coat on and the veil over his head.

Scouts for the bee swarm had been sent out to find a place that would be suitable for their new home, so Tom had to work fast. He prepared the smoker, and getting as close as he dared to the swarm, he pumped the bellows to blow smoke all around the crowd of humming honeybees. It took only seconds for the noise to go down.

Setting the bee smoker on the ground, Tom began to saw the branch. Carefully, he cut as fast and as calmly as he could, until the branch began to fall into his hand. He steadied the limb, and as it broke into two pieces, he held it as motionless as possible. Almost before he realized it, in his hands were the makings of his first beehive.

Placing the limb in the open drawer, he laid the lid over the branch to enclose the bees as completely as possible. Slowly he carried the section of the hive toward home. The sound of buzzing was low for awhile, but just as he reached the trail that led around to the spring, the noise became louder. Sweat broke out on Tom's forehead.

Finally, he reached his destination without mishap, and placed the section in the slot for which it was designed. Gathering his nerve, he slowly leaned over the beehive and opened the cover of the box. To his relief, he found that the bees were accepting their new home. Almost all of them had dropped their hold on the limb and were on the floor of the section of the hive. He would wait awhile longer before removing the limb. The danger of losing the swarm was now small. The workers were clustered around the queen bee—bringing a delighted smile to Tom's face. He had been successful!

Just as Tom straightened up, he felt a sudden pain in his right hand. Looking down, he saw a bee just as it stung him. Knocking the bee from his hand, he scraped the stinger off immediately, but a puffy knot was already forming. The pain was intense and continuous.

Tom walked quickly to the cabin, where he knew Retter would have something to put on the sting. Wal, he thought as he walked, it was a small price to pay. The little bee that had stung Tom would pay a bigger price. He had lost his stinger, and in a few hours, would be dead.

Retter was waiting for Tom when he came through the door of the kitchen. She had seen him come running in from work, grab his bee equipment, and run back the way he had come. So, she had begun preparing a poultice as soon as he had left—knowing that he'd probably be stung. She could remember, that back when she was small, one of her relatives had almost died from a bee sting. So, she wasn't going to take any chances.

The poultice she had prepared contained, among other things, tobacco—and the mixture looked terrible. But she knew that it worked.

After seeing Tom's hand, she took out some of the tobacco and placed it over the sting. Almost immediately, Tom felt the bite get cooler, and there was less pain. He breathed a sigh of relief and smiled at Retter, saying, "Wal, Retter! We have a beehive now! Them bees took to that there hive slicker'n a whistle!"

"Are we gonna have honey right away? Or will it take awhile?" asked Retter as she began to clean off the table where she'd been working.

"No, Retter. It'll take quite awhile before the bees make

enough honey," replied Tom as he looked at her. He'd noticed how lovely she looked in her pink dress and dark hair. With a twinkle in his eyes he continued, "'Sides, I have a honey what's sweet enough as she is . . . and my honey don't have any stingers!"

Catching her to him, he wrapped his arms around her and nuzzled her in the neck.

Playfully, Retter laughed and tried to push back a little, which only inspired Tom to tighten his arms around her even more.

Mica, who had been sleeping by the stove, raised his head, opened his sleepy eyes, and yawned loudly. This display was nothing for Mica to get excited about. It happened too often.

Tom could relax now, knowing he had finally pulled off a major accomplishment. Holding Retter in his lap, he contentedly ran his fingers through her hair and spoke softly into her ear, "Now I have two queen bees."

The rest of the spring and summer flew by as Tom watched his bees and built the rest of his barn. By the end of summer, he had his cow in her own stall. Now his daily chores included milking. With the fresh milk for the boys and soft butter for their hot biscuits, all the hard work had been worth it.

In her younger days, Retter had always milked her goats, so milking the cow became her chore for the summer.

Winter howled its way to the mountains, and the warm fire drew the family together during the long cold evenings. It was during these evenings that Tom began to teach Bryson and Jim their letters and numbers.

Retter would sit in her rocker, sewing and mending, and listen to the boys toil over the teachings of their father. She was so proud of them all.

Mica hardly ever left Retter's side. It seemed he couldn't keep his eyes off her. When Retter would tire of her needle, she would lean back in her chair and pat the brown head that was constantly there.

The dog was not young, but was steadfast and loyal to the family. Even Tom admired the patience he showed with the boys. At times, they would ride him, pull his ears, and hide his food—and Mica allowed it all—because of the other times, when Retter or Tom would find dog and boys sleeping together, all rolled up in arms and paws, the boys' faces glowing from the wash job Mica had given them.

For the winter months, Tom took over all the milking. However, when the spring of 1917 arrived, Retter informed her husband that she could now take care of this chore again. Deep down inside, she loved the quiet of the barn, the coolness of the shadows, and the smell of straw and warm milk. Sitting on her stool as she milked, she would relive days gone past. She believed Charlie was there with her as he'd promised. If she thought real hard, she could still see his faint smile and the kindness in the lines on his face. Retter loved the shadows of the barn and of the past.

Tom was gone the day it happened.

Retter had risen early, happy and full of energy. After feeding the boys and Mica, she had sat churning on the porch, singing all the folk songs she knew, keeping time with the dasher.

She worked hard, and before long she had churned a large amount of butter. Taking the now soft whitish-yellow solid from the churn, Retter added a little cold water and began to work the butter until it was free of milk. Draining off the water, she added a little fine salt and just a pinch of sugar to help preserve it. Humming to herself as she worked, Retter formed small flat balls of butter with her hands and placed them in a wide-mouth gallon jar. Over the top, she tied a piece of muslin.

In another jar, she poured the buttermilk from the churn, and covered it also. Then, still singing to herself, Retter was out the door and on her way to the spring, where she would store the milk and butter in the spring box that Tom had built for her. Mica was close behind her as she walked.

David F. Ammons

The spring went deep into the side of a mountain, with a huge rock formation going back into a crevice where the mountain water flowed out in an icy-cold stream. There was quiet magic around the coolness of the spring as the wet green moss and ripples of water seemed to whisper to her.

Setting one of the jars down, she stepped on the wet rocks and opened the lid of the spring box that was situated in the deepest part of the water. She arranged the jars in the box, placed rocks on the lids of the jars, and covered the box carefully. Mica was below her, lapping up the cool sparkling water. Leaning over to the porcelain cup that hung upside down on a stick beside the mouth of the spring, Retter filled it, and drank slowly. There was nothing so deeply refreshing as cold mountain water.

Suddenly, there was a crashing sound overtop the adjacent hill. Tom's beehive was over there. Retter began to run up the hill, with Mica at her heels. As she gained the top and went over the crest, she came almost face to face with the biggest brown bear she had ever seen. The beehive had been ripped open, and the bear was standing on his rear legs, honey spread from his nose down over his forelegs and chest. Bees swarmed around his head. He was batting at the buzzing insects, and from the roar that came from his mouth, it was plain to see that he was very angry. He had short, strong legs and large feet. Each foot had five toes, and each toe ended in a long, heavy claw undisguised by any hair. The long, thick fur of the animal protected him from the sting of the angry bees, but the buzzing around his head excited him. His short temper had got the best of him.

All at once, he saw Retter. He moved quickly in spite of his great size. He loomed up in front of her and swung his powerful front paw, grazing her arm and ripping the material of her dress. He moved closer, both sticky paws spread out—Retter seemed to be frozen in her tracks as her frightened hazel eyes grew wide in fear!

Just then, a brown streak came between the girl and bear. Mild-mannered Mica had turned into a snarling wild dog, with white gnashing teeth.

As the teeth of the dog sank into the bear, the big animal hit

Retter alongside her head with the back of his powerful paw, knocking her down the hill. Later she didn't remember rolling down the incline, nor the briar bushes she fell into at the bottom. All she could hear was the awful sound of flesh being torn open and the quick sharp yelps of pain.

She didn't know how long she lay there in the briars, but when she finally came to, her first thought was of Mica.

Struggling to her feet, Retter gazed up the hill, but could see nothing. Painfully, she made her way up the slope, dread filling her, calling, "Mica! Here, Mica! Where are you, Mica?"

At the top, the wrecked beehive was standing alone. The bear was gone. Retter's eyes searched the ground all around, and then she found him.

There at the foot of the old pine was Mica's ripped and torn body. He was lying in a pool of blood; his faithful eyes would see no longer.

Retter dropped to her knees, sobs racking her sore body as her tears fell on the dog. He had died saving her life. She reached out and stroked the lifeless head. All she could think of was that she could no longer drop her hand and stroke the smooth coat of her friend as he lay beside her. She drew her hand away and looked at it—it was covered with blood.

Dropping her head to her knees, she rocked from side to side silently, as her grief consumed her.

Sometime later that night, the white drawn face of Tom gazed down at a dirt-covered grave. He had buried Mica under the pine where he had died. Freshly carved in the bark of the pine were the words . . .

MICA, A HERO

CHAPTER TWENTY-THREE

The Girl Baby

"Retter," said Tom, helping himself to another biscuit, "I figger to be gone 'most all day. I'm going out past where they're talking about building the power house."

Tom opened the biscuit on his plate and dipped gravy into the fluffy white texture. Then he cut the moist crust of the biscuit with his fork and raised the fork to his mouth. The smell of the rich brown bacon gravy brought a smile to his eyes as he quickly consumed the complete biscuit and then cleaned his plate with another.

"Yummm," came his voice again. "Yore gravy is the best I ever ate!"

Retter smiled at Tom as she poured him another cup of coffee, while she fanned herself with her apron. It was midsummer, and even though it was early in the day, the heat of the morning sun slipped through the open window, warmly caressing Retter. When she leaned over Tom's coffee cup, the aroma of the freshly poured brew enveloped her, bringing a nauseating sensation to her stomach. Her dark eyes narrowed as the importance of this struck her. At first, she was skeptical of her suspicion. But, then, after going over in her mind the events of the past couple of months, especially the last one, she accepted the fact. She was pregnant.

She set the porcelain coffeepot down on the stove. It was crusted at the bottom with the burnt grease of a hundred brewed potsful. Pushing back the loose strands of her dark hair, Retter sighed and walked to the open window. She stood quietly gazing out, overtop the barn, up at the tall pine that stood to one side of the spring. She stood here often, thinking of the soft brown eyes of the dog that had loved her so much. She would never forget him.

Then she glanced back over her shoulder at Tom, still sitting at the breakfast table with their sons. Retter's eyes rested upon the boys, one by one.

There was Bryson, who was now seven. He was going to be tall, she could tell. He had dark hair and a dark complexion, and he put her in mind of Tom.

Next to Bryson sat five-year-old Jim. He looked so much like Bryson, yet his frame was much thinner. He still couldn't outtalk his brother.

And then, there was little Albert. He was three years old, but was still so small that he had to sit in a special chair Tom had built for him. Albert never said too much to anyone, but his smile flashed often.

In the high chair near the open window was Thomas, the one-year-old baby. Retter could tell he was another talker. He laughed and jabbered constantly.

Retter shook her head, and gathering her nerve, she walked over to Tom, laid her hand on his shoulder and began, "Tom, I have something to tell you."

Tom, not seeing the look on her face, stood up, wiping his mouth on the back of his hand. "Retter, that there was a mighty fine breakfast, but I'm late now leaving. I've gotta git acrost the mountain and over to where they're offering the jobs I told you about. The sun's been up fer a spell already."

Tom reached for an old gray hat that hung on a nail near the window. Above the band of the hat, the fabric was discolored with the sweat of a hard-working man. As Tom adjusted the hat on his head, he spoke as if in afterthought, "What wuz you gonna tell me, Retter?"

"'Tis of no never mind, now, Tom. You best be moving on down the mountain and quit yore lollygagging around." She smiled as she straightened her back and began using her apron as a fan again. Then, more quietly she said, "I'll tell you tonight."

Tom had begun to swing around to go out the door when he caught the tone in Retter's last statement. He stopped, and turning, he took a long look at his wife. "Retter, you look a bit quair, and yo're nigh on to looking peaked. You ortn't be doing too much in this heat."

Tom walked over to Retter and put his arms around her, squeezed her, then tilted her head up with his hand under her chin. His warm eyes drank in her beauty. He kissed her tenderly, and spoke softly, "I love you, Retter."

Retter laughed as she pushed Tom away, saying, "You quit yore sweet talking, you varmit! You'll have me taking on cuz yo're leaving me fer the day."

Smiling, Tom turned to go, then stopped by the door. "Retter, yo're not feeling porely, are you?" he asked.

"No, Tom! Now, git!"

Retter watched Tom from the front door as he began his journey down the trail that wound its way around the creek below the cabin. As he crossed the split log that was their only bridge, he swung up his arm and waved once to her. Then the trees and bushes hid him from her view.

Standing there in the doorway, Retter once again felt the sun's heat. Today was surely going to be a scorcher, she thought. There wasn't even a breeze blowing. As she turned to go back to her children, she made up her mind that she would definitely tell Tom her news tonight.

The day dragged on, just as it started—hot! Tempers flared up among the boys. Retter's nausea continued to fill her throat until it was almost unbearable. To make matters worse, she had decided that this was the day she was going to make her new supply of lye soap. It was a hot job for a hot day.

Telling Bryson to watch the boys, she rolled up her sleeves, carried out the iron pot, and hung it on the tripod Tom had long since fashioned for her. She was using the area she used for her weekly wash—in the backyard near the chicken house. In building a fire under the pot, Retter accidentally burned the thumb of her right hand. With her thumb in her mouth, she felt like crying, but instead, she threw herself into her work with even more zeal.

When the pot was hot enough, she put her can of rendered-down lard into the old black pot. While the lard was melting, Retter poured in the lye she had made previously out of ashes, stirring constantly. With steam from the hot liquid rising all around her, Retter's hair slid down from the usual bun on the back of her head. The loose strands clung to the wetness of her red face and neck. She was so engrossed in her task that she'd forgotten the sick feelings she had all morning.

Retter dipped cold water overtop the flat pans into which she intended to pour the soap. The pans needed to be as cool as possible.

After pouring the liquid into the cool pans she'd prepared, she was finished, except for cutting the lye soap into squares when the concoction was cool and set.

Before sitting down to rest, Retter picked up the water pail and walked to the spring. In the coolness of the wet rocks that enclosed the water back in the mountain, Retter stooped down to the softly rippling spring and splashed the water over her flushed face. Then, filling her pail, she walked home, greatly refreshed by the warm air on her wet face.

Reaching her kitchen, Retter lifted a dipperful of water to her lips and drank deeply. What a delightfully cool sensation it brought to her body! She closed her eyes and relished the feeling.

All of a sudden, she felt a shadow fall over her. Her eyes flew open! There, in front of her, in the doorway of the kitchen, stood a man she'd never seen before. He was almost bent double as he tried to breathe. Behind him was a teenage boy, almost in the same condition, but trying to hide from her eyes.

Retter stood still, and motioned for Bryson to stay where he was. She grew very calm as she waited for the man to catch his breath. Then he spoke.

"Missey, I need help. My wife's with chile—and there's nobody to help her!"

An urgency began to grow inside Retter, and also a feeling of fright. "Where, man!" she cried.

"It's quite a far piece over the other mountain. We'uns jest moved here about a month ago. Missey, I'd be much obliged fer yore help!"

"Wal, don't let's stay here and gab. Let's git going! But wait! I cain't leave my boys alone!"

"My boy here will take care of them. This is John right here. Come on, boy, say howdy."

The frightened boy barely nodded his head and eased into the doorway. He walked in slowly, then leaned against the wall.

Retter's eyes went back to the father as she said, "And who might you be?"

The older man nervously fingered the battered hat he held in his hands. "My name is Jeb Reeves. I jest moved here to work fer the railroad that's coming through up near Grassy Creek Falls. Ah, Missey, cain't we please hurry?"

Without further questions, Retter rushed to ready herself, and before long, they were on their way across the upper side of the pasture. Then they dipped down through the dense wooded area Retter had never traveled. The urgency of the older man that led her was real—so it affected Retter even more deeply. It seemed to her that they had walked miles when they finally reached a small clearing.

Hound dogs began to bark, causing a few scattered chickens to cackle. From the back of the roughly built cabin, Retter could see underneath the floor because of the logs that elevated the small structure. A screen door slammed, and Retter could see the brown legs of children as they ran. She couldn't tell how many there were, but she could see that they weren't used to having visitors.

It was dark inside the house, so it took awhile before Retter's eyes could adjust to the dimness. When she could see, she took in a very sparsely furnished room. It looked as if there were many people living here, but there were none in sight. The door to the back room was covered with a dirty drab-looking cloth. It was through this doorway that Jeb Reeves went with Retter at his heels. It was even darker inside this room. Faintly, Retter could make out a figure lying on the bed. She heard a deep and painful moan.

"Mary Ellen, I've done brung our neighbor, Miz Ammons, to help you," said Jeb as he leaned over the woman in pain.

"Ohh, thank you, Jeb. I hurt so bad!" came a muffled voice from the shadowed bed.

Retter swung into action! With a commanding voice, she spoke as she scurried around the room. "Mr. Reeves, lessee how fast we kin git some light into this here room. Git some clean rags and some hot water—and I mean RIGHT NOW!"

The old man hurried out to do as he was told.

Flinging open the heavy curtains at the windows, Retter stirred the dust of many months. She could tell that this room had been dark for a long time. The whole room needs a good scrubbing, she thought as she dusted off her hands.

Now that she could see the patient, Retter stopped beside the bed and gazed down at a woman who looked to be close to her own age. She was surprised. She guessed she was so stunned because Jeb was a much older man—even older than Tom.

Frightened eyes looked back at Retter. The woman was much too thin to be having a baby. Dread began to fill Retter. She'd never before delivered a child by herself; she had just assisted midwives in the past. Now, it was up to her. She reached out and laid a reassuring hand on the woman called Mary Ellen, and spoke softly. "There now, Miz Reeves, I'm here to help."

The trembling woman moistened her cracked lips, hesitated, and then spoke, "Are you a granny woman?"

"No, I sure ain't. But I have helped at a plenty of birthings in my time! Don't you fret none, now. I'm gonna take care of you." Retter hoped she sounded as confident to the woman as she sounded to herself.

A pain struck Mary Ellen again, and she bit her lip to keep from yelling.

"Now, that's enough of that! When you have the pain, beller

like a stuck pig! You hear me! I said, BELLER!" Retter almost yelled at the woman.

With the next pain, Mary Ellen opened her mouth and obeyed Retter. From then on, time flew. After Retter received the hot water and rags from Jeb, she cleaned the table beside the bed, washed Mary Ellen as best she could, and prepared a clean area for the forthcoming baby. Jeb had made a swift exit from the room, and Retter forgot him entirely.

Before long, perspiration covered Mary Ellen and Retter. The pains were coming at shorter and shorter intervals, and Retter knew the baby would be here at any moment. She and her patient were ready.

Then, the time arrived!

The birth of the little baby drew the two young women together in gratitude. The mother was grateful for Retter's help and encouragement—and Retter returned gratitude to the mother—thankful to have been a part of this ever recurring miracle.

It was a girl—tiny, and light in complexion. Retter's heart pounded as she gazed at the baby in her arms. She had had four boys of her own, and she loved them dearly, but her heart still longed for a little girl.

As Retter held the baby, absorbed in her own desires, she began to notice, out the corner of her eye, a movement in the cloth that hung over the door. Suddenly, she realized that she hadn't told the father of his good fortune.

Covering the baby with a clean cloth, Retter smiled at the sleepy-eyed mother and walked to the doorway. Pushing aside the door cover, she stepped into the other room. Her eyes grew big at what she saw. Slowly, she surveyed the room, counting as her eyes swept the faces she saw. "The Lord have mercy!" Eight! She had counted eight children. She couldn't believe it. That poor woman in the back room couldn't be the mother of all these! And there was one still back with her boys—that would be nine, and the baby made ten!

Recovering her voice, Retter spoke to the father, "Mr.

Reeves, you have a new one . . . this one is a girl baby. Mother and daughter are both doing good. Would you care to see her?"

Retter handed the baby over to him, and stood looking at the rest of the frightened and uneasy children. They were dirty, poorly dressed, and plainly scared to death of her.

Smiling, she took a step forward, intending to speak to the children. But before she could get a word out, they were gone, running through the door without a backward look.

Sadness consumed Retter. If she could just talk to them, she thought. Shaking her head, she turned and went back to Mary Ellen's bedside.

That night as they sat in the kitchen, Retter told Tom of her adventure. It was something she would never forget.

Tom listened and sympathized with all Retter had to say. "Shore is a pity about the Reeves' young'uns. But, Retter, all them young'uns don't belong to the new wife. Reeves wuz a widder man. This new woman's only been with him a few years. I met this Reeves feller down to the store some time back. He struck me as a mighty quair feller." Tom leaned back in his chair as he spoke, stretched his arms up over his head, and smiled at his wife. "Retter, I have some news fer you! Today, peers as if I got myself a new job. Yo're looking at the newest railroad man! I start from the ground up, but my boss allows that I'll be a foreman soon!"

"Oh, Tom!" Retter was instantly happy. Now, she could tell him her news. "Tom, I'm so proud of you!"

Retter leaned forward and took Tom's hand, her eyes shining. "Tom, I have news of my own to tell you. You better save some of that there money yo're about to make. Near as I kin figger it, you'll be a poppa again in about eight months or so. You'll need all that money to buy it some 'play-purties!'"

Later, lying in Tom's arms, Retter was remembering the eyes of the girl baby she had helped bring into the world that day. Her whole being longed for a girl for herself. She went to sleep praying for a daughter.

On April 5, 1918, the first little girl was born into the Ammons family, making Retter about the happiest woman alive.

As she lay in her bed, holding the dark-haired, hazel-eyed beauty in her arms, tears of joy rolled down her face. She had been blessed—and she called her blessing "Martha Jane Ammons."

CHAPTER TWENTY-FOUR

The Man Among the Boulders

It had been unseasonably cool for July, and it had rained the night before, so when Tom left for work that morning, a damp mist filled the air. The leaves of the trees were still shiny with dew, dripping water on the forest floor. In the distance was the sound of the waterfall. He shivered.

As he walked on down the mountain over the washed-out rocky road, the sound of his own footsteps echoed in his ears. Tom had to keep his eyes on the road in front of him to avoid walking through the streams of water that ran across his path.

Since he had had to leave so early in order to get down the mountain and across the river to catch his ride, it was hard to see very well in the semi-darkness. But, by the time he reached the river, the sun was coming up, causing the water on the leaves to sparkle like diamonds and the spider webs along the trail to look like spun silk.

He reached his destination. He was early, so he sat down on a rock. Lighting a cigarette, Tom pushed back his hat and gazed down the road, watching for the wagon that was to carry him over to Grassy Creek Falls. Then he stretched his long lanky frame and yawned loudly. Shaking his head to clear his thoughts, Tom drew on a cigarette, inhaled deeply and then, holding his head back, blew smoke rings in the air. Through the circles, he could see the orange and gold sunrise in the sky above the treetops. He smiled. It was going to be a good day. The warmth of the sun's rays touched his uplifted face.

Then, in the distance, Tom heard the clank of the heavy

supply wagon. As it approached, he stood, and placing the cigarette in his mouth, he hitched up his pants and tucked his shirt in.

"Howdy, Doc," grinned Tom as the wagon pulled up and stopped. "Looks to be a good day."

"Morning, Tom," replied the young driver. "Climb aboard!"

The ride to Grassy Creek Falls wasn't long. They reached the path Tom was to take, and jumping down from the wagon seat, he went around to the back and threw out the tools and other material he was to use that day. He thanked Doc for the ride and instructed him to be back around noon with more material. It was going to take more than what he had to repair the damage to the trestle. Lifting a heavy black tie, he placed it on his shoulder and set off down the trail.

The high steel trestle that Tom had been sent to work on that morning soon loomed up in front of him. The trestle, spanning a deep valley, was made of tall, closely spaced posts connected by ties and braces. Underneath the trestle, down in the valley, were boulders of all shapes and sizes strewn among the underbrush.

The route through the mountains the train took to reach this trestle had so many curves that travel along the route was extremely slow. Tom would be able to hear a train long before it reached the bridge. The many curves reduced the train's speed, but didn't prevent it from carrying heavy loads. These loads and weather conditions produced the need for constant repair and frequent inspections of the steel trestle. This was Tom's job, along with the help of a co-worker.

As usual, his helper wasn't here yet. As Tom surveyed the area, his lips grew tight, and he shook his head impatiently. This type of work called for two men just for safety's sake. The man who would help him was Jeb Reeves, the father of the little girl Retter had delivered last year. It was no picnic working with the man. First of all, he was lazy and had to be pushed to get the work done, and then he was jealous of the fact that Tom had been promoted over him. Tom dreaded working with the sullen man. He had decided that at the end of the week, he was going to request that Jeb be replaced as his co-worker.

Throwing down the tie, Tom turned to go back over the trail he'd just come down—to get the rest of the material. He worked for the better part of an hour transferring the material and the tools he needed. Just as he was carrying the last load down the trail, he spied Jeb up ahead. sitting on the ties that he had already dropped. Jeb was nonchalantly rolling a cigarette, a smirk on his lips as he spoke. "See you got it all brung down from the road. I'd been here afore now, but the ole woman needed fer me to fetch 'er some kindlin'." The laugher in his eyes taunted Tom. He continued, "I walked acrost the trestle. It's a closer way from the house."

Tom said nothing. His face was grim as he threw the load he was carrying down on the ground. Turning his back on Jeb, Tom strode over to the edge of the ledge, and placing his foot on a rock, he leaned over and looked for the best place to start the repairs.

Jeb watched Tom with a slow, burning hate in his eyes. More and more, Tom seemed to be ignoring him. Jeb thought that the job Tom had should have been his—he'd been with the railroad company for years, and Tom had just walked in a year ago, and already Tom was his boss. Jeb was holding his tobacco pouch so tight that the knuckles on his hands grew white.

"Jeb," came Tom's voice, "git one of them ties and lessus git to work."

The sun climbed high in the sky as the two worked together. Tom had to keep pushing Jeb all morning. The sullen man grew more and more antagonistic, and Tom's patience was wearing thin.

It must have been around eleven in the morning when Jeb's wife and daughter showed up. They stopped at the other side of the trestle, and his wife called, "Jeb, Lillie May ain't feeling good at all. Won't you help us acrost this here bridge, soes I kin catch the supply wagon back to town?"

David F. Ammons

Tom felt sorry for the woman as she stood holding the young child in her arms. The concern for her daughter could be heard in her voice.

"Woman," came the hostile voice of Jeb, "cain't you see I'm right busy now. Yore bothering a hard-working man on his job. Jest holt yore hosses."

"All right, Jeb," called his wife. "I didn't go to bother you none."

At first Tom had watched the man and wife as they talked, but during the conversation his eyes had wandered to the child. Even though he was at some distance, Tom could tell the little girl wasn't feeling well at all. He threw down his hammer and started out across the trestle. Upon reaching the other side, he spoke quietly to Jeb's wife, "Howdy, Miz Reeves. You been doing okay lately?"

"Fair to middlin'," answered the woman. "How's yore good wife, Miz Ammons? Ain't seen her fer ever so long."

"She's fine, thank you." As he talked, Tom held out his arms for the child. "Let me hold the baby, Miz Reeves. You go on out the trestle before me, and I'll carry the baby."

Smiling her appreciation, the young woman did as she was told, and the three made their way across the trestle without mishap.

Jeb had stopped what he was doing and stood watching them with malice in his eyes. His hands were clinched as he held them close to his sides.

The woman looked at her husband as she took her child from Tom's arms. The intense look on Jeb's face scared her. Without a word to him, she thanked Tom and hurried on up the trail toward the road.

They stood together, the two men, and watched the woman and child disappear out of sight.

"You should let my family, be, Tom!" Bitterness clung to each word as Jeb glared at Tom.

"Now, Jeb! All's I did wuz to carry that baby across," Tom turned to go back across the trestle. "'Sides, it's good that I did. I saw that mallet I lost over to the other side."

Jeb watched Tom's back for a minute, and then, picking up a rusty iron pipe lying beside the rail, he hurried to catch him. As he neared Tom, his fingers tightened around the pipe. He grew cold and clammy all over. Then using all his strength, he swung the pipe and hit Tom squarely on the back of the head.

Uttering no sound at all, blood flowing over his face and down his back, Tom tumbled off the railroad trestle. The silence of the woods was broken with the thud of Tom's body as it landed among the boulders below.

Jeb stood looking down, something like glee on his face. Then, slowly realizing just what he had done, fear began to grip the man. Hurling the blood-stained pipe out over the ravine, he began to move across the trestle, looking stealthily around him. Nearing the end of the clearing he began to run. Soon he disappeared into the dense forest.

Down among the boulders there was no movement. Clouds began to cover the sun, and the wind began to feel its way through the valley. A faded gray hat, stained with blood, lay alone on the trestle.

When the supply wagon arrived sometime later at the top of the trail, the driver greeted Jeb's wife and child. He assured the woman that after making his delivery, he'd take them to town with him. The driver was a boy who couldn't have been more than fifteen. He looked down the path, expecting to see Tom coming to help him. But seeing no one, and impatient to get back to town, he began to unload the wagon.

Just then, another wagon pulled up, and two men climbed down and approached the driver.

"Hello Doc, how are you today," said Jim Ammons as he held out his hand to the boy.

Shaking hands with the older man, Doc said, "Howdy, Mr. Ammons, and you, too, Robert! I reckon yo're looking fer Tom."

"You reckon right, son," answered Jim. "Why ain't he up here helping you?"

"Don't rightly know! I wuz fixing on going down to git him. I have these womenfolk here who's heading fer town."

"You hold on, Doc. Robert and I'll jest go on down and git him," said Jim, starting off down the trail with his son Robert right behind him.

As Jim and Robert got to the trestle, they could see no one. Looking at each other in surprise, they began calling, "TOM! TOM! WHERE ARE YOU?"

There was no answer.

Robert began walking across the trestle, trying to see the other side, calling back over his shoulder, "Daddy, ain't there supposed to be a man working with Tom?"

"If there's one about, he ain't to be found!" answered the father.

Suddenly, Robert stopped. He had spotted something lying on the trestle ahead of him. It was Tom's hat. With a feeling of dread growing inside him, Robert's eyes traveled from the hat, down—down to the boulders underneath the trestle. He stared at the crumpled figure of a man lying motionless on the rocks below. Swallowing his fear, he began to run back along the trestle, calling to his father, "Daddy, looky there! There's a man amongst the rocks!"

Father and son both headed for the ledge. Straining their eyes to see beneath the high steel structure, they could just make out the body sprawled out on the rocks. With a sinking feeling, Jim muttered, "Oh, my God! Robert, lessus git down there!"

The two men began to descend the slope, gravel flying as their feet slid before them.

Robert cried, "It looks to be Tom! My God!"

When they reached him, it looked as if he wasn't breathing, but upon closer inspection they could hear a faint gurgling sound. Jim could see that Tom's body was broken in numerous places. His jaw was cracked and hung low, and blood was oozing from the side of his mouth.

There was a cough.

Jim straightened the broken jaw with his fingers, pulling

clotted blood out of Tom's mouth. The breathing improved, and Tom moaned softly.

Robert was crying and cursing at the same time. "Daddy, where's that son of a bitch that's supposed to be his helper?"

"Robert, hush up! Git up there and git Doc. Gittin' him up from here is gonna be a trick!"

Tom opened his eyes. They were glassy and filled with pain. He said only one word, "Jeb!"

Hours later, Tom lay in the hospital in Sylva. Jim sat slumped over in the small dimly-lit hall, waiting for word on his son. He had sent Robert to tell Retter and to keep her home until he found out about Tom.

Finally the doctor came out and approached Jim. The conversation was short.

When the doctor left, Jim slowly sat down and put his face in his hands. How long he sat there, he didn't know, but he was still there when two feet stopped in front of him. Slowly Jim looked up into the pale, anxious face of his daughter-in-law.

"Where is he? Tell me! What have they done with him?" Her words tore into Jim.

"Retter, you shouldn't have come. You cain't do nothin'."

"How is he? The doctor fellers are caring fer him, ain't they?"

Jim stood up and placed his hands on Retter's shoulders. Tears formed in his eyes, and began to overflow down into his bushy white beard. He spoke softly, words that hurt him so deeply that his voice could hardly be heard. "Retter, the doctor says jest about every bone in Tom's body is broke." And with a sob, Jim concluded, "He won't live a week."

CHAPTER TWENTY-FIVE

Leaves of the Chestnut

The room where Tom lay was dark, and the smell of medicine hung in the air. Retter sat sideways in a hardback chair in a corner of the room, her head resting on the wall. Through the window near her, she could see the sun coming up. Her body was sore from sitting in the chair all night, and her eyes were red from crying and lack of sleep.

Slowly, she stood up, her hands resting on the small of her back, and stretched. "This place shore needs Tom to fix up some resting chairs," thought Retter, walking over to the window. She looked outside with unseeing eyes. She was deep in thought, remembering Tom as he had looked when he'd left the house the morning before. As he had gone out the door, he had kissed her good-bye, and had teased her about the baby. She would always remember how he had laughed and told her that she was spending more time with Martha than she was with him. But he had only been playing with her. Since she had wanted a girl so much, she had not even wondered how Tom felt about having a daughter. Before, he had never mentioned his feelings, but after Martha had come, Retter could see a change in Tom. He had become softer. He would sit and hold the baby, just looking at her.

With a deep sigh, Retter turned and looked at the still figure lying in the bed across from the window. The doctor had told her that he wasn't sure when Tom would come to . . . or even if he would wake up or not.

She had five children to care for, the youngest being only

three months old. Tom had to live—he just had to! What would she do without him? Uncertainty filled her eyes and then overflowed. She uttered no sound, just cried softly. She loved him so much that she couldn't stand to think of life without him.

Retter sat all day with Tom, but he didn't move once. Jim and Robert had come in for awhile, but they didn't stay long. Tom's mother was also ill and had to be cared for. As for Retter's children, they were all staying with her mother. She didn't want to leave Tom, and have him wake up and not find her at his side.

The first day came to an end, and still Tom slept. The nurse who took care of the patients on the floor brought Retter a more comfortable chair and a blanket. This night Retter finally got some sleep.

In the morning of the second day, Retter awoke with the sun shining in her face. Her first reaction was to look at Tom. He was staring at her.

Happiness flooding through her body, Retter jumped up and ran to his side. The only part of Tom's body that moved was his eyes. They seemed to cry out to her.

Tom tried to move his lips, but only moaned. Since his jaw was broken, he couldn't move his mouth. Retter thought she saw something close to terror in his eyes as he discovered that he couldn't move. His eyes grew wide with fear as he stared at her. Then uttering a low whimpering sound, he tried to move his arms. The pain was too much, and he passed out.

"Oh, Tom. My poor Tom," whispered Retter, laying her hand overtop his, tears rolling down her cheeks.

Suddenly, the door opened, and the doctor walked into the room. He was older than Retter, and looked tired. "Wal, how's the patient today? Is he awake yet?" he said as he laid down the pad that he was carrying.

"Not more'n five minutes ago he opened his eyes and stared at me. But, 'pears he passed out again. Ain't there anything you kin do fer him?"

"Mrs. Ammons, I'm afraid there isn't much at all we can do for your husband. I have never seen so many broken bones!"

The tone in the doctor's voice telegraphed to her the hopelessness he felt for Tom's condition. He was giving up without even trying! From somewhere deep inside her, there was born, at that moment, a determination! As the feeling climbed, Retter's hands turned into fists, her eyes began to flash, and when she found her voice, she said with feeling and certainty, "Mister doctor man, my Tom is tough. He has been all across this here United States—and he's a man who doesn't give up easy! And I don't go to argue with you none, but all yore book-larning doesn't tell you how to save my Tom." Retter's voice had gotten louder as she spoke, until she almost yelled at him. "My Tom WILL NOT DIE!"

Turning on her heel, Retter ran from the room, down a hallway, and out the front door of the little hospital. Outside, she looked all around her, and then, fighting through her tears to see where she was going, Retter ran around to the back. There she found a path that led away from the building. She ran through the lilac bushes and pines, up to a knoll. There, trees with wide branches hid Retter from the bright sun. Dropping to her knees, Retter sat back on her heels and stared up through the leaves of the trees into the blue sky. Her tears were gone now, but the tragedy that was changing her life had all but consumed her soul. Through her mind flashed scenes of another time in her life—a time when she had lost her grandfather, Charlie. She had not understood it then, either. "Oh God, I need yore help." The words seemed to crawl over one another as Retter spoke aloud.

All of a sudden, a chill went through her body. Her hands became clammy. With wide eyes, Retter looked around her. Clouds had covered the sun, and a light wind seemed to come from nowhere. Some of the leaves on the limbs overhead, pushed by the wind, came falling down on her. Retter leaned over and picked one of them up and absently brushed her hand over it. It was a chestnut leaf.

Then, it seemed as if she were years younger, and she could hear the words again. "Retter not forget—Great Spirit lives in chestnut tree. Someday Retter have big trouble in life. Take leaves, soak in water, Great Spirit help Retter. Charlie see."

Retter's heart almost stopped. Charlie had told her what to do. A feeling of peace began replacing the sorrow in her soul.

Hours later, a composed Retter sat beside Tom's bed. He had regained consciousness, and Retter had talked quietly to him. His eyes were full of understanding as he watched his wife's face. He was in her hands now, and he trusted her.

Weeks passed. To the surprise of the doctors, Tom lived. The determination of Tom and his wife was amazing to the townfolk. As soon as he could be moved, Retter had begun bathing Tom in an aluminum tub of hot water and her special herbs. She wrapped his body in chestnut leaves that had been boiled in water. Retter would leave the hospital only to go see her children, and to gather more herbs for the hot tub baths. Tom lost so much weight that Retter could lift him herself to and from the bathtub.

The bones in Tom's legs were set, but the hipbones were left to heal as they were. Thus Tom's body showed scars where the skin had healed, and the crooked curvature of the hip and upper leg bones was all too evident. The right hipbone protruded slightly and worried Retter considerably. She knew that Tom would have trouble walking again.

Before long, she decided that she could do much more for Tom at home. She wanted to expand the treatment of the chestnut leaves. Getting Tom home was a chore that only his father and Robert could handle. They prepared a wagon with straw and blankets. It was such a painful trip for Tom that again and again he passed out from the pain. But when he regained his senses, at last, he was home in his own bed. The children were all in the room to welcome him. They hardly recognized their father and were just a little afraid of him—until he spoke and held out his arms to them. They would have piled on him if Retter hadn't stopped them.

Retter sent the children back with her mother at the end of the day. It would be a long convalescence for Tom, and Retter needed to devote all her time to his care.

Immediately, Retter increased the number of chestnut leaves

so that she could cover Tom's body completely. As she positioned the soft hot leaves, she would wrap them to Tom's body with cloth to hold them close to his skin. Soon, his skin began to turn red with the stain of the leaves. Tom continued to improve.

But although Tom's broken bones were healing, his patience did not. Although the pain he had endured seemed to grow less and less every day, the idea of not being able to care for himself began eating at him. He had always been such a carefree and jovial person. But now, he began to withdraw into himself, and he wouldn't talk to Retter at all. He began to snap at her for no reason, and soon her life with him grew to be almost unbearable.

One day, Retter brought a tray of food in, and set it down beside the bed. Tom gave Retter a sullen look and turned his head.

"Tom, this here is yore favorite—beef stew." Retter tried to smile. She had had to wash him that morning, and he always became hard to live with after that. "It's here beside yore bed. It's real good! Cain't you smell it?"

As Tom turned back toward her, she could see the frown that covered his face. With one sweep of his arm, he brushed the bowl of stew away from him, hitting it against the wall, breaking the bowl. The stew ran down the wall and onto the wooden floor. As Retter watched, her eyes grew wide with rage, and her mouth dropped open with astonishment. Her fiery temper exploded.

"TOM, yo're addled in the head! Yo're the aggervatinist man I ever knowed! If you don't start to act human again, I'm gonna go off and leave you be! And I mean it!" With her hands on her hips, she continued, "I have nussed you like a young'un . . . and seems yo're all taken up with yore troubles and ailments. With the misery yo're giving me with yore carryings on, I'm the one what's gonna have to git a stiffiket from the doc to say I'M all better!"

Tom turned his head from Retter again. She was hot all over by now, and this only made it worse.

Without another word, she turned and stomped out of the room. Her anger drove her to do as she said she'd do. She made herself ready and walked to the doorway of the living room. "Tom, while I'm gone, you kin take care of yoreself. Good-bye!" And off she went, down the mountain, and over to her mother's house. She needed her children.

She explained to her mother and father what she was doing, and convinced them that it would be all right to leave Tom alone overnight.

Retter stayed away as long as she could stand it—two days and one night. When she went back, she was almost afraid to find how Tom had fared. She walked to the door and quietly peeped into the room. Tom was lying where she had left him, and his face was still turned to the wall.

"Tom, I'm back." Retter spoke softly. And as Tom turned to face Retter, she could see the tears on his face. He had been crying awhile because his eyes were red and swollen. "Oh, Retter! I'm so glad to see you. I'm sorry fer being such a pain to you!"

Retter was so happy to see Tom and so relieved that he was his old self again that she too burst into tears. The two put their arms around each other and cried together.

Later, Retter asked Tom the question she had been wanting to ask for quite awhile. "Tom, what are you gonna do about Jeb Reeves? Are you set on puttin' him where he belongs—in the jailhouse?"

Tom was quiet for a moment before he answered. "No, Retter. Let the Lord punish him. He'll git his come-uppance someday."

Retter tried to argue with Tom, but there was no talking to him about it. Tom had made up his mind. Jeb Reeves had got off scott-free—for now.

It took many months, but Tom's body, eventually, completely healed—however, when he could finally stand, Retter saw that Tom had dwindled to only around five feet. The broken bones had taken a foot of height from his now frail body. He walked, but only with a cane.

Tom would be a cripple the rest of his life.

CHAPTER TWENTY-SIX

Corn Liquor

It was early morning. Tom opened the door and walked out onto the porch. He moved slowly, his cane tapping on the wooden boards. Since his left leg was now shorter than his right, he walked a little bowed, with most of his weight on the right side. He stopped at the edge of the porch, and putting the cane out in front of him, he propped himself up, placing both hands on the handle, and gazed out over the foggy mountains. Tom's breath rose like steam in the crisp morning air. He looked different—his handle-bar mustache was gone!

It was still painful for him to walk, but the pain he felt now was nothing compared to the pain he had endured for the past seven months. He was thankful that he had lived; however, during the first few months after the attempt on his life, he had, at times, wished he had died.

Tom's thoughts turned to his wife. A smile played on his lips as he thought of the love and patience Retter had displayed in caring for him. She had literally saved his life. It was a gift that she had—her knowledge of herbs and the cures they could produce. He knew that the knowledge had come from Charlie—the Indian that had taught Retter the world of plants. It was after Charlie had died that Tom had first learned of him. And because Retter had never talked of him after that initial discussion, Tom had forgotten him almost completely.

Now, seven months after his fall, Tom had begun to believe in the quiet whisperings he had heard from Retter during his convalescence. She had often called Charlie's name, asking for his help in choosing the right herb for each different symptom that Tom had displayed. Retter insisted that Charlie had known—back when he was teaching her—that Tom would have trouble. She explained that Charlie had carefully prepared her for this crisis. When Retter talked about this sort of thing in whispers in the wee hours of the morning as Tom lay abed, cold shivers had run up his spine. Staring at the light in Retter's wide eyes, at times like that, Tom's belief that Retter was a special person was compounded. Even now he was still watching her with awe in his eyes. When Tom had married Retter, he had not known how much strength she had. If it hadn't been for her—well, he just didn't think he would be here now. Tom sighed. For whatever reason, and no matter how it was done, the bottom line was that Retter had proved all the doctors of Sylva wrong. He had lived, and now, he walked.

Standing on the porch, Tom pulled himself up as straight as he could. It was good to see another morning—even the fog that hung in thin layers, drifting and softly fingering its way among the pines.

A rooster crowed.

The door behind him opened, and Retter emerged, buttoning her jacket. "Morning, Tom," she said. "How are you a-feeling this day?" She walked over to him as she spoke and kissed him on the cheek.

"Fine and dandy! Think I'm up to milking the cow this morning," said Tom, looking at her from the corner of his eye.

"Tom! If I told you once, I've told you a million times—wait till the first of March, and then the chore's all yours." Shaking her head, Retter crossed the porch to the door of the kitchen, and went in to start the fire in the cookstove.

Tom moved slowly over to the chair near the kitchen door, and painfully sat down. Sensing eyes on him, he turned his head and stared into the beak of a dominecker hen. But seconds later, her head bobbed, and then she ruffled her feathers, giving up hope that this human had any handouts. She slowly strutted off, clucking, her head turning from side to side. Tom chuckled.

If there's anything on earth that lives fer food, it's a chicken, thought Tom.

It wasn't long before the aroma of fresh brewing coffee filled the air, along with the tantalizing smell of frying bacon.

Tom's weight loss had been great, his loss of appetite the main cause. But since he had been able to move around more, his appetite was returning—and this morning the smell of breakfast in the making was most welcome! He was actually hungry!

Retter had left the door ajar, so Tom leaned over slightly and looked into the kitchen. Retter was just putting her large biscuits into the oven. Tom smacked his lips. Yummm, he could just see the hot delicately browned biscuit come out of the oven and into his hand. Then he visioned whipped butter between the two layers of fluffy white texture, melting and dripping drops onto his plate! He could hardly wait!

"Hullo! Hullo, the house!" the sudden call of an approaching visitor caused Tom to jump in surprise. It had been awhile since they had had callers.

"Hullo, yoreself! Come on around back," called Tom in return.

Boot heels echoed hollowly as they hit the rock that protruded out from under the back porch. From around the corner of the house came a man dressed in a black and red wool jacket, faded denims, and a black cap pulled down tightly over his abundant grayish hair. Under bushy white eyebrows, dark eyes flashed, indicating pleasure at seeing a friend. A beard covered most of the man's face. He was breathing heavily.

Stopping just at the porch and resting one foot on the edge, he gazed at Tom. "Wal, Tom! How the dickens are you?" His voice was deep and raspy.

"Bless my britches, if it ain't Ben McCall!" Tom raised himself, grinning broadly, holding out his hand in welcome. "It's good to see you, Ben!"

Ben McCall stepped onto the porch, the smell of the woods clinging to his clothes. He reached for Tom's hand, and the hearty handshake that followed felt good to both of them.

"Ben, yo're jest in time fer breakfast! Come on in and sit a spell," said Tom.

"Don't mind if I do," Ben replied.

Reaching for his cane, Tom pushed the kitchen door open and followed the rugged-looking older man into the warm aroma-filled kitchen.

"Retter, yo're still the best-looking cook in these here parts!" Ben said, holding out his hand.

The smile on Retter's face upon seeing this man plainly showed that the warm welcome she extended to him was deeply felt.

"Ben, yo're climbing the mountain early this day," she said as she poured the two men a cup of coffee.

"Yep! 'Specially with the trail all kivverd up with fog! Never seen the likes." Ben sipped his hot coffee, and then, wiping his beard with the back of his hand, he turned to Tom and continued, "But, Tom, I'm here with a proposition fer you!"

Ben leaned back, one arm draped over the back of the chair, gazed intently at Tom, and then spoke, "Tom, what do you plan to do now since yo're all stove-up?"

Staring at Ben, Tom hesitated before he spoke. This question had been on his mind almost continually while he was lying all those months in bed. He swallowed, and then spoke quietly, "Don't rightly know, Ben. I done give it a lot of thought—but I ain't come up with nary a thing."

Retter was taking plump hot biscuits out of the oven, but she was also listening intently to the conversation at the table.

"Wal, Tom—what's yer thinking on corn liquor?" Ben's question was forthright and brassy.

Retter gasped and stared at Ben, her mouth dropping open, the start of a frown on her pretty face. "Lord have mercy!" she exclaimed.

Tom said nothing. He seemed to be turning it over in his mind. Slowly, he spoke. "Wal, Ben, I don't know—"

"Tom, jest listen a bit. I'll do all the work. Alls you have to do is make the recipe right. I'll haul the corn and sugar up till we kin grow our own corn in the spring. It pays good, Tom!"

"TOM! Yo're gonna make a—still?" Retter stared at her husband, dread beginning from deep within her and slowly rising.

Tom's eyes were clouded with deep thought. It did make sense to him. He wouldn't have to go down the mountain too often—he had worked at a distillery for a time in his younger, carefree days—and it did pay well, even if it was illegal. Tom glanced at Retter's disgruntled face, but his mind was already made up.

"Wal, Ben! You got yoreself a deal! Lessus do it!"

Ben's hand met Tom's in a handshake that cut Retter's heart to the quick. She could feel it in her bones—there was trouble ahead for the Ammons family!

And trouble there was! After the still was built, Tom spent most of his days there—and part of his nights—working at making the strong drink. The terrible stench of fermentation hung around Tom whenever he came home—and then, his breath began to smell of the whiskey.

Retter's life was changing fast. There seemed to be nothing she could do about it. More and more, her eyes would be puffed and swollen from crying. Tom no longer listened to her. He seemed to be possessed with proving that he could still make a living. He grew sullen and seldom talked at all. There were times when Retter would find Tom drinking from a jar out in the shed before every meal, and then there came times when she had to put him to bed because he was so drunk.

Retter knew that the reason for Tom's lapsing into this state was the physical damage he had endured—and his fear. Since he had been knocked off the railroad trestle, Tom had not tried to make love to her at all, even though she had given him lots of opportunities. She believed that he was afraid to try. She had wanted to talk to him, and give him confidence, but these things Retter had trouble discussing.

Time passed.

The day that Retter took her first drink of corn liquor dawned cold and dreary. Tom had come home and was in bed. A growing feeling of helplessness consumed Retter. Her children took up most of her time now—they were so confused over the change in Tom that each of them had grown more quiet as time went on. When Tom was home, Bryson would stare with wide eyes at the stranger that was his father.

As the morning turned into afternoon, Tom finally arose—ate only lightly—and limped off with his cane.

Retter stood by the cabin and watched him until he was out of sight. "Why?" she thought. "Why is he doing this?" Going into the kitchen, she suddenly spotted a quart jar of the "home-brew" behind the water bucket on the table. She walked over slowly and stared at it. Maybe she would just taste it, and see what the hullabaloo was, over the awful-smelling stuff. But how could she stand the smell long enough to drink it? Holding her nose, Retter raised the open jar to her trembling lips. She felt as if she were committing a terrible sin—but she took a sip anyway!

"My God!" gasped Retter. It burned her all the way down. It was a horrible taste—and yet, it warmed her stomach, and made her feel hot.

Hurriedly, Retter replaced the jar behind the water bucket, and continued with her daily cleaning. Every once in awhile, she would stop and stare at the liquor. Somehow, the small taste she had taken had intrigued her—it was awful—yet, warm.

It was late in the day when Retter finally faced the fact that she wanted to taste the liquor again. She had told herself all the reasons not to drink the strong brew, but temptation finally won out.

She sat down at the kitchen table, and placed the jar in front of her. Then, slowly, she took another drink, holding her nose again. It burned just about as much, but it didn't seem to be as severe.

The next drink came easier.

As darkness fell, Retter was laughing and talking to herself.

Putting the children to bed proved to be a delightful time for them. They hadn't seen their mother laugh in so long that they went to bed happy and laughing at her attempts to walk in a straight line.

When Tom came home, Retter was waiting for him. His surprise at her condition was only heightened when she made overtures to him for the first time since he had been crippled. As usual, Tom had been drinking, and for some reason this night seemed to bring everything to a head. Tom accepted Retter's forwardness, and they came together in a freedom they hadn't known in over a year.

When Retter woke the next morning, her throat seemed to be so dry that she could hardly speak. She was thirsty! She moved—and the pain in her head seemed to hit her between the eyes. She moaned aloud. Well, she had to get up—there were the children to care for. How she made it through the day was a mystery to her. That evening she decided to have another drink . . . just to help clear her head. She had heard Tom say that.

Weeks passed.

Tom began to watch Retter as she drank. At times she would be sweet and lovable—then again, at other times, she would become ill-tempered and quarrelsome. Black circles began to form under Bryson's eyes, as he came to understand what was happening to his mother. Little by little, Tom quit coming home drunk. But he didn't know what to expect from Retter when he arrived.

Each day, Tom pondered his problem. Finally, he thought that if he would just be tolerant with his wife, she would, herself, surely see what she was doing. Retter had always hated drink in the past. He decided to be patient, and wait until Retter came to her senses.

CHAPTER TWENTY-SEVEN

Empty Jars

But as time went on, things got worse instead of better. Retter began to gain weight. She didn't tell Tom that she'd discovered that she was pregnant again. She let herself go until she looked ten years older. Her dresses had to be let out, and she wore no belt. It felt much better just to let the dress hang. Then, it even became a chore for her to wear anything underneath her dress. When she began to sleep in her clothes, Tom finally decided that she had gone too far.

On his way home from the still one evening, Tom practiced the speech he intended to give to his wife. He knew from his own experience with strong drink that he'd have to be careful in his choice of words—and he knew also that she'd probably not listen to him. But he had to try. Retter no longer looked like his love of long ago—she was entirely different now that she drank. He longed to have his wife back—he didn't want this stranger.

During the day, the boys were getting little supervision from their mother, so they were growing wild—to the point of fighting among themselves and forming habits of laziness and talking back. Something had to be done.

As Tom opened the door to the family room, a damp musty smell floated up to him. Grimacing, and moving his head as if to dodge the offensive smell, he swallowed, and stepped inside the door.

It was dark. Tom stood quietly as his eyes adjusted to the evening light. Dimly, he made out a form lying on the bed. Some of the dirty covers had been kicked to the foot of the big brass bed, and others hung partially off the edge, touching the wooden floor. Empty quart jars lay on the floor—some turned over and their contents spilled on the covers.

Retter was passed out, one arm dangling over the edge of the bed. Her dress had inched up during her sleep and barely covered her body. Her rounded stomach pushed at the disheveled dress.

The boys were nowhere to be seen—but Tom could make out Martha Jane sleeping on a pallet near the bed.

Tom felt sickness rise in him—it swam up only to stick in his throat. Tears of anger came to his eyes as his fingers clenched—becoming fists of helplessness.

"Oh, my God," Tom moaned to himself as his tears rolled down his cheeks and dried up almost as fast as they came.

He crossed the floor, and leaning over his wife, he shook her. "Retter! Retter! Wake up!" Tom's anger made his voice quiver. "Retter! I said, wake up!"

Retter heard Tom's voice, but it sounded as if he were far away from her. She had to come from deep inside herself to try to reach the top. A part of her struggled to get out and up to Tom—while another part of her wanted him to just leave her alone.

Tom was shaking her roughly now and yelling, "Retter! I cain't take it no more. Retter! Git up!

"Tom—jest leave me be . . . 'er git me a drink—'er somethin'. My throat feels like I swallered a chinquapin hull."

Retter moved to sit up—and then, moaning, she fell back onto the bed—her hands holding her head.

"Tom—my head is killin' me!"

"Retter, I don't know you anymore. What's got into you? This here drinking has got to stop. The whole family's suffering from it."

Tom limped over to his chair beside the fireplace as Retter pulled herself up and dropped her legs over the side of the bed to touch the floor with her bare feet. Her back was bent over and her hair hung in clumps around her neck. Through blood-shot eyes she tried to see her husband's face. There was still so much whiskey in her that she swayed from side to side. Suddenly, she almost fell forward on her face.

"But Tom, I have quit—therz no more left."

She tried to keep a straight face, but when she realized what she had said, she giggled aloud—then quickly covered her mouth, swaying again.

Tom sat staring at the empty fireplace, still too sick to look at her.

"Tom, lessus talk 'bout it—but first, I hafta go pee."

Retter stood up, holding onto the brass bedpost, and walked shakily, hanging onto the wall, toward the door to the back porch.

Tom couldn't stand to look at her. He caught a whiff of her as she pulled the door open. His skin crawled.

Feeling her way along the outside wall, Retter made it to the rock that stuck out from under the porch. She had to relieve the pressure inside her, but also knew that if she squatted down, she'd probably never be able to get up. So, she just spread her legs apart, and covered the rock with urine—the splashes hitting her legs and ankles.

As a warm vapor rose, Retter pulled her dress up and looked down at her feet. She giggled again as she drunkenly envisioned the face of her mother-in-law. If she could only see Retter now.

She decided that she didn't want to hear Tom yell anymore and that she wanted another drink. She knew where to find another jar. Moving unsteadily, Retter made it out to a shed just beyond the wash area, and pulled at the latch on the door. Feeling around in the darkened leanto, she finally found the half-full bottle she had hidden. Tilting her head back she relished a long drink—then another—and another—until the liquor was gone. Dropping the empty jar to the dirt floor, Retter stumbled out into the light and made her way back toward the house. When she reached the porch, she raised her foot stepping up, swaying slightly. She missed the porch. Losing her balance, she fell forward, hitting her stomach on the edge of the porch flooring and then on the hard rock underneath.

Pain shot through her body, but she allowed no sound to come through her clenched teeth. Just before she passed out, she felt the warmth of the blood that coursed its way down between her legs.

Days later, Retter lay between freshened bedclothes, crying softly. She had lost her baby, and she had herself to blame. It had been too great a price to pay for her mistakes. How could she look at herself in the mirror again—how could Tom look at her?

But she had learned something about herself and her weaknesses—she had learned that everyone has weaknesses—and she was no exception.

Tom came into the room, his cane steadying him as he walked. He carried a bowl of soup in his free hand.

"Mornin', sleepyhead. Feel up to snuff today? Fetched you some tater soup."

As Tom limped to her bedside, Retter gazed with tears in her eyes at his weathered face. Whatever he had thought of her drinking, it seemed not to show now. Only concern and love were evident as he pulled up a chair with the crook of his cane.

Through the open window by her bed, a soft cool breeze came stealing over Retter's wet face.

"Oh, Tom, I'm gonna be all right—but what about my dead baby?" The tears now came full force as Retter buried her face in her pillow.

A scarred hand rested on her arm, and her husband's voice soothed her tears away as he spoke quietly, "Retter, listen—when the Lord closes a door—somewhere, He opens a window."

Catching Tom's hand in hers, she drew the crooked fingers to her cheek, and turning her head to the side, Retter gazed out the open window, through the boughs of the balsam, to the blue of the morning sky.

It was a new day.

CHAPTER TWENTY-EIGHT

The Mattress Factory

The warmth of the fire touched Tom's face as he sat in the shadows. He was dozing, his arms folded, with a hand underneath each arm—his chin resting on his chest.

Big hazel eyes watched him, gazing with love at the face with the stubby beard. She wanted to play, but her father just sat there.

The only light in the room was the light from the fireplace. For quite awhile now, her mother had allowed only one lamp to be lit in the evenings, and that one was now in the kitchen where the boys were taking their bath. Martha had already taken hers, and stood clean and warm near her dozing father.

Retter sat in the rocker close by and watched the baby gaze up at Tom. There was a smile on her face—she was happy that Martha showed such interest in her father. She seemed to be fascinated by him.

The little girl moved closer to Tom, and placed one chubby hand on his knee, still watching him. "Daddy—" she said quietly.

Tom opened one eye and looked at his little daughter. Her hair hung in brown curls, and her hazel eyes showed up in contrast to the whiteness of her ivory skin. The likeness of Martha to her mother was striking.

Reaching down, Tom picked up Martha and hugged her. "Yes, my little sweetheart?"

"Daddy—pay horsy?" Martha said as she rocked back and forth on Tom's lap.

Laughing, Tom moved her down his leg, onto a seat on the top of his shoe. Then he began to bounce her, as well as he could. She loved it, giggling as her curls bounced all about her head.

The firelight flickered and danced, almost in tune with the motions of the little girl and her father.

Retter smiled. Tom was himself again, and to see him play with Martha was a joy. The children had forgotten the days that had been filled with drink. Home life was so much better now. The family had been made even closer by the troubles that had befallen them.

But more than ever before, Retter had problems trying to make ends meet. Tom still made the liquor, but the trips up the mountain by prospective buyers had grown fewer and fewer in recent months. There was just not enough money to buy the supplies needed for the months ahead—when going down the mountain in the snow would be impossible. Without telling Tom, Retter had decided that tomorrow she would venture down and try to find herself a job. That seemed to be the only solution to their money problems.

As Retter got up to check on the boys in the kitchen, she felt a twinge of fear—fear of the unknown—the people she would have to face tomorrow! But Retter had made up her mind, and that was that! She was twenty-seven years old and in the best of health—so there had to be a job for her somewhere.

It was November, 1920, and cold weather had again come creeping up the mountain, covering the world around her with spectrums of frost. It was early morning, and Retter was already halfway down the mountain—on her way to Tuckasegee Valley. She had told Tom that even though she had little money, she was going to visit her mother and on the way back stop by the store for a little fatback and flour. He had been satisfied with her explanation and had promised to look after the children. Bryson was ten years old now, and helped a great deal in caring for his brothers and sister, so Tom would have help.

As the sun moved higher in the sky, Retter watched the

wonders of nature unfold around her. She could hear the birds chirping and see the squirrels jumping from limb to limb. The waterfall down below was like continuing music to her ears. She began to hum, and swing her skirt as she walked. It was as if she were ten years old again, and wandering along the mountain trails she had loved so much. At any minute, she half expected to go around a bend in the road and find Charlie waiting for her.

Suddenly, as she realized anew that she would never see Charlie again, tears welled up in her eyes. It almost seemed to Retter that her childhood had died with Charlie.

Wiping the tears from her eyes, she experienced determination—determination born out of responsibility. She was going to meet the challenge of a problem that had, in the past, been Tom's.

When Retter reached the main road, she caught the supply wagon on its way back to Tuckasegee. There were only two stores in the small town, and both were general stores. The larger was owned by Don Moses—it was called the biggest because he sold more clothing than the other. Don also took care of the mail that came and went in the small town, so he was not only the proprietor of a store but, at the same time, the postmaster.

On this day, Don was sweeping out the store when Retter entered, "'Pon my word, if it ain't Retter Ammons! Shore am proud to see you, Retter!" Don Moses was sincerely happy to welcome her. She was his first customer of the day, and it had been months since she'd come down to the store.

"Right nice to see you, too, Don! You got any fatback and flour?" Retter stood by the counter and watched Don bring the slab of fatback out from the back. Taking the butcher knife that had been lying by the cash register, Don placed it on the slab and spoke, "Retter, how big a slice do you 'spect you want?"

"Wal, now, jest about a pound will do. Cain't even afford that much, to tell you the truth."

As he cut the meat, Retter continued to talk. "Don, I'm in need of gittin' myself a job. Being's Tom's all stove-up like he is, I need to see about earning some money fer supplies fer the winter. Do you know where I could find a place to work? I'm a mighty good cook, you know!"

Don finished cutting the meat, and while wrapping it in plain brown paper, he started to shake his head, but suddenly, he smiled as if remembering something. "Retter, I did hear of some jobs opening up down to the mattress factory. You might jest ketch the wagon before he pulls out and ride over to the other side of Shook Cove and see if they're still wanting help. I'll hold yore meat till you come back." And then, just before Retter moved to leave, Don said, "Oh, say, Retter—did you hear about Jeb Reeves? He fell off'n the railroad trestle over to Grassy Creek Falls—and died last week!"

The shock that Retter felt was short-lived. She heard Doc call from the wagon that he was leaving. Retter left hurriedly, thanking Don over her shoulder.

The driver of the supply wagon was just climbing up into the seat.

"Wait there, Doc! Wait fer me!" called Retter.

Sometime later, Retter came out of the shed that was the office of the mattress factory, a large smile on her face. She had a job, and she was to start immediately. She disappeared into the doorway of a huge square, barn-like building.

Don Moses was happy to see Retter when she walked into the store later that day and told him of her job. She was tired and she showed it, for she had worked all day, and like the determined person she was, had put her heart into it. It had been backbreaking labor—but it would be worth it when she showed Tom the money she would get at the end of the week.

Oh, but she was tired as she started her journey up the mountain. As she reached home that night, she realized that the lamp in the window had been her beacon. Darkness had fallen and Tom was pacing the floor, worried about why she was so late.

"Retter, where the dickens you been? I've been most worried to death over you!" Tom was angry when he could see that she was all right.

Retter pulled her rocker over to the fireplace, and sat down, holding her hands out to the warmth of the flames. She slipped her shoes off and set her feet on the warm hearth. Through the heavy stockings, she moved her toes.

Looking at Tom, she said softly, "Wal, Tom—I didn't go to scare you any. I jest went and got myself a job down to the mattress factory. I'm to work there five days a week. Now don't go gittin' mad, Tom—we do need the money!"

Retter could see that Tom was unhappy about what she had done, but he said nothing. He accepted it with his face averted from her. His pride was hidden deep inside, but he agreed with her that they needed the money. He agreed to look after the children while she was working, and on the weekends he would run the still to maintain his supply of moonshine.

Suddenly, Retter remembered the news about Jeb Reeves, and catching Tom's hand, she spoke, "Tom remember when you said that Jeb Reeves would git his own someday? Wal, last week, he fell off the same trestle he knocked you off of! He's dead, Tom!"

Tom's face was still. Then he said, "There's no joy in my heart over him dying, Retter. There's shore a lot of young'uns down to his cabin that's gonna need some help. We best be doing what we kin."

Love for Tom grew even more in Retter's heart. He was such a good man! She leaned over and kissed him on the cheek and smiled.

A month of hard work went by. Retter's legs, at first sore from climbing up and down the mountain, soon grew strong and sturdy. The walk and the work seemed to agree with her. Each day, she brought more supplies up with her to the cabin. Then, the day came when she no longer brought any packages with her, and she wore a worried look.

It was a week later that Retter came stomping into the kitchen where Tom was preparing supper. She was earlier than usual, and he could see that she had been crying.

"Retter! What's the matter?" said Tom.

"I'm so put out, Tom! I've been working fer that there factory the best I kin—and what do you reckon they went and done?" Retter's temper was showing, as her voice rose and fell with the words of her story. "'Twas the other day when I knowed that they wuz setting to soft talk us outta something! They said we wuz gonna have a sharing of the profit! You ever heard the like? They wanted to give me a piece of paper, in place of my money! You hear me? NO MONEY! Wal, I waltzes up to the bossman and I says that I wanted my money, not that there paper. Bless me, if everybody don't foller me! Wal, I took on something fierce—and I sets my mind to not giving in to them!" Retter had been talking fast and furious, then pausing in her speech, she went over to the water bucket, dipped out some cold spring water, and drank, the water dripping off her chin.

"Wal, to make a long story short—I got fired from my job, Tom!"

Tom had to turn away to keep Retter from seeing the grin on his face. Fortunately she didn't see his expression.

But with his back to Retter, Tom didn't see the look that covered her face either. It was a gleeful vengeful look! He barely heard her next statement. "I don't care, I got back at them!"

"Retter! What did you say?" exclaimed Tom, turning back to gaze at her in surprise.

"I said I got back at them! When they wuz to dinner, I took my wages out in mattresses. I had Doc tote them up here on the back of the supply wagon. Wouldn't gonna pay me, they says. Wal, now you kin sleep good. With yore back gittin' all stove-up on that straw we've been a-sleeping on, I swore I'd git you a good mattress. I know it's good! I made it myself!"

Tom laughed until he cried, and then moving close to her, he said teasingly, "Retter, why don't we try it out tonight and see if it'll take a thrashing!"

CHAPTER TWENTY-NINE

Franklin Lee Ammons

From the day Retter discovered she was pregnant with her seventh child she knew this was to be a special child. Together, she and Tom had been through a lot of strife, but through it all, they had come together in a union of love and laughter—and this child was the result.

Winter came—then spring. Due to her experience at the mattress factory, Retter was in fine physical condition to carry her child. In addition, there was a lot to do, so Retter worked like a man. In the fields she raised cabbage to sell, and closer to the house, she began raising as many chickens as the henhouse could hold. She would get a decent price for good frying chickens from Don Moses down at Tuckasegee.

Life on the mountain was hard—but satisfying to Retter and her family. Everyone pitched in and helped, and the months flew by. Retter was happy.

But summer was hot and as each day passed, it grew hotter. There was no rain.

The long dry spell brought more hardships. The cool spring under the tall pine trees had almost dried up—there was but a trickle where there had been plenty. Thus buckets of water had to be carried to all the livestock, and the vegetables in the garden slowly began to wither and die.

Hard work and the heat made tempers flare. Every day, all faces would be turned toward the sky, praying for rain.

August came—and still there were only cloudless skies and hot sunny days. This was Retter's last month of carrying the baby, and she knew that this would be the hardest time she'd ever experienced with any of her children. She had gained less weight with this child than the others, but the strain of all the extra work and the unusual heat had finally pushed her almost to exhaustion.

As her time drew near, Retter's kitchen grew most unpleasant. The heat from the wood stove enveloped her tired body as she cooked for the family. Perspiration soaked her clothing, the cotton fabric clinging to her. To make matters worse, through the open windows on either side of the stove came scores of flies: they became Retter's constant companions.

"Oh, God!" thought Retter, "if it would only rain!"

From deep inside Retter, the pains began. She opened her eyes immediately, her hands going to rest on her stomach. She felt her water break, and the bed beneath her was instantly soaked.

"Tom, Tom! Wake up!" she said urgently.

"What?" came the sleep-filled reply.

"Tom—there's no time! This here baby's coming!"

The now wide-awake Tom sat up in bed, lifted his legs over the side with his trembling hands, and reached for his pants.

"Oh, my God, Retter—guess I'm all you've got to help you this time."

Tom found his pants and hurriedly pulled them on.

"I helped plenty of critters birth their young'uns—I reckon I know a little bit."

Using his cane, Tom limped as fast as he could out of the room, still talking, "Shore hope I know enough to help birth my own chile."

Tom had left the door open. A musty smell floated in to Retter. With surprise, Retter realized that it was just beginning to rain—the raindrops stirring the dust of many months. "Thank you, Lord, fer the rain," muttered Retter as she turned her head toward the sound. Light from the oil lamp in the kitchen found its way out onto the porch, casting long shadows through the doorway and onto the far wall of the room Retter occupied.

The pain came again—more intense. Retter gritted her teeth and clenched her hands. There would indeed be no waiting for a granny woman tonight. Her time was here.

Outside, thunder grew from a low murmur into a roar—then died, as the pouring rain began to dance on the tin roof above her.

It was now only minutes between the pains. Retter knew that the baby would be born very soon. "Tom!" she cried. "Hurry!"

Tom appeared in the doorway, the oil lamp shaking in his hand. "Retter, I have the water on the stove. It took me awhile to git the wood burning to heat it."

Setting the lamp on the table across the room from the bed, Tom hurried over to his wife. "What do I need to git, Retter? Tell me quick!" he said, his words falling out in a rush.

Retter laid her hand on his, and tried to smile. "Tom, don't you go gittin' flustered now. All you need is my good scissors, and some clean cloth."

Another hard pain interrupted Retter and her fingers clamped themselves into Tom's hand. She moaned behind tight lips. Then, taking deep breaths, Retter slowly relaxed. Tom caught her hand with both of his, gazing at her with deep concern.

"Look in my sewing box over yonder by the lamp fer the scissors, and there's some sheets in the closet under the stairs in the back room. All's you need then is some disinfect . . . maybe some of yore corn liquor will do."

Perspiration began to gleam on Retter's forehead as Tom scurried around doing as she had instructed.

Suddenly, a voice spoke from the doorway of the back bedroom, "Dad, what's going on?"

Bryson stood in just his pants, wiping the sleep from his eyes.

"Son! Here, help me with this here table—yore ma's gittin' set to have her baby."

Bryson stumbled as he ran to help his father, glancing over his shoulder at his mother's bed in the corner.

"Now run to the kitchen and fetch the hot water in here—and both of the water basins from the table."

The boy ran out, and was back almost instantly, his bare feet hardly touching the floor.

Lightning flashed—followed by a clap of thunder. Bryson's wide eyes grew even wider. "Dad—I'm askeered. . . ."

Tom was watching Retter. Because of her pain, she could no longer help him. Then, from somewhere, help came—and Tom suddenly felt a calming sensation. "It appears to me, son, like it's about to happen. You go on over and sit down while I help yore ma."

Tom dropped the scissors in the basin full of hot water, and quickly poured corn liquor over his hands.

"Oh, Tom. It's COMING!" Retter's voice rose and dissolved into the music of the dancing raindrops.

As his mother screamed, Bryson hid his face in his hands.

Retter's body was convulsed with pain. Her breathing came in short puffs. Reaching over her head, she caught the rails of the bed in her hands. The knuckles of her fingers grew white as she went through the pain of another contraction. It felt as if her eyes were going to jump out of their sockets, and as if her back would explode. The pain consumed her whole body. Yet the baby still didn't come.

Fear engulfed Retter. The baby should have already been born. Retter's thoughts became jumbled as she began to believe that something was wrong. As the contraction subsided, her eyes found Tom's worried face in the dim lamplight. Fingers of fear traveled across her body and her heart raced.

"Oh, my God! Please help us," prayed Retter silently, closing her eyes tightly, forcing tears to roll down the side of her face into her already damp hair.

She felt Tom close to her, and opened her eyes as he wiped her face with a washcloth. She caught his arm, allowing him to see the fear in her eyes.

"Tom! There's something wrong. It's taking too long now. My water's been gone fer nigh onto an hour."

"No, Retter—everything's gonna be all right. Listen to the

rain on the roof—ain't it purty? You know the Lord wouldn't stop with jest one blessing—He's gonna give us two."

Tom's quiet voice calmed Retter. He was leaning against her bedside, holding her hand in one of his, and brushing back her damp hair with the other as he talked. Retter listened, and she relaxed—her eyes never leaving Tom's face.

Another pain came—harder and stronger. Retter screamed. This time the pain didn't go away—it continued, growing so quickly that her whole body began to push.

Once again, she held onto the rails of the bed. And, although Retter could feel nothing but the pain, she could hear, floating above her, Tom's voice—his soothing words becoming her life-rope. Her spirit reached out and clung to the sound.

The storm outside intensified. Black clouds rolled and tossed, streaks of lightning reaching across the sky—and along the path of each lightning flash ran footsteps of thunder.

Retter felt her skin tear, sending a burning sensation throughout the lower part of her body. Then suddenly, a great relief came flooding up and the head of the child appeared.

Minutes later, Tom's crippled hands cradled the baby boy as his mother pushed him out into the early morning.

No one in the mountain cabin was listening to the storm that raged outside. The darkness of the room was interrupted only by the flickering lamplight in the far corner of the room—the light that caressed the miracle of birth.

Quickly, Tom cut the cord that bound mother and son—tied the end attached to the baby's belly, and laid him on Retter's stomach. She looked down at the small form, tears covering her face. Another boy—and he looked fine. Tom had been right—the Lord had given them two blessings tonight.

The afterbirth came fast and was caught in one of the basins, and set aside. Tom would bury it later.

Then, with Retter watching, Tom turned the baby over and shook him. The newborn whimpered and gave a weak cry.

Tom looked at Retter with a question on his face. She answered his look with a tired smile.

Very carefully Tom wrapped the baby in a piece of torn sheet, and laid him in Retter's arms.

"It's a boy baby, Retter," softly came Tom's voice.

"Fetch me something to wipe his face, Tom," said Retter, gazing at her newest son.

As Tom turned, Bryson edged around his father, straining his neck, trying to see his brother.

"Look, Bryson, ain't he precious? He puts me in mind of you when you wuz borned." As she spoke, Retter was wiping the baby gently with the edge of the sheet.

There was a look of wonder on Bryson's face as he gazed at mother and son. What he had witnessed this night, he would long remember.

"Here, Retter," said Tom as he handed her a warm wet cloth. "Are you all right?" he continued earnestly.

"All I want, Tom is some catnip tea. And I need to break the hives out of his body. Oh, and you need to git some sweet'ning fer the baby to git the phlegm out of his throat."

"Okay, Retter—but are you all right?" Tom's eyes were concerned as he gazed at his wife.

"I'm fine, Tom. I'm fine—now."

Later, as Retter lay in bed, her baby held tightly in her arms, she gazed with glistening eyes at Tom as he sat near her. Softly and carefully, she spoke, "Tom, we shore do be a pair! We've been through jest about everything together. What would I have done without you tonight?"

Retter paused, and wiped her eyes with the edge of the torn sheet that covered the baby. Then she continued, "Tom, you may have crooked bones and look crippled-up to the world, but to me, I still see you a-standing there, six feet tall, holding open yore coat fer me to snuggle up to you. And even though I'm growing old, you still look at me with love in yore eyes. There ain't nobody in this whole wide world that kin be as happy as me."

Quietly, Tom slipped off his chair and knelt down by the bed. Taking Retter's hand in his, he held it up to his lips as tears fell from his eyes. Slowly, he spoke, "Retter, yo're right, we shore do be a pair."

On August 29, 1921, there was born to Tom and Retter, their seventh child—a rosy-cheeked boy baby—and they called him Franklin Lee Ammons.

CHAPTER THIRTY

Nekkid as a Jaybird

The strawberries stained her fingers. She brushed her fingers on her apron.

Retter was on her knees, the half-full pail beside her as she picked the luscious wild strawberries. They were so good that Retter had sampled one every so often, and the taste of the berries lingered in her mouth.

She was smiling—there were enough berries in this patch for at least a dozen quarts of jam. In her house, strawberry jam went faster than any of the other jellies.

Sitting back on her heels, Retter stretched her back. The only trouble with picking strawberries was the need to bend over close to the ground. Retter tugged at the scarf that covered her hair. It had slipped, and she pulled at it until it was once again covering the dark strands of her hair.

It was early morning, and the dew still covered the leaves of the plants. The rays of the sun flowed softly over Retter, quietly bathing her in warmth. She enjoyed this time alone. She usually did not hear the clamor of the children that accompanied her household chores. But sometimes, on certain days, and for no apparent reason, all of a sudden it would hit her—she just couldn't stand the noise, and she had to get away by herself. This time she had climbed a hill to the strawberry patch.

As she stood, she felt her legs stiff and sore from kneeling so long, so she slowly stretched again. Taking her bucket with her, Retter walked over to the stump of an old oak and set the bucket on the stump. She was on top of a hill that had been partially cleared a few years before. The trees that had been cut down lay in a pile a little way from her, close to the edge of the woods. Wild strawberry plants flourished in and around the stumps and dead limbs of the trees.

There was a movement at the bottom of the incline—someone was climbing up the path. Retter stared hard at the slight figure, straining her eyes to see. She raised her hand, covering her eyes from the sun.

"Oh, it's Frank. Now what's that young'un doing? Guess he's follerin' me again," Retter spoke aloud, shaking her head. Ever since Retter had lost her eighth baby a few months back, Frank had followed her and watched her closely. Although he was six years old now, he was still her baby and seemed to want to take care of her. To Retter, it seemed that Frank was becoming more like her Tom every day.

Retter had carried her eighth child the full nine months, and had had no problems with the delivery, but the child had been born dead. She had cried for days—it had been her second little girl, and the deep grief she'd felt had been evident to all her children—but Frank had especially noticed it. So, in his small way, he had tried to stay close to her and ease her grief.

As Retter watched the short legs of Frank climb the incline, she started to smile again. This fifth son of hers was just as she had thought he would be—someone special. Even at such an early age, the evidence was already there. Frank was quiet, yet loud when necessary—he was soft-hearted, yet strong and stubborn when he thought that someone was being taken advantage of—and the underdog was usually his sister, Martha. He had become her champion.

As Frank drew nearer, Retter could tell something was wrong. There was a stormy look on his face, and his thin legs seemed to almost push him as he climbed. Both his hands were balled-up fists that swung out stiffly as he moved. His dark curly hair hung down over his forehead, and his lips were pressed together tightly.

"Son, what're you frettin' about?" said Retter as he approached her. She stood with her feet apart, her stained hands on her hips, watching him.

"Momma, Thomas and Jim—and Bryson, too—jest askeered Martha to death. She's down there crying." The words rushed out from between Frank's lips as he spoke, disgust written all over his face. "Momma, I git so tired of them making her cry!"

"What did they do now?" said Retter.

"Wal, Martha wuz making up the beds like you told her to do. Jim and Thomas done ketched a little ole snake in a fruit jar. Then them and Bryson snuck in whilst Martha wuz doing yourn and Daddy's bed and put the snake in her bed. When she went to make up her bed, she pulled down the kevvers, and I never heard such a hollering in all my life. She took on something fierce!" Frank paused in his speech, and shook his head. "Momma," he continued, "it jest about askeered me to death, too. Martha still is down there crying—and them boys are still laughing! It wuzn't nothing but a little old garden snake, but it slithered jest the same."

Retter was amused as she listened to Frank relate the story—he sounded so grown-up and responsible—just like his mother.

"Momma, I aim that them boys are gonna be sorry fer doing it this time. I'm gonna git them fer it!" Frank's eyes took on a glint that surprised even Retter. She had a feeling that those boys had better watch their step.

"Frank, don't you git in Bryson's way again. You know a seventeen-year-old boy is too big fer you to tangle with. I cain't be watching you both all the time." Retter turned, picked up her bucket, and returned to where she'd stopped in her berry picking. Kneeling, she resumed her chore.

For a minute, Frank stared at his mother with unseeing eyes, his thoughts on brotherly revenge. Then shaking his head, he moved over beside his mother and began to help her.

Later that day, Retter stood over the hot stove in her kitchen, stirring the jam as it boiled. Her sterilized jars stood on the table, ready for the hot red liquid. The jam came to a rolling boil, and after a minute, Retter moved the pan to the table. The rolling boil settled down, leaving a bright pink foam floating on top.

As Retter removed the foam with a metal spoon, Frank and Martha watched with heightened excitement—waiting for the dish with the foam. When it cooled, it was so sweet and delicious—they loved it.

"Okay, kids. You kin have it." Retter handed the dish to the two and began pouring the hot jam into the jars.

The aroma of the sweet-smelling liquid moved out from the kitchen onto the porch, where Tom sat whittling. The smell tickled his nose. His well-worn cane lay at his feet, shavings clustered all around the chair and overtop the cane. He was making an axe handle. Don Moses had told him that he would buy all he could make, so Tom had began working at a job that he loved—creating things with his hands. During the last few years, Tom had grown proficient at whittling just about any kind of wooden furniture and tool handle. He'd always loved to work with wood—now he had the time. He was happy. He still operated his still, but the boys were doing most of the work.

Life on the mountain was going along evenly and without any great upset. In the spring, Bryson had taken on the chore of plowing the fields and planting the crops. Thomas and Jim helped him a little, but it was mostly Bryson's job. Jim and Thomas milked, and cared for the livestock. Albert helped Retter and Martha in the house, and Frank helped them all.

Retter had been talking about raising more laying hens and selling eggs to help with the income. Tom laughed a little—knowing that Retter would do exactly what she said she would do, once she made up her mind.

Retter came out onto the porch, wiping her face with her apron.

"It's gittin' hot now, Tom, ain't it?" her voice was soft and low, just loud enough to reach Tom's ears.

"Yes—guess it's gonna be a hot one," said Tom.

"Where's the other boys?" asked Retter, gazing around her.

"They're out in the upper field, putting in some late corn," answered Tom. He was smoothing out the axe handle he'd just finished.

"When the time comes fer them to come home fer supper, jest send 'em on down to the creek to wash up. Make 'em feel better anyways."

In the doorway, Frank stood, a sudden gleam in his eyes as he heard his mother's statement. He turned and went back into the kitchen.

The day grew even hotter as the sun moved across the sky, not a cloud to create even the slightest cover. The three boys were tired and dirty when they arrived home close to milking time. Their father didn't have to tell them more than once to bathe in the creek. Grabbing their change of clothing, they ran off down the path, batting each other around and laughing. A little ways behind them walked a small lone figure.

The sun was going down when Retter finally had supper on the table and went to call everyone to come and eat.

Tom and Frank were playing checkers on top of an overturned nail keg on the porch. Martha stood by, telling Frank which move to make.

The boys were nowhere in sight. Retter walked over to the living room and called Albert, asking him if he had seen the other boys come back from the creek.

Laying down the book he was reading, Albert answered, "No, Momma, I ain't seen 'em. Want I should go look fer 'um?"

"I think you best do that. Supper's gittin' cold."

Albert left, taking the same trail the boys had taken earlier. It wasn't long before he was back, laughing so hard he could hardly walk.

"Albert. What on earth. What's so funny?" Retter said, her hands on her hips.

"Oh, Momma. It is so funny!" Albert began to laugh again.

Tom couldn't help smiling, even though he didn't know what was so funny. Frank moved back into the shadows of the porch so no one could see the devilish grin on his face. He said nothing.

"Albert. Tell us," said Martha, tugging at her brother's sleeve.

"Wal—the boys are still in the creek, almost blue from the cold, since the sun went down. They went into the creek, left their clothes on the bank and when they come out there were no clothes. None. And no towels, either. They are as nekkid as a jaybird, and freezing!" Albert started to laugh again as he spoke, "They're yelling fer their britches!"

Retter watched them all laugh, and then slowly sought out Frank in the shadows.

"I guess you finally done it, huh, Frank. You got back at 'um. Where's their clothes, son?" she turned eagle eyes on Frank, and waited for him to speak.

"But, Momma, I didn't take no clothes— " he began, and then in a lower voice, he continued, "I jest moved 'um."

"Wal, where DID you move 'um, boy?" questioned Retter.

"They're over on the other side of the creek—right out where they kin see 'um—hanging in the trees," he answered. "They ain't thought to jest look over their shoulders."

Retter and Tom looked at each other and grinned. Frank never saw this exchange—he was digging his toe in the boards of the porch, his head hanging low.

"Albert, go show them boys where their clothes are," said Retter, and glancing at Frank, she said, "I'll talk to you later!"

As she went back into the kitchen, laughter grew louder behind her. With her back to the others, Retter couldn't help but have a satisfied look as she grinned also.

"Wal," she thought, nodding her head, "the war is jest commencing."

D.Ammons

CHAPTER THIRTY-ONE

The Spirit of Cooweesucoowee

The sun was going down, sending out soft feather-like reds and oranges into the darkening sky. Tom sat in his chair on the porch, and Retter stood watching the beauty of the sunset. Somewhere there were big cities, bright lights, loud noises, and bustling crowds.

But here, there was the song of the cricket, the light of fireflies as they softly glowed here and there above the damp grass—and the sound of laughing children in the cabin.

A sudden breeze in the pines above the cabin bent the boughs, and the swishing of the pine needles on the roof sounded like the soft scratching of a cat. The breeze touched Retter's face.

"Charlie's here," she thought. "He's here waiting and watching."

She looked up—the colors of the sunset were fading now, and the clouds that filled the sky made her think of Charlie's snow-white hair flying in the wind, the color growing darker with the end of the day.

As she gazed around her, a realization suddenly filled her. She wondered why she hadn't thought of it before. The evidence had been there all the time.

Charlie was not only her grandfather, and a Cherokee—but, to her, he was the spirit of the mountains. He lived! His voice was the cry of the cat in the darkness, and the roar of a hidden waterfall—he moved with the wind in the tall pines, and with the sweep of an eagle's wings.

The spirit of Cooweesucoowee was in the first golden rays of the morning climbing over the mountains—and in the rainbow of the sunset.

He was all around her—life was all around her.

Retter turned and gazed at Tom. He was growing old—the hair mostly gone from the crown of his head. He was diminished in stature now, but the goodness of the man shone on the loving tenderness of his face.

Retter sighed. It was a contented sigh.

"What are you sighing fer, Retter? And yo're turning a quair look on me. Are you finally gitting tired of me and my cane?" Tom spoke quietly, looking at her with questioning eyes.

Retter slowly walked over to Tom, and taking his face between her hands, she said, "There never has been and never will be any man fer me but Tom Ammons."

RETTER AND TOM AMMONS
Years after the accident.

EPILOGUE

Retter

Even though times were always financially hard for the Ammons family, they continued to flourish and grow.

Retter had three more children after Frank. On September 1, 1928, Lillie Mae Ammons was born; on May 23, 1931, Corie Elendar Ammons; and on December 15, 1934, Nealie Roosevelt Ammons arrived.

Tom and Retter were able to pull together in a life full of obstacles. Together, they had blazed out a path through their troubles and had led the way through rocky terrain so that their children and grandchildren could follow in their footsteps.

However, their troubles were not over—they were just beginning. In the years to come, their sons would grow up and acquire the reputation of the "mean, fighting Ammons boys." And the girls would receive their share of mountain gossip.

But these are other stories . . . stories that I will tell in *CANNIE.*

★ ★ ★ ★ ★

RETTER is based on a true character—my grandmother. She was a most memorable and remarkable woman, who, I hope, will always be remembered by her many descendants.

When I began this novel, it was very exciting to me just to be able to finally put down on paper what I had longed to say for many years. As each chapter developed, the admiration I felt for my grandmother grew—and grew.

As the oldest grandchild, I suppose I do remember more of the family's history than any of the other grandchildren. I remember sitting at the feet of my grandfather, on the warm hearth in the cabin on top of the mountain. There, by the light of the oil lamp, he told me story after story about his and Grandmother's life together. These stories were lovingly stored away in the memory of a wide-eyed girl—until a dream awakened them.

Retter was a big woman, in more ways than one. When she entered a room, there was no mistake—you knew she was there. I will never forget her eyes—hazel in color, but piercing—eyes that seemed to see right through you. But she had a smile! And ample room in her arms to enfold you in about the softest resting place in the world. To my knowledge, Grandmother's hair was never cut in all her adventuresome years, and when she died, it was entirely snow-white. She wore it draped around the crown of her head.

Tom Ammons, my grandfather, died of a stroke in 1956, at the age of seventy-five. Retter lived eighteen years longer, dying on May 17, 1974. She was eighty-three years old. To me it was remarkable that a woman who had struggled through so much earlier in life, could live such a long time. In fact, she lived long enough to hold her great grandchildren on her knee. Her face would light up with pleasure, just holding and watching her "babies." She was always alert, and up to the very end, never lost her faculties—her mind was sharp and clear.

In my mind, I can still see the kindness that was written on Grandpa's face, and the tenderness he continually showed my grandmother. They never mentioned to the people around them the love they had for each other, but no one ever questioned it. It was self-evident.

Years after Grandpa died, Grandma came down from the mountain to live with her daughter, Corie, but she never quit talking of going home. Happiness to her still lived in the cabin on top of the mountain.

And even today, climbing the mountain to the cabin is an adventure! Grass and brush have covered the once worn paths that led to the door of the Ammons home. Only part of the dwelling stands—but inside lives memories.

Shadows roam the cabin—the cabin that is almost no more—whispering of a time that is gone forever. The wind still whistles through the pines outside, the boughs scratching no more on the tin roof.

But there are footsteps—Retter's footsteps—footsteps that will never be blown away with the wind of time. As long as there is someone who remembers and someone who cares, she will always be there.

Stand on that mountain, look over your shoulder, turn your face to the wind—and listen . . . listen.

There are footsteps following—crackling in the browned leaves of yesterday, echoing on the pavements of today. Listen to the next generation—the footsteps of Franklin Lee Ammons . . . my father.

Amy Ammons Garza